DARK TOMORROW
RISE OF THE CROW

JEREMIAH FRANKLIN

Month9Books

Month9Books

This book is dedicated to my amazing wife, Jodi, and to my wonderful children, Jackson Thomas and Haylie Ryann, whose unwavering love and support made this all possible.

DARK TOMORROW

RISE OF THE CROW

1

The boy stood at the top of the hill and stared straight ahead, his green eyes narrowing in the hazy afternoon sun. His throat was dry, as always, and he unscrewed the cap of his water bottle and tilted it up to his mouth. He took a single, measured sip from the bottle, the faint taste of bleach bitter and lingering on the back of his tongue. He swallowed the water quickly but took his time as he replaced the cap, careful not to waste a single drop. He clipped the bottle to the side of his backpack and raised his eyes once again.

The boy had been to this neighborhood only once before, sometime just before the blackout, and there was no denying that it looked very different now. He forced a smile as he spoke out loud to no one but himself, his voice quiet but loaded with sarcasm.

"Another beautiful day in paradise. How the hell did I get to be so goddamn lucky?"

It felt good to use the kind of language that would have earned him a smack in the face had his father been around, but the smile was not long on his lips. Since the beginning, he had held on to the hope that the estates on the hill had somehow escaped the looting and the fires that had followed the blackout, that the rich people's money, and the tall gates that money had bought, had proved their worth. But now, when the boy finally arrived, he knew that he had been wrong, and, worse than that, he had been naïve. In the end, the gates had not held, and the pristine homes that once lined the street were now little more than blackened skeletons of charred wood and metal.

The boy was not exactly sure why it bothered him so much this time. He had seen it all before. It had been the same in almost every neighborhood he had come across in the last year—the withered bodies of those few who had dared to stay behind, the homes burned, the roads littered with abandoned vehicles and debris. He knew that it was simply the way it was now, but for some reason, this time it felt different. This time it hurt more.

The truth was that the fall of humankind had been nothing like the boy had been told it would be, and in some peculiar yet uniquely teenage way, he felt as if he had been cheated. His generation had been conditioned from birth to expect the spectacular, to always presume the fantastic, but Armageddon had not come with a brilliant flash or the blockbuster finale. The machines had not taken over. There had been no zombie outbreak, no hostile alien invasion. There had been no global thermonuclear war, no doomsday meteor, no Four Horsemen of the Apocalypse. In reality, the final days had been nothing like Hollywood had promised him they would be, and as the boy looked over the burned-out homes and the piles of garbage that would hopefully contain his next meal, he knew firsthand that the end of the world had been anything but spectacular.

He continued walking down the street for another full block before he finally came to a stop beneath the shredded fronds of a dead palm tree. A dozen or more crows were picking through a pile of garbage a short distance away, and they stopped to eye him suspiciously as he bent down and picked up a good-sized rock. It seemed amazing to the boy that of all the creatures who had survived the virus, the blackout, and the chaos that ensued, it was the crows that had fared the best. And while the boy had not seen anything more than a single living dog in more than a month's time, the number of crows seemed to have multiplied exponentially, and the boy stood up and tested the weight of the rock in his hand. The nearest bird was at least forty feet away, but the boy was deft with the throw, and he took several steps forward and let the rock fly. The stone hummed past the head of the largest crow, missing by mere inches, and the boy laughed out loud, his green eyes flashing brightly.

"Ha! Just missed! Next time you won't be so lucky, filthy crow."

Despite the gnawing hunger in his belly, the boy had no intention of eating any crow he might kill that day, or any other day, for that matter. The bird's meat was technically edible, but the boy had discovered early on that raiding houses and rummaging through the trash was a much more efficient means of feeding himself, and he continued moving forward.

The boy had no idea how or why the heaps of garbage had come to rest where they now were, but he approached the nearest pile with unabashed hope and slipped his arms deep into the muck. His hands moved in tandem, unseeing fingers feeling, sifting, sorting, and it was not long before he felt something round and familiar roll across his palm. He closed his fingers tight and pulled his find up from the garbage and into the sunlight. He had found nothing more than a single, shriveled apple, its skin now brown and desiccated, but the boy smiled nonetheless, his mouth watering. He whispered quietly to himself, his words drawn out, his voice mimicking the announcer on an old game show he remembered watching as a child.

"Jackpot. We have a winner."

He shoved the apple into his backpack without hesitation and continued searching, reciting one of his father's familiar sayings as he worked.

"Take whatever you can get, whenever you can get it. Isn't that what the old bastard used to say?"

The boy had only begun to talk to himself in the last month or so, and he was growing more comfortable with the idea each passing day. At first, he thought it meant that he had begun to go mad, but the boy had seen firsthand what that looked like, and even what that smelled like, and he figured that at the very least, he was no more insane than anyone else who had stayed alive for this long. In truth, the boy was remarkably stable for all that he had seen and done, but it was also true that he had been uniquely well-prepared for such an existence. For better or for worse, the boy's father had substituted military-style training and discipline for love, and the lessons had been both simple and painful. Follow your instincts. Compartmentalize your feelings. Train to exhaustion. Survive at all costs. Some would have called it abuse, but to the boy, the intense physical and mental training that he had been put through at such a young age was all that he knew, and in that respect, even he could not deny that his father had prepared him well.

The boy's name was Sawyer. He was big for his age, and although he was thin from lack of food, his wide shoulders and large frame were built to carry muscle. He was attractive in a rugged way: his hair an unremarkable brown, his nose a bit crooked, his lips a half-size too big. However, it was his eyes that truly distinguished the boy. Set widely across his face, they were a sparkling shade of emerald green that seemed to glow in the vanishing light, and although the boy was barely sixteen, one look into his eyes betrayed the fact that deep down inside, he felt much, much older.

He was dressed in the only clothing he had—a pair of worn, dark-blue denim jeans and a black t-shirt with the outline of a redwood tree and the words "Renew-Reuse-Recycle" emblazoned in faded green on the front. He thought his t-shirt's mantra was humorously ironic, considering it was now his only option. His feet were wrapped in duct-tape-covered hiking boots, and the bill of his baseball cap was torn and slightly crooked. On his shoulder, he carried a Mossberg pump-action shotgun, and on his back a brown leather pack loaded with gear. A long, dull machete knife was tethered to one side of the pack, and a dented, gunmetal gray water bottle hung from the other.

Inside the backpack, he carried a variety of items that he had deemed essential, including a bottle of bleach, a small flat-edged crowbar, a hatchet, a pair of binoculars, some random hand tools, and a makeshift grappling hook with thirty feet of knotted rope. Wrapped in a plastic shopping bag was a roll of duct tape, a roll of electrical tape, a flashlight, a thin plastic tarp, some clean bandages, several cotton rags, and a nearly full box of double-zero shotgun shells. The two small pockets on the side of the pack were equally loaded; one contained a stainless-steel buck knife, a Leatherman multi-tool, a 9-volt battery, and a sewing kit. The other pocket held a length of aluminum wire, a handful of steel wool, and a single flashlight.

Of all of the items that he carried, it was only the ammunition, the shotgun, and the water that truly mattered to him. The single box of double-zero shotgun shells and the 12-gauge had been among the few items that his father had not taken with him when he left, and the boy carried the loaded weapon both out of necessity and as a cold reminder that he was quite literally all alone in the world. And while it was true that in the beginning he had used the weapon only in self-defense, it had taken only a few days without water before the boy had been forced to take more extreme measures.

Right or wrong, Sawyer had discovered that taking the precious liquid from one of the few remaining survivors was often his only option, and more than a few men had either given up their water or taken their last breath looking down the barrel of his shotgun. In truth, the boy took no pleasure in the act of taking another's life, but if he had learned only one thing over the past year, it was that water was not only something to hope for, and something to search for, but also, when it came down to it, something to kill for.

Nevertheless, the boy also needed to eat, and he continued scavenging for another half hour before he finally gave up and wiped his hands down the front of his jeans. He could see that the fading sun would soon be dipping below the horizon, and he was thinking of the long walk back down the hill when he slowly became aware that the crows had gone uncharacteristically silent. He looked around and saw nothing—no signs of movement, no obvious threats, only the dead palm trees swaying quietly in the warm, dry wind. Still, the boy could feel that something was not quite right, but before he could reach over to slip the shotgun into his hands, he was suddenly and violently spun off his feet, his right shoulder erupting in blinding pain. Sawyer fell beside the pile of garbage and looked over at his shoulder in confused horror, gasping in utter disbelief.

"What the hell? What the hell!"

Buried deep in the meat of his shoulder was a heavy, one-hundred-grain broadhead, the long black shaft protruding into the sky, the bright red and blue fletchings of the arrow bobbing up and down with the heaving of his chest. Sawyer was more than just surprised to see an arrow lodged in his arm—the boy had not seen another living human being in over a full month, but it was not until a second arrow whipped by only inches from his head that he realized he was in very serious trouble. His mind was spinning, and all he could think was that he had to find cover, and fast. He peeked above the mound of trash and tried to think.

There was a burned-out Chevy truck resting twenty yards to his right and a cluster of dead palm trees about ten yards to his left. He could easily make it to the trees, but they offered little cover. He looked back at the truck and noticed that there was a break in the wall just beyond the vehicle. The boy took a deep breath. He had no good options, but he knew that he had to move. He counted down from three, got his feet underneath himself, and then burst out from behind the pile of garbage, sprinting the full twenty yards and reaching the truck just as another arrow skidded off the vehicle's hood and whistled into the sky above him.

Sawyer crouched down behind the truck and tried to catch his breath. Against his better judgment, he looked over at his injured shoulder once again. The arrow was still there, dangling grotesquely from his arm, and a steady flow of dark red blood was now leaking out from under his sleeve. There was no question that the boy was scared, but he tried to fight the rising panic, to control his thoughts like his father had taught him. He closed his eyes for a moment, ignoring the pain, focusing his mind. Sawyer had been taught at an early age that his fear could be channeled into controlled action, and as he took a single calming breath he could feel the rush of adrenaline coming on—the familiar tingling in the tips of his fingers, the quickening of his pulse, the hairs standing up on the back of his neck. It was almost as if a switch had been flipped somewhere inside the boy, and, buzzing with a burst of energy, he slipped the shotgun off his shoulder and peered through the one unbroken window of the truck, his eyes scanning every inch of the street.

A minute ticked by. Then another. He was so keyed up that he was almost shaking, but still he saw nothing. Another minute passed. Sawyer looked down at his shoulder. The adrenaline was masking the pain, but blood was now running freely down his arm and collecting in a small pool at his feet. He knew right then that he could not wait much longer, but he suddenly caught a flash of movement at the end of the street, and the boy's eyes instinctively narrowed. It took him another minute, but then, just as he was about to give up, Sawyer saw him. Crouched in the shadows below a cluster of dead eucalyptus trees was the fuzzy, yet unmistakable, silhouette of a man holding a bow and arrow, and the boy whispered quietly under his breath.

"I see you now, Bowman. I see you now."

The tree line where the Bowman lay in wait was at least fifty yards from where Sawyer now stood, and the boy quickly began to calculate his options. He could either stand and fight or cut and run, and even though the boy wanted nothing more than revenge at that very moment, he was no fool. The break in the wall was just across the street, and he had lost more than enough blood already. He was not happy, but he had made his decision. It was time to run. He took the Mossberg in his one good hand and sighed.

"All right, Bowman. Let's see if you can hit a moving target this time."

Sawyer took one last breath and quietly counted down from three.

"Three, two, one. Go."

With every last ounce of speed he could muster, the boy exploded out from behind the truck, raising the shotgun with one hand and firing blindly toward the trees as he ran. He knew that the single spray of buckshot was useless except to buy him a half-second of time, and he could only hope that it would be enough as he put his head down and raced toward the break in the wall. At the end of the street, the Bowman barely blinked as the shotgun blast spread out harmlessly in the trees above, but seeing that he had one last chance to hit his target, the man took in a deep breath, pulled back on the bowstring, and let the bolt fly.

With the arrow cutting through the air at more than four hundred feet per second, Sawyer had no time to react, and there was little he could do but flinch as he felt the arrow strike home. Still, the break in the wall was only steps away, and before the Bowman could draw his bow again, the boy slipped behind the wall to safety, one bloody shaft still dangling from his shoulder, another fresh arrow lodged deep in the side of his backpack.

2

The girl stared out of her bedroom window and picked at the fraying strip of duct tape that lined the edge of the frame, the dull scraping of her fingernails the only sound in the otherwise silent house. She gazed for what seemed like a long time before she pulled her eyes from the window and looked down at the open journal resting beside her, the pages heavy with ink, the edges of the cover worn and threadbare. She had not written a single word in the journal since sometime before it all began. Reading it now had been like throwing gasoline on a fire.

Emotions that she thought she had buried many months ago suddenly resurfaced, scabs torn free. She hated herself for the selfish words she had written, for the childish thoughts that she had put down on paper. Mostly she hated the terrible things that she had written about her mother, the exaggerations, the outright lies.

She had written those words out of immaturity, out of misplaced teenage angst, and to read them now only stoked the anger that smoldered just below the surface.

She closed the cover of her journal and took the book in one hand as she slid her legs off the bed, her bare feet barely making a sound as they touched the cool, hardwood floor. She stood there for a long moment before she moved at all, her eyes slowly rising to the full-length mirror that stood just across the room. She walked forward until she stood just before it. One hand holding her journal, the other clenched in a fist. She looked at herself for a long time, studying her own body, her own face, her own eyes. With each passing day, she looked more and more like her mother, the resemblance impossible to ignore. Every time she looked in the mirror she was reminded of her, reminded that she was now dead and gone, reminded that it was too late to tell her that she was sorry.

Her name was Sara, and just like her mother had been before her, the girl was undoubtedly beautiful. Her face was feminine and soft, her olive skin smooth and nearly unblemished. She wore her hair in a simple ponytail, just like her mother had, but with sharp bangs that hung like a dagger over one eye. Still, the girl was not accustomed to staring at herself in the mirror, and after several seconds she looked down at the journal in her hands, her dark eyes bright and intense. It was too late to take back what she had written. It was too late to say that she was sorry, and before she could stop herself, she reached back and threw the book as hard as she could at the heavy mirror, her reflection exploding into a thousand tiny pieces as she turned and walked out of her room.

She took her time as she came down the spiral staircase, the warm sunlight subdued and dull as it filtered in weakly from the outside. Thick sheets of translucent plastic had been taped across every window in the house, and as always, the air on the ground floor was stale and dry. The plastic had been her father's idea; he had told them that it would keep them safe. But, like so many other times in her life, he had been wrong. The day after her mother had died, Sara had ripped the plastic from her own bedroom window in a fit of anger, hoping to God that she too would fall ill and die, or, at the very least, prove her father a fool. He was furious when he discovered what she had done and replaced the plastic almost immediately, only to have the girl rip it down again the very first opportunity that she had. Her father was so angry that he did not speak to her for two full days, but when neither of them became sick, he could not deny the facts, or his daughter's will, and he did not replace the plastic a third time.

For the next few months, they had rarely spoken, and even now, almost a full year after her mother's death, their conversations were few and far between. On most days, her father was simply not there, leaving well before she woke up and coming home after she was sound asleep. She did not know where he went, what he was doing, or when he would return, and that was just fine with her. In Sara's mind, her father was only concerned about himself, and she refused to worry about anything he did as she opened the door to the pantry and took a reluctant look inside.

There had been many months when the girl had been able to survive on a strict combination of Goldfish crackers, mineral water, and a pantry full of Top Ramen noodles, but that time had passed. Now there was little left except for whatever her father could scavenge from day to day, and of course what the soldiers had left behind. She opened the walk-in pantry and stepped inside. The shelves that had once been lined with junk food and Diet Coke were now filled with at least a dozen cardboard boxes of military rations and at least as many jugs of purified water. Another dozen or more boxes were stacked at the rear of the pantry. Sara picked up a box from the nearest shelf and held it up, scowling as she read the thick black lettering printed on the side of the cardboard.

"*Meals ready to eat, MRE. Individual, thirty-six-count. Do not rough handle when frozen. Property of US Army.*"

She smirked and spoke directly to the cardboard box.

"Like we even have an army anymore."

Sara did not know all the facts, except that her father had made some type of a deal, and when the last of the soldiers had pulled out he had taken possession of a large cache of military supplies. She flipped through the silver packages, not stopping until she found the one labeled "*Beef Ravioli*," the meal that she hated the least. In Sara's opinion, all the vacuum-sealed packs of ready-to-eat-meals could barely be considered edible, and a few were absolutely horrible. Once, after eating the Pork *Chow Mein*, she told her father that it tasted more like puke *Chow Mein*. The look that he had given her from across the table only reinforced the idea that it was best not only for her to keep her mouth shut, but also to take her meals alone.

Sara opened the package of ravioli, activated the small chemical heating pack, and waited for it to heat up. She ate the ravioli quickly, finishing as the last rays of the sun seeped lazily into the kitchen. The girl looked out the window. It would be dark within the half hour. She knew that her father would be returning home soon, and she picked up the box of MREs and returned it to the pantry. She turned and was about to go upstairs when she suddenly stopped and looked back.

Sara had never really given much thought to how much food and water they had; she had taken it for granted when her father told her not to worry, that they had enough food for years. Nevertheless, her father had been acting even more strange than normal for the last few weeks, leaving earlier each morning, staying out longer each night, and skipping meals in between. Despite their lack of communication, she could tell that something was up, and she re-opened the door to the pantry and stepped back inside. Sara took a good look at the stacks of boxes. Something about them did not seem right. They were lined up too straight, the rows too perfect, the stacks in the rear too high. Sara thought that it almost looked staged, like a bad advertisement for a military surplus store.

Sara put a finger on the nearest box and pushed lightly, her eyebrows rising as it slid backward with ease. She slid it to the side and let it fall to the floor. It was obviously empty. She scowled, pinched her mouth to one side, and kicked the box closest to her, sending the whole stack tumbling to the ground. Confused, she began checking each box in the pantry, finding that only four of the two dozen unopened boxes of MREs were full. The others had been re-taped to appear full, but they were clearly empty. She turned and put her hands on her hips.

For a moment, she wondered if the soldiers had cheated them, but then, as she thought about the type of man that her father was, she knew the truth. They had not been cheated—and not only had her father done something with the rations, he had tried to hide it from her, as well. Sara closed her eyes and did the calculations in her head. It did not take long for a mind as sharp as the girl's to see the writing on the wall. There were four boxes left and thirty-six meals per box. Divide that by six meals per day for the both of them, and even if they began to ration right away, they had no more than a month's worth of food left. Sara shook her head and scowled.

"I don't believe it. We're totally screwed."

An hour later, Sara was sitting in the nearly dark living room waiting for her father to come home when she heard the key hit the lock. She had stacked the empty boxes of MREs in the middle of the entryway, hoping to shock her father into some type of apology or explanation, but as usual he did not take the bait. Her father shut the front door behind him and casually looked over at the stack of boxes, ignoring Sara's stare as he walked into the living room and sat down directly across from her. If Sara's father was anything at all, he was known to be both impulsive and rash, but on this rare occasion, he bought himself a few moments of time as he sat down and took off his shoes. Finally, the man named Jacob looked over at his daughter, his voice tired and raspy.

"So, now you know. We only have enough food for about three weeks, maybe four. Our bottled water will last longer than that, but not by very much."

Sara had been so angry about the food that she had not even though about the water. She frowned. Her father looked away and stammered on.

"I know what I said before—what I had promised you. But, Jesus Christ, Sara, we can't stay here forever. I have been out looking for food and water every day and there is nothing left for us here. I have made up my mind. The tank in the Rover is almost full. That's four hundred miles, if we play our cards right. At least it's enough for us to take a chance on the road."

He waited for her to say something. She just stared at him. He kept talking.

"I know you think that you know better than I do, Sara, but there is no reason for us to stay here any longer. It's time for us to go. We'll head south in the morning."

Sara stared up at her father, her soft, round face swollen with emotion yet held perfectly still. She did not move. She did not say a word. She only looked up at him, knowing that she was impossible to read, and that anything she said would only make him angry. Jacob stood and sighed.

"Only bring what you really need, Sara. I mean it—only what you *really* need. We are leaving first thing."

The girl was a statue. She could see him growing more frustrated with each refusal to respond, and she liked it.

"I'm *speaking* to you. We are leaving in the morning. Do you understand me, Sara?"

She would have continued to ignore him even longer, but she saw no reason to delay the inevitable. Sara looked up at her father and spoke to him for the first time in many days, her voice quiet and calm.

"I understand you perfectly. But how did you get so much gas? Is that why our food is gone? Did you trade it? Do we ever plan on coming back? What about Mom? What about her grave?"

Jacob kept his eyes fixed on a small, white scuff mark on the hardwood floor.

"I traded out most of the MREs not long after the blackout. Those boxes have been sitting empty for months. Believe me when I tell you that I didn't have a choice, it was our lives or the food, let's just leave it at that."

Sara stared over at her father. Jacob was not known for telling the truth, but the girl saw no point in digging any deeper. There were still other questions she wanted answered.

"OK. Even if that is true, where did you get the gasoline? And what about my mother? We can't just leave her here all alone. And where is 'south,' exactly?"

Jacob reached his hands to his face and rubbed his eyes, clearing his throat several times before he finally answered.

"South is south. California, Mexico, Central America, wherever I decide it is. As for the fuel, I found a gas station with some unleaded left in the underground tanks on the other side of the city. That's what I've been doing for the last two weeks. And for your other questions, I don't know the answers, Sara. Not at this exact moment in time."

Sara stood up. Her voice grew suddenly louder and high-pitched, her dark eyes burning bright in the dark room.

"You don't seem to know anything, do you? Why can't you just tell the truth, for once? You don't plan on ever coming back here again, do you?"

Jacob kept his eyes fixed on the floor. The white scuff seemed to have grown longer and wider, the edges spreading like a crack in the hardwood. Sara kept her eyes locked on Jacob's face. She was finally losing her cool, her voice getting louder with each word.

"It was your idea to stay here in the first place. Mom and I wanted to evacuate along with everyone else, and you promised us that it would be all right. You promised us that we would never have to leave. You promised that we would be safe!"

Jacob turned away from her, and with the rare opportunity to say something hurtful right in front of her, the girl aimed as low and as deep as she possibly could. Her voice was as cold as ice.

"And now Mom is dead because of you—because of your decision to stay here. Now you've decided that we are leaving and going 'south' to who knows where? Sounds like a good way to get me killed, too. But I guess I shouldn't be so surprised; maybe that was your grand plan all along. Then you could do whatever the hell you want all the time, instead of sneaking behind my back."

She said it with such callous satisfaction that Jacob could do nothing but let his jaw drop, and suddenly Sara wished that she had not said a single word. Although she hated her father for many reasons, most of them justified, at that moment the little girl inside of her wanted nothing more than for him to reach over and take her in his arms, to kiss her on the forehead and tell her that he was sorry, that everything was going to be all right. But deep down the girl understood that Jacob was not that kind of father, and she was no longer that kind of girl, and she quickly sat back down and closed her mouth.

Jacob stared down at her and waited until he was able to speak, his body literally shaking with anger. Finally, he pointed a tobacco-stained index finger straight at her face, his words spoken through gritted teeth and tight lips.

"You speak like that to me again and you will regret it, do you get my meaning, Sara? I have made my decision. We are leaving in the morning. Get your crap together. End of discussion."

Sara could see the rage simmering just behind her father's eyes, and she knew better than to say another word. Instead, she walked calmly out of the room and up the stairs without a sound, closing the door to her bedroom softly only because she knew he was expecting her to slam it.

3

It was more than a full mile of switchbacks before the boy reached the bottom of the hill, but with enough distance between him and the Bowman, he finally took a quick moment to catch his breath. He looked over at his wounded arm and scowled. The arrow was still protruding from his shoulder, his shirt sleeve soaked with blood, but he knew better than to pull it out quite yet. His camp was still another several miles from the base of the hill, and with the sun beginning to set, he needed to keep moving.

An hour later, he finally came upon his tent, and Sawyer collapsed on his bedroll completely spent. The adrenaline that had carried him this far was now long exhausted, and the throbbing of his shoulder was the only thing he could think about. Still, the boy had no painkillers of any kind. No extra-strength aspirin. No Knock-You-On-Your-Ass Vicodin. Not even a bottle of whiskey like they had in the old Westerns that he had watched with his father. Still, there was no way around it—the arrow had to come out, and he pulled the pliers from his pack and repeated another one of his father's favorite mantras.

"No pain, no gain; no thorn, no throne."

With a final sigh, the boy clamped the teeth of the pliers around the shaft and closed his eyes. A single, hot tear rolled down his cheek in anticipation. His voice was shaky as he sucked in a huge gulp of air and counted down from three.

"Three, two, one. Go."

The boy squeezed the pliers closed and yanked on the shaft as hard as he could, ripping the arrowhead straight out of his shoulder with one swift and severe motion. The pain was like nothing he had ever felt before, and Sawyer could muster little more than a dull whimper as the wound split open and began to gush fresh blood. A tremendous wave of nausea rolled through his body. There was nothing in his stomach to throw up, and he dry-heaved a mess of spit and bright yellow bile into his lap. For a moment, he told himself that the hard part was over, but then he looked over at the wound. It was wide and gaping, and he half cried, half laughed out loud.

"Damn it. I don't think duct tape is going to cut it this time."

The boy could see that the wound would need to be stitched closed, and he opened the pocket of his backpack and pulled out the sewing kit. Sawyer had used the kit only a few times, to repair holes in the tent and his clothing, and it took him several attempts just to thread the needle. He cleaned the wound as well as he could, and when he was finally ready, he whispered quietly to himself.

"Here goes nothing."

Sawyer bit down on his lip hard enough to draw blood, and, feeling as if he were somehow detached from himself, he slipped the needle beneath his skin. Twice the boy lost consciousness from the pain, and although the patch job was jagged and excruciating in its creation, at the end he could not help but look down at the black stitches in morbid satisfaction. Somehow, against amazing odds, the boy had once again lived to fight another day, and as he fell back on his bedroll, thoughts of revenge were already heavy on his mind.

It took him two full weeks to recover, and on the night before he planned to return to the hill, the boy once again had the reoccurring dream that he was being attacked by ravenous crows. However, in this particular dream, the crows' sharp beaks were twisted into long, silver arrowheads, and the birds stabbed and tore at his flesh as he tried to fight them off. In the dream, Sawyer had nothing but his bare hands to fight back with, but when he awoke the next morning and saw the shotgun resting beside him, he knew that the time had finally come. Taking the shotgun in his hands, he stepped out of the tent and looked up at the sky. Dark cumulonimbus clouds were gathering in swollen pockets along the horizon, and the boy's eyes narrowed.

"Better watch out, Bowman. There's a storm coming your way."

Sawyer took his time ascending the hill once again, and as the skies opened for a rare summer shower, he kept a watchful eye out for the Bowman. The first day, he saw no signs of the man, but the boy was patient, and he filled his bottle with rainwater and waited. When he finally caught a glimpse of a lone figure slipping from shadow to shadow on the eve of the second day, the boy smiled, whispering under his breath.

"Ready or not, here I come."

Without a second's hesitation, Sawyer dropped from his rooftop perch and hit the ground running. He had wanted to wait and control the adrenaline rush until the perfect moment, but as soon as he saw the curved bow in hand and the quiver of arrows strapped to the figure's back, he let the adrenaline wash over him, his heart suddenly racing, every muscle engorged with blood. He flipped the safety off the shotgun and exhaled slowly. The Bowman was only a dozen or so yards away now, and coming toward him, and as was his habit, the boy counted down from three once again.

"Three, two, one. Go."

In a flash, Sawyer rushed out from behind cover, his adrenaline at full tilt, the Mossberg leveled and ready. The Bowman looked up in absolute shock at the boy coming toward him, but before he could reach for an arrow, Sawyer took careful aim, and pulled back on the trigger. The double-zero buckshot tore through the man like he was made of rags, and the wooden bow splintered in his hands as he was blown backward by the blast. The sound of the shotgun was like a bomb going off in the otherwise silent street, and the crows took to the air by the hundreds, the sky suddenly black. Sawyer slowly reloaded the weapon and walked toward the wounded man.

The heavy steel buckshot had torn through the Bowman's chest and neck, and small fountains of blood were leaping from his exposed skin. Sawyer lifted his sleeve and showed the man the jagged, purple scar on his shoulder.

"Remember me?"

The Bowman looked up at him and nodded, but his windpipe was shredded, and he could not speak. The boy bent down beside the man and shook his head.

"I'm not sure why you tried to kill me in the first place, but I do know that payback's a bitch. I'm sure you understand. That's just the way it is, right? No hard feelings."

Sawyer instinctively racked the shotgun to load another round, but the boy had no intention of firing the weapon again. He had seen enough men die to know that the Bowman was not long for this world, and he waited only a few seconds for the man to take his last breath before he began to search the body. He quickly found that there was nothing much of use on his person—some matches and a decent knife, but the bow was ruined, and Sawyer had no use for the arrows.

There was one item that caught the boy's eye, however. Inside a back pocket, the man was carrying a single photo of a smiling, blond-haired girl, and Sawyer held it up and studied it in the waning light. He could only assume it was the Bowman's daughter, but he had no way of knowing for certain. She looked so happy, so carefree, and for a moment the boy wondered if anyone would ever feel that way again. He let out a long sigh, but as he reached down to put the photo back in the dead man's pocket, he suddenly had the uncanny feeling that he was being watched. The boy spun around with the shotgun ready, but there was no one there, not even a single crow. Still, Sawyer knew better than to ignore his instincts this time, and without so much as another look back, he dropped the photo on the Bowman's chest and quickly headed back to his camp.

The boy had chosen his campsite for the simple fact that it was well off the beaten path and very well concealed, and by the time he reached his tent, he was no longer feeling uneasy. He had done what he had set out do, and without remorse he fell back on his bedroll, letting his heavy eyelids fall shut. It was not long before the boy fell asleep, but just as he was about to enter another familiar dream, Sawyer suddenly awoke, and he sat up in his sleeping bag and rubbed his eyes. The unmistakable smell of lighter fluid was suddenly heavy inside the small nylon tent, and for a moment the boy was convinced that he must still be dreaming. Nevertheless, only a moment later, a flash of bright light unexpectedly bounced off the top of the tent, and before Sawyer knew what was happening, the roof suddenly burst into orange flames and began to melt down on top of him.

Instantly wide awake, Sawyer kicked his legs free of his sleeping bag and scrambled to his feet, closing his eyes and launching himself through a hole in the burning tent. He landed on his hands and knees, but as he tried to stand up he was suddenly attacked from behind, a heavy wooden axe handle smashing into the back of his head. He heard the sickening thud of the wood bouncing off his skull, and he fought to remain conscious as a half dozen more blows rained down upon his back, the sound of the wood cracking bone ringing in his ears. He somehow managed to get to his feet just as he caught the glint of a large knife reflected in the moonlight, the heavy, curved blade whistling in his ear as it came inches away from his face. His attacker came at him with relentless abandon as Sawyer scrambled back to his feet and raised his arm to block the plunging knife, the blade hitting his forearm at an angle and rebounding hard off his elbow, blood spraying as he screamed in pain.

Sawyer staggered and fell backward over the melted tent, landing heavily as the dark figure above him rushed forward with the knife. With only a split second to react, Sawyer put all of his strength into a single sweeping kick, swinging his leg in a powerful, low arc. A loud crack shattered the night air as the assailant's shinbone was snapped in two by the kick, and the attacker crashed to the ground, the knife lost somewhere in the darkness. Sawyer did not waste another second. Like an animal, he launched himself on top of his assailant, landing a series of devastating blows with his fists, his knuckles ripping open as they smashed through teeth and bone. He groped wildly in the darkness until he found his attacker's neck, clamping both hands around it with brutal force, the boy ignoring the sharp nails tearing at his face as he shifted his weight forward to crush the windpipe.

Blood and spit poured from his mouth as he pressed down with all his remaining strength, struggling to hold his grip as the attacker writhed like a serpent underneath him. For what seemed like eternity, they wrestled in the darkness, but just as he felt he could fight no longer, the body underneath him went suddenly limp, and after one final shudder, Sawyer knew it was all over.

As soon as he was able, Sawyer lifted himself to his feet and stared at the body lying beside him. The night was dark, but as the clouds moved across the sky, the moon was nearly full, and as Sawyer's eyes began to adjust, he leaned in close, his brow furrowed. He shook his head in confusion as the moonlight illuminated the bloody corpse, his voice shaking.

"What the hell did I do?"

A tendril of long, dirty blond hair was draped across the face, the fingers on both hands tapered and thin, gold and silver rings reflecting dimly. Even in the faint light of the moon, he could now see clearly what he had done, and his mouth fell open as he stepped back in horror and disbelief. At his feet lay the body of a teenage girl, her dead eyes staring up at him. Her delicate features had been smashed into a bloody pulp, but the boy thought of the photo of the blond-haired girl, and suddenly he knew exactly who she was and why she had come to kill him.

"Goddamn it all to hell. The Bowman's daughter."

Sawyer had killed men before, but he had never laid a hand on a girl in his entire life, and suddenly he felt as if he were going to be sick. He sat down and put his head in his hands, ignoring his wounds as he tried to fight back the tears. It took him some time to compose himself, and by the light of the moon he started collecting anything that had survived the fire, trying but failing to ignore the body of the dead girl resting only a few feet away.

Despite his refusal to accept it, the boy was in bad shape himself, the burns on his face and scalp weeping and painful, the cut on his forearm dirty and bleeding. His head and face were covered in contusions and cuts, a series of long, deep scratches running from his forehead down to his chin. He could not be sure, but he felt that at least a few of his ribs had been fractured, and every breath he took sent sharp pains through his chest and back. He took what seemed like an eternity to gather up what was left of his supplies, and as dawn began to break, he finally looked over at the Bowman's dead daughter and sighed.

"I can't leave her like this."

Sawyer wanted nothing more than to simply walk away and put it all behind him, but he knew that he could not just leave the girl where she was, her bones left to be picked clean by crows. He had no shovel, or the strength to dig a proper grave for that matter, but he covered the girl with what was left of the tent and stacked heavy stones over her body. He never took the time to look for the knife, or to search the girl's body, and he took nothing of hers when he left. The boy knew that he had already taken everything he could from the girl, and the scars from that day would be more than enough to remind him of her for the rest of his life.

4

Neither Sara nor Jacob had slept for more than a few fitful hours before they woke at daybreak, once again ignoring each other as they pulled back onto the main highway and began to drive. They had been traveling now for several days, and though they had covered a good distance, Jacob was beginning to get nervous as the low fuel light lit up on the dash. He had expected to find fuel in at least one of the hundreds of abandoned vehicles that lined the freeways, but for the last fifty miles they had stopped beside each derelict automobile, and just like Sara had warned him, one after another the tanks came up dry. As the vehicle began to sputter, she picked her head up from the single roadmap they had brought along and looked over at the fuel gauge.

"Awesome. Almost out of gas and still miles away from the nearest town. What a great plan you've put together. I can't wait to start walking."

Jacob ignored her sarcasm as they used up their last few drops of fuel to coast into the outskirts of a small resort town not far from the ocean. Once they stopped, he took the keys from the ignition, looked over at Sara, and scowled.

"Just grab your gear and keep your smartass comments to yourself, Sara. There has got to be gas somewhere in this town."

They put on their packs and walked the last few miles into town, Sara carrying an empty five-gallon plastic gas can and Jacob carrying a loaded .38 caliber Smith and Wesson revolver. Sara was not exactly sure how or when Jacob had come across the weapon, but she knew that the six bullets in the gun were all that they had. They kept off the main roads and out of sight as much as possible, passing ransacked homes and vehicles as they made their way downtown. Jacob checked each car for gas, but it was always the same—fuel tanks sucked dry, windows shattered into spider webs, tires and wheels flat or missing.

Every mile they traveled south the number of crows seemed to multiply, and Sara found herself hating the black-feathered birds as they eyed her from every angle. Still, the girl was an expert at ignoring things that she did not like, and she refused to pay the crows any attention as they walked into town. Most of the homes and businesses had been looted and burned to the ground, and finding no fuel before nightfall, they slept in the bed of a random pickup and woke early the next morning to begin searching again. Just before midday, they finally came upon a detached garage that appeared to have escaped the fires, and Jacob peered through the window and looked over at Sara.

"We may actually have something here."

Jacob used a hammer to break the window and opened the door. A 1969 Ford Mustang sat in the center of the garage. It was in perfect, restored condition, and Jacob opened the door and searched inside. There was no sign of any key, but Jacob opened the hatch to the fuel tank and stuck his nose inside the hole, the unmistakable scent of gasoline burning in his nostrils. He gave Sara a smug look.

"I was right. We do have something here."

Trying to contain his excitement, he quickly went to work. He grabbed the rubber tubing he had brought and slid it into the tank. He put his mouth on the other end and sucked in hard. Within a few seconds, the gas was flowing steadily through the tube and into the five-gallon container in Sara's hands. Jacob grinned at her, but the smile on his face slowly began to fade as the precious liquid quickly began to reach the top of the container. He had not expected more than a few gallons in the tank, and he began to look around the garage, panic written on his face. The gas was nearly spilling out of the top of the container when he turned and yelled at Sara.

"Don't just stand there, Sara! Go find something, quick!"

Sara had no idea what to do, and she just stood there.

"What? Where should I look?"

Jacob was frantic. He screamed at Sara.

"Just go find a container, any container! Hurry up!"

Sara began to search the garage for anything they could use, but after a few seconds she knew that it was now too late. She watched without a word as her father fumbled to stop the flow of gas out of the tank, the rubber tubing slipping from his hands, his pants and the ground below soaked with gas. By the time Jacob pulled the tube free, it was too late, and the last several gallons of fuel had spilled onto the cement below his feet. Sara stepped back from her father as he threw the rubber tube across the garage, the gasoline dripping from his pants, the vein on his forehead purple and distended. She looked down at the full container of fuel and smiled weakly.

"At least we got the five gallons. That's better than nothing, right?"

Her father looked at the wasted pool of spilled gas at his feet and shook his head in disgust, his nostrils flaring wide as he turned and screamed at her.

"Five gallons won't get us anywhere!"

Sara had had enough, and she screamed right back into her father's face.

"You're the one who spilled the gas; you're the one who's not getting us anywhere!"

Sara turned and stormed out of the garage before he could answer, but she had only taken a few steps outside when he grabbed her by the arm and spun her around. Sara pushed him away and looked up with hatred burning in her eyes.

"Just leave me alone! I hate you!"

Jacob was not moved by her outburst and screamed back at her.

"You hate me? What a surprise. You are so much like your mother it makes me sick."

Sara's eyes narrowed at the mention of her mother, and Jacob knew he had made a mistake. He tried to backtrack, but Sara stopped him before he could speak, her reply delivered with unbridled spite.

"That's right, I am just like my mother, and if I could have one wish, it would be that I'm nothing like you, Jacob."

She had never called her father by his first name before, and she could see that the disrespect hit him like a punch in the face. Jacob's voice cracked as he tried to control himself.

"So now I am 'Jacob' to you—is that what you think, Sara? Well, you can think again, because I am your father, and you will show me respect. Am I clear? Do you understand me, Sara? I don't want to hear another damn—"

Sara was confused as Jacob abruptly stopped speaking midsentence, his eyes suddenly growing wide. Slowly, he moved his hand to the gun in his belt and whispered quietly in her direction.

"Shhh. Walk slowly toward me, Sara. We need to get out of here right now."

"I don't understand. What's wrong?"

Jacob pressed a finger over his lips and whispered a single word.

"Dogs."

Sara could hear the fear in her father's voice, and she turned to see a huge, reddish-brown dog staring at her from across the street, a distinct ridge of bristling hair running along its back. Two brindle-coated pit bulls were standing behind the first dog, their thick noses tilted up to the wind. For a moment, Sara thought that she must be hallucinating. They had not seen a single living, warm-blooded animal in as long as she could remember, but here they now were, looking at three very large, very alive dogs. The girl's instincts told her to turn and run, but she had barely taken a step backward when the two pits came running straight for them. In an instant, the two dogs were halfway across the street, their massive jaws clicking in anticipation as they closed the distance with astonishing speed. Jacob yelled something unintelligible as he grabbed Sara's hand and pulled her into the garage, barely closing the door behind them as the two dogs hurled their bodies against the wood.

The air inside the garage was heavy with the smell of the spilled gasoline, and Sara could hardly breathe as she inhaled a deep breath of fumes. She could see that the dogs were already beginning to tear through the wooden door, and Sara began to think. There was one small window above the workbench on the opposite side of the garage, and Sara grabbed a hammer from the nearby tool rack and threw it straight through the window, the glass shattering just as the first dog thrust its jaws through a crack in the door. Jacob pointed the revolver straight at the dog's head, but Sara grabbed him by the arm before he could pull the trigger.

"No! Don't do it. This garage is full of gas fumes, and we need to save the bullets. I have an idea. Please trust me. We have to get out through the window, right now. Go!"

Jacob did not understand what she planned to do, but he was very aware that the six .38 caliber bullets resting inside the cylinder were all that they had, and he shoved the revolver in his belt and climbed onto the workbench. Sara pointed to the window.

"You have to go through first! I'll be right behind you. There's no time to argue, just go!"

The first dog was already halfway through the door, and Jacob pulled himself up and dropped out of the window, the air knocked clean out of him as he hit the ground hard. Despite the pain, he scrambled to his feet as fast as he could, surprised that Sara was not right behind him. He stood up and yelled into the broken window.

"Sara! What are you doing? Get the hell out of there!"

Sara heard him yelling, but there was no time to respond, and she reached into her backpack and turned to face the two dogs on her own, a cigarette lighter in one hand, her journal in the other. She had assumed that the workbench she stood upon was high enough to be safe, but the two dogs were mad with bloodlust, and they flung themselves at her like wild beasts, their jaws snapping closed only inches from her legs. Sara knew the dogs would soon find a way to get to her, and there was no more time to hesitate. Knowing she had nothing else to burn, she hung one leg out of the window, touched the lighter to the edge of her journal, and boldly tossed the book over the dogs' heads as the pages caught fire.

Even before the flaming journal hit the ground, the fumes from the spilled gasoline instantly ignited, and a massive fireball suddenly erupted inside the garage. The force of the explosion blew

Sara clean out of the window, the flames singeing her hair and clothes as she came tumbling to the ground at Jacob's feet. He bent down and put out the small flames that were smoldering on her pants leg.

"Sara! Are you all right?"

For a moment, Jacob sounded almost like a concerned father, and Sara sat up with a half-smile, the smell of burnt dog hair and gasoline heavy in the air. She cleared her throat and spoke.

"Don't worry. I'm OK. Thanks for trying to catch me."

Jacob leaned over and gave her a small hug. His voice was a bit shaky.

"I am not sure that I did anything at all, but you are welcome anyway."

Sara stood up and looked back at the garage. Thick black smoke was now billowing from the window, a few small flames coming from the roof.

"Do you think they're dead? The dogs, I mean."

As if he suddenly realized what she had just done, Jacob looked down at his daughter and scowled, his voice now stern and unforgiving.

"Yes, I think they must be dead, Sara, but that was a dangerous stunt you pulled in there, and you are very fortunate that you were not killed along with them. Next time you need to follow my lead, not the other way around, do you understand? I could have just shot them and been done with it."

Sara faked a laugh.

"Ha! What a great idea. Let's start wasting our only bullets the first chance we get."

Jacob was about to start yelling at the girl when Sara suddenly took a step back and stood perfectly still. She whispered as softly as she could.

"Never mind. I was wrong. You can go ahead and use the bullets now. The other dog is right behind you."

Jacob slowly turned around. No more than twenty feet away stood the massive ridgeback, its black lips curled into a vicious snarl. The animal stood as tall as Sara's hip and outweighed her by a good margin, and she instinctively slipped behind her father, squeezing his arm as the canine took a step closer. The dog made a deep guttural growl that sent shivers down the girl's back, and she yelled in her father's ear.

"What are you waiting for? Shoot it! Shoot it now!"

Jacob slowly raised the revolver toward the dog. To his surprise, at the sight of the gun the animal suddenly sprang out of the line of fire and backed away from them, circling around to their left before coming to a bristling stop. Sara was dumbfounded.

"Did you see that? Do it again. Point the gun at it again."

Jacob took a step forward and once again leveled the gun in the direction of the dog. Just like before, the ridgeback leapt to the side, baring its long canines as it backed up, eyes locked on the weapon in Jacob's hand. The man was astonished, and he muttered under his breath.

"Well, I'll be damned. Smart dog. No wonder it's still alive."

There was no longer any doubt in their minds that the dog understood exactly what the weapon could do, and Jacob decided that he was done playing games. He took a step toward the dog and cocked the hammer.

This time the dog knew to retreat just out of the revolver's range, daring Jacob to take a shot before it finally sauntered off and disappeared out of view. Jacob looked down at his daughter and shoved the gun into his belt, his voice sounding tired.

"Come on, Sara. Let's get the hell out of here before it comes back."

He turned and took a step to leave, but Sara did not move an inch. The girl was suddenly smiling, and he looked over at her and shook his head.

"What now, Sara? Why are you smiling?"

Sara took a deep breath and let it out slowly as she spoke.

"I was just thinking that if those dogs could stay alive for this long, if they could somehow survive the virus and everything else that happened, that means there might be other survivors out there, too. Not just us."

Jacob sighed.

"We haven't seen a single sign of another living human being since we left home, Sara. I wouldn't get your hopes up."

The girl twisted her mouth to one side.

"But don't you think it's possible that we aren't the only ones who survived? Isn't the whole idea, the whole reason we left home, to find other people? Don't you wonder if anyone else is out there?"

Jacob shook his head and started to walk toward the Rover, his eyes focused somewhere in the distance.

"No, Sara, I don't, and there is no point in wondering about something we will probably never know."

Sara just shook her head at him and frowned.

"I'm sorry, but that is where you are wrong again. The whole idea is to wonder, to someday know what's out there. Otherwise, what's the point of even surviving in the first place?"

5

For the next two weeks after the incident with the Bowman and his daughter, Sawyer did little but rest and tend to his wounds, scraping by on almost no water and even less food. The scar on his shoulder had ruptured, and with the wounds to his forearm, head, and at least two broken ribs, he knew he was lucky to be alive. Nevertheless, he also knew that he was literally beginning to starve, and even more dangerous, his thirst was once again growing increasingly severe with each passing day.

It would not be the first time since the blackout that the boy had known what real thirst felt like, his throat burning, lips cracked, his mind playing tricks on him. On each previous occasion, he had somehow found water before it was too late, but it had often come at the cost of another survivor's life. The boy took no pleasure in such facts, and he felt no guilt. It was simply the way it was now, and remorse was a luxury he could not afford.

With no rain in sight, the boy widened his search for both food and water, eating insects and robbing birds' nests, emptying garden hoses and raiding water heaters. He pulled fetid water from toilet tanks and the bottom of swimming pools. He climbed onto roofs and checked the rain gutters, sipping at stagnant puddles, but it was never enough, and with each passing day he was growing more desperate.

One such morning, he awoke to find that his mouth was so dry that he could not swallow, and while he walked through the tall grass with cotton rags tied to his ankles in hopes of collecting a few precious drops of dew, he suddenly heard a quiet voice echoing through the trees. With his heart beginning to race, Sawyer dropped to the ground and peeked his head up above the grass. No more than twenty yards away, a living, breathing human being walked across the open space, the man's face fully bearded, his long hair matted into thick, brown dreadlocks. He was talking to himself in low whispers and looking down, a heavy walking stick held tightly in one hand, a holstered pistol on his right hip. Most importantly, he had several plastic jugs filled with cloudy water slung over one shoulder, and Sawyer could not help but touch his finger to the trigger on the shotgun, a dark smile crossing his face. The boy whispered under his breath.

"Looks like we have another lucky contestant ready to play."

To the boy, it was all a deadly game, and although there was a small part of him that wanted to shout out to the Whispering Man, to believe in the goodness and generosity of others, he knew that was not how the game was played. A much larger part of the boy understood that all that really mattered was that the Whispering Man had water, and the boy was absolutely prepared to kill him in order to get it.

Still, despite his first inclination to rush forward and kill the man before he could leave the clearing, something told the boy to wait, and he kept his distance as he decided to follow instead. The Whispering Man kept true to his moniker as he walked a narrow trail that led out of the foothills, quietly talking to himself the entire way. Eventually, he came to a paved road, and from there the boy watched as the man disappeared into the front doors of a long-abandoned elementary school.

The school itself was half-covered in overgrown bushes and ivy, its roof ringed with a crown of screeching crows, but the boy paid the birds no mind. For several minutes, Sawyer waited outside the playground of the school, deciding what he should do, but the dryness in his throat was unbearable, and the boy realized that there was no reason to wait any longer. It was very simple. The boy needed water, or he would die, and he took a deep breath and looked down at the Mossberg. His voice was raspy and weak.

"Here goes nothing."

With the shotgun in hand, Sawyer sprinted across the playground and pressed his back against the brick wall of the school building. He slid along the wall slowly, ignoring the tiny flakes of brick dust bursting red-orange in the sunlight, his mind focused on the task at hand. He could see that the lock on the entrance nearest to him had been destroyed, and he slowly opened the door and peered into the hall. It was dark and very quiet, and the boy stepped inside and let the door close behind him. For a full minute, he did nothing but remain still in the dark hallway, his ears on, his eyes open. Hearing and seeing nothing, he moved silently down the length of the hallway until it opened into what looked like the main office.

The boy moved slowly through the office, shaking his head in surprise as he looked around the room. Unlike every other building he seemed to come across, the school had completely escaped the fires and the looting that had followed the blackout, and everything was in perfect order. Computers resting on desks, papers neatly stacked in color-coordinated piles, pencils sharpened to a point. It was clear that the teachers and students had planned on returning someday, and the boy frowned in the knowledge that such a future would never come to be.

After another long minute, Sawyer came to the end of the office and listened once again, and this time the sound of muffled whispers came drifting out of the darkness. There was no question that the Whispering Man was close, and Sawyer peered around the corner and saw that there was a door ajar halfway down the next hall. He inched closer. Another murmur. Another muttering. A flicker of candlelight. Sawyer took a deep breath and held it. The Whispering Man was on the other side of the door. The boy knew that it was now or never, and before he could change his mind, Sawyer pushed through the door and leveled the shotgun squarely at the man's chest. The Whispering Man froze, and Sawyer spoke, his voice calmer than he felt inside.

"Don't move, or you're a dead man. Trust me on this one. I'm not bluffing."

The Whispering Man took a step back and stared blankly at Sawyer, one hand dangling at his side, a burning candle held fast in the other. The boy warned him again, this time louder, every nerve ending buzzing, his heart racing.

"I said don't move, man. Stay right where you are, or I'll blow your goddamn head off."

The Whispering Man simply stared at the boy, his weathered face glowing orange in the candlelight. They sat in utter silence for several seconds before a wicked grin began to spread across the man's lips. Sawyer saw the man's free hand begin to slowly move toward the gun on his hip, and the boy shook his head.

"Don't be stupid. I told you already. I'm not bluffing."

The man's long, dirty fingers stopped an inch away from the gun, and he paused for a moment before he spoke, his voice quiet and melodic.

"All right, man. No reason to get excited … the thief he kindly spoke. James Marshall Hendrix. Ever heard of him?"

Sawyer was confused. He took a step forward and squared his shoulders, his voice low, the shotgun held still as he moved into the candlelight.

"I don't know what the hell you're saying but move that hand again and you're a dead man. Last warning."

The Whispering Man appeared unfazed by Sawyer's threats, and he licked his lips and continued to smile as he spoke again.

"Hey, man. Take it easy. All we need is love. John Winston Lennon. James Paul McCartney. Ever heard of them?"

Sawyer took a step closer. Adrenaline had flooded his system, and he could feel the blood rushing in his ears, his finger stroking the trigger.

"Look, I don't know who or what you're talking about. All I want is your water. Tell me where it is."

The man continued to smile.

"Water? How about some wine? I'm just here for the show, man. It's whispered that soon, if we all call the tune, then the piper will lead us to reason. James Patrick Page. Robert Anthony Plant. 'Stairway to Heaven.' Ever heard of it?"

Sawyer was close enough that he could smell the man's unwashed body and rancid breath and see the unhinged look in his eye, and he knew right then that he was not dealing with a sane mind. The boy shook his head, and his green eyes narrowed.

"I won't ask again. Where's the water?"

The look in the boy's eyes was nothing less than frightening, and the Whispering Man's smile finally faded from his lips. He stared at the boy for a few seconds before he spoke.

"You're going to kill me no matter what. Isn't that right, boy?"

Sawyer took one last step forward, the barrel of the shotgun now only an arm's length away from the Whispering Man's face. It was the first thing the man had said that made any sense, and the boy saw no reason to lie to him.

"Depends."

The Whispering Man nodded. For a long moment, there was nothing but silence, but then suddenly the man's eyes narrowed, and he looked up at the boy.

"So, this is the end? My only friend, the end. Of our elaborate plans, the end. I'll never look into your eyes ... again? James Douglas Morrison. Ever heard of him?"

Before the boy could answer, and without as much as another whisper, the man dropped the candle and went for the gun on his hip. He was surprisingly quick, but the boy was quicker, and with a single pull of the trigger and a bright flash of light, the Whispering Man's head was nearly blown clean off his body. For several seconds, the boy did nothing but wait in the dark for the smoke to clear and his ears to stop ringing. Finally, he picked up the candle and opened his backpack.

Crouching in the darkness, with his heart still pumping, the boy pulled out a pinch of steel wool, a scrap of paper, and a single 9-volt battery from his pack. Like many of his possessions, his flashlight and matches had both been lost in the tent fire, but the boy still had a few tricks up his sleeve. Among the many skills his father had taught him, creating fire was among the most useful, but unlike the ancient art of rubbing two sticks together, the method Sawyer planned to use was both modern and quick. The boy had learned that simply touching the live terminals of the battery to the steel wool was enough to heat the fine metal filaments to the point of ignition, and Sawyer had only to add the paper to make a flame. Within moments, the wick was relit, and the boy held the candle high and looked around the room. There was only one thought on his mind, and he voiced it out loud.

"Now, if I had lost my mind and reeked like piss, where would I stash my water?"

Sawyer could see that he was in some type of storage room, and that the space was lined with tall, metal cabinets that reflected dimly in the light of the candle. Although he saw no sign of the water bottles the dead man had been carrying, he was still intrigued. He walked down the first row and found that most of the cabinets were locked, but that each one was labeled. He read them out loud as he walked down the row.

"Paper goods. Tape and glue. Writing utensils. Art supplies."

He turned the corner and continued down the next row.

"P.E. equipment. Gardening. Maintenance. Custodial supplies."

He turned the corner again.

"Emergency supplies. Emergency supplies. Emergency … supplies?"

Sawyer stared at the row of cabinets as his mind began to race, his heart not far behind. He had been so focused on collecting a few gallons of dirty water from the Whispering Man that he had not really considered what else he might find inside the school. But now, as he stared at the locked cabinets, he finally dared to wonder, and Sawyer set the candle on the ground and pulled the crowbar from his backpack. He slipped the edge between the door, and with a quick snap, the lock was broken. The door swung open, and Sawyer stepped back, his mouth falling wide open.

"Holy crap. I don't believe it."

The cabinet was stacked from top to bottom with emergency food rations, the shelves lined with enough freeze-dried meals, canned goods, and powdered milk to feed him for a half-year at least. Sawyer stared ahead as if mesmerized, his face blank as he continued to move down the row. He used the crowbar to pop open the next few cabinets, discovering that each one was stocked with invaluable items: more food, medical supplies, pain meds, tools, search-and-rescue gear—almost everything he could want, except for the one thing he needed most. He tried to swallow, but his throat was too dry, and he shook his head in frustration.

"Really? No goddamn water?"

There was only one cabinet left, but it was already cracked partly open, and Sawyer approached the doors and closed his eyes. He had long ago stopped asking for help from anyone, including God, but at that moment, Sawyer put his hand against the cool metal of the cabinet and looked up as he spoke.

"Please, God, just this once. That's all I'm asking."

With no one else to pray to, and nothing else to lose, he grabbed the handle of the cabinet and swung the door open. Sawyer's heart sank. He had hoped to find shelves full of bottled water, but instead all he could see was stack after stack of unfamiliar white boxes, each one marked with bold blue letters. He reluctantly picked up a box and read the label.

"Aquatabs? What the hell are Aquatabs?"

He picked up the candle and held it close to read the smaller print. He read the first few words, and a sudden chill washed over his body, his voice growing more excited with each word that he read.

"Aquatabs. Water purification tablets. One hundred and sixty-seven milligrams, five hundred-count. Each tablet treats up to six gallons of water. No way."

The boy tore open the box with his teeth, his heart pumping inside his chest. Inside were several silver foil packages, and he ripped one open, taking one of the white tablets between his fingers and holding it up to his nose. The tablet looked like an aspirin and smelled exactly like chlorine bleach, but to Sawyer it was the scent of life, and hot tears began to irrepressibly roll down his face.

It was at that moment that Sawyer truly realized the magnitude of what he had discovered, and for the first time in well over a year, the boy felt true hope. Not only did he now have enough food to potentially last him for years, if he could find a way to collect enough water, he would never go thirsty again. He could not be sure if it was God that answered his prayer, or simple blind luck, but the boy knew better than to tempt fate, and before he went in search of the Whispering man's water, he wiped the tears from his eyes, and smiled up at the heavens.

"Thanks. And yeah, I know. I'm going to owe you for this one."

6

After leaving the dogs behind, Sara and Jacob returned to the Rover and poured the gas into the tank, careful not to spill a single drop. They soon found the highway and began to drive, but they had covered no more than few miles before Jacob was forced to quickly slow down, a dense concentration of abandoned vehicles suddenly blocking the road. He pulled onto the shoulder and continued ahead slowly, squinting through the dirty windshield. Sara rolled down her window and hung her head out as they passed the first few cars.

"What do you see, Sara?"

"I don't know. It looks like there's some type of checkpoint ahead, but just keep on going."

Jacob accelerated and began to weave through the vehicles, but as the checkpoint came into view he slowed again and peered through the windshield.

"What are those, Sara? Are those …?"

Suddenly Sara gasped, and Jacob slammed on the brakes as he realized exactly what they were looking at.

"Holy Mary, mother of God, what in the hell happened here?"

Sara did not answer, and both father and daughter stared ahead as if transfixed. It was like a scene out of terrible nightmare, the road before them littered with hundreds of human bodies, the scattered remains of men, women, and children baking cruelly in the sun. The checkpoint itself was covered in red and black spray paint, and multiple images of ragged-feathered crows were emblazoned on the walls. Above the symbols of the crow, dozens of severed human heads were impaled on tall poles along the fence line, their yellowed teeth poking out of black, lip-less mouths.

They sat idling in silence for only a few seconds before Sara finally looked over at her father and whispered.

"We should go now. Can you please get us out of here?"

Without another word needing to be said, Jacob hit the gas and sped past the bodies and through the barrier, but even as the checkpoint disappeared in the rearview mirror, they both knew it was a place they would never forget.

For the rest of the day, they drove on in complete silence, until the Range Rover began to shudder and lose speed as the engine devoured the last fumes of their gasoline. Jacob wrestled the vehicle to a bumpy stop alongside the highway and looked over at his daughter. She looked up from the map and frowned.

"We're in the middle of nowhere. There's nothing here. The

next town is not for another ten miles at least, and there's no way I'm going back the way we came. What are we going to do now?"

Jacob scowled and looked out the windshield.

"We can walk to the next town. We can search for fuel there."

Sara shook her head.

"You have no idea what you're doing, do you? Why are we even going south in the first place? Nothing you do makes any sense. Do you have any plan at all?"

Jacob squeezed the steering wheel, the veins bulging on his forehead as he turned to Sara.

"Just shut up and get your gear, Sara. We walk for now. That is the plan."

They walked one in front of the other, Jacob pulling a wagon loaded with the last of their supplies, the girl following close behind with the map. They had found that most of the road signs and identifying markers along the highway had been cut down for some reason, and even with the map, the girl could still only guess where they were. They walked in silence until the sun went down, sleeping for only a few hours on the side of the road before they began again. They followed the highway for several miles until they came over a low rise, finally stopping just outside the next town. The town was little more than some trailers, a gas station, a few stores, and a streetlight, and Sara pointed to a small dot on the map and held it up for Jacob to see.

"I think we're right here."

Jacob looked at the map and frowned.

"We should take a look around, at least. Maybe we will get lucky."

Sara began to fold the map when she suddenly thought she heard something. She stopped what she was doing and looked up.

"Do you hear that?"

Jacob stopped and turned, straining his ears. He shook his head.

"I don't hear a single thing, Sara. Come on."

Jacob started to walk away, but Sara did not budge. She closed her eyes. She could hear something for certain now; it was coming from somewhere behind them.

"No, I hear something, for sure. It's like a humming sound. Can't you hear it?"

Jacob stopped. He turned and scowled down at his daughter.

"No, Sara. I told you that I don't hear anything. Now can we please keep moving?"

Suddenly, Sara's eyes grew large, and she spun around and grabbed his hand.

"We need to get off the road. Right now!"

Jacob was confused, but he could hear the panic in her voice, and he let go of the wagon and stepped off the highway.

"What? What is going on, Sara?"

There was no time for the girl to say another word, and before Jacob knew what was happening, she reached up and yanked him down to the ground beside her. Jacob hit the dirt hard and immediately spun to face Sara, his face contorted with confusion, her face white with fear. She looked at him and pressed her finger to her closed lips. It was in that moment of silence that he finally heard it, too: the low rumbling of an engine coming fast. He pressed himself to the earth just as the vehicle raced by, leaving a trail of strange-smelling black smoke that settled all around them. Jacob looked over at Sara, but her eyes were following the truck as it continued down the highway. She spoke quietly, her voice shaky.

"They had to have seen the wagon. What if they come back? We have to hide."

Jacob looked around. There was a row of low-lying bushes behind them. There was a chain-link fence behind the bushes. There was nowhere else for them to go. He tried to sound reassuring.

"Maybe they didn't see it. Maybe they will just keep driving."

Sara nodded hopefully as they watched the truck continue down the highway, and for a moment it looked as if Jacob might indeed be right. He smiled weakly.

"See? They never saw a thing."

He was just about to stand up when the truck suddenly came to a stop in the middle of the road, a black cloud of exhaust momentarily obscuring the vehicle like a ship lost in the fog. Sara bit her lip as the taillights switched from red to white and the truck began to slowly reverse in their direction. Sara grabbed Jacob and pulled him down beside her.

"We have to hide, now!"

They quickly turned and crawled behind the row of bushes that lined the side of the highway, their panicked breaths falling into sync as the truck came to stop directly in front of them. Sara held her nose and tried not to cough as the heavy smell of the truck's exhaust permeated the air around them. Jacob could see that the truck was an older model Ford or Chevy, something American, the exterior a dull, primer gray, a heavy tint on the windows. He pulled the revolver from his waistband and waited, his heart racing as he heard the driver's-side door creak open. Jacob gave Sara a strange look that made her even more frightened than she already was. He dared to whisper in her ear.

"I will not let them take you. Do you understand? Even if I have to do it myself, I will not let them hurt you."

Sara had no way of knowing that her father had a made a promise to himself that he would rather kill his own daughter than allow her to be raped and tortured, and she put her finger to her mouth and whispered.

"What are you talking about? No one is taking me anywhere, just shut up and be quiet."

Sara peered through the bushes and held her breath. She could see the driver of the truck clearly now. He was younger than her father, but his face was equally worn, a patchy beard beneath a thinning head of greasy, black hair. He was carrying a length of pipe in one hand, and Sara noticed that his arms were scarred and inked with tattoos. A faded black AC/DC t-shirt hung loosely from his wiry frame, and the Driver's camouflage pants were adorned with various military-style patches that Sara did not recognize. A shiny silver 9mm pistol was cradled in a leather holster on his right hip, and a large knife hung menacingly on the left. The Driver stepped over and poked at the wagon, tapping the end of the pipe against the metal.

Sara looked over at her father, and for the first time in her life, she saw him begin to panic, his chest heaving, his face flushed. Sara reached out to calm him, but her touch only seemed to make him more apprehensive, and he batted her hand away as he struggled to catch his breath. Sara did not know what else to do, and she watched in disbelief as her father pulled his knees to his chest and tucked his head down, the revolver slowly slipping out of his fingers and falling softly to the leaves beside her.

The contents of the wagon had been secured with a tarp and bungee cords, and the Driver reached down for his knife, the heavy blade slicing through the cords with an audible snap that made Sara flinch. He pulled the tarp away and leaned down to investigate the wagon, a crooked smile spreading across his lips. Sara's eyes narrowed as she noticed the tattoo of the black crow on his arm. It was the same symbol she had seen spray painted on the walls of the checkpoint, and the girl swallowed hard and shuddered.

Inside the small metal wagon were nearly all of their vital supplies: a plastic container three-quarters full of bleach, a dozen sixteen-ounce bottles of water, their sleeping bags, several miscellaneous tools, two pairs of spare shoes, and, of course, all of their food. Sara looked over at the gun resting in the leaves beside her, and she understood that they would die without those supplies. She looked over at Jacob one last time. He was shaking, and it was at that moment that Sara realized just how weak her father truly was. She looked back at the Driver, and seeing no other choice, Sara picked up the gun and stood up from behind the bush. Her voice was barely above a whisper.

"Drop the pipe and back away from my stuff. If you come any closer, I'll shoot."

The Driver's smile instantly fell from his face as he looked up to see a skinny teenage girl pointing a large .38 caliber pistol directly at him, and he let the pipe fall from his hand without her having to say another word. They stood motionless for several seconds before he finally flashed the same crooked smile as before, speaking with a faint accent from somewhere that she could not quite place.

"Just take it easy, sweetheart. Why don't you put the gun down and let me introduce myself? My friends call me Axel. You sure are a pretty little thing. What's your name?"

Sara kept her mouth closed, trying to keep the gun as steady as possible. The Driver looked down to her right and nodded.

"You got a friend down there with ya? Tell 'em it's OK to come on out. It's great to finally run into some decent folks. Heck, I got some good, warm food and clean water in the truck that we can all share."

Sara's lips parted slightly, but she said nothing. She was caught off guard by his friendly demeanor, and the mere mention of warm food made her mouth water. She glanced down at her father, a single line of clear mucus running out of his nose. The sight of Jacob cowering made the girl's blood boil, and she scowled over at the Driver.

"There's no one else. I'm all alone, and if you don't want to die, you need to get back in your truck, and leave it that way."

The man laughed.

"All alone, is that right, sweetheart? Awfully strange for a girl your age to be alive in the first place, much less on the road all alone. It's even stranger for you to be carrying around a pair of men's size-ten shoes in your wagon."

Sara swallowed hard, her heart pounding in her chest. She was feeling a unique mixture of fear and anger like at no other time in her life, and she cocked the hammer back on the Smith and Wesson. The man laughed at her again.

"Now just hold on there a minute, good-lookin'. You got me all wrong. I'm one of the good guys. I don't think a sweetheart like you would really shoot a good guy like me."

He took a step toward her, and Sara stiffened. She wanted to shout, but instead her voice was chillingly quiet, her chin quivering with growing rage.

"I don't care what you think. You need to turn and around and leave. I'm not playing. If you come any closer, I'm going to kill you."

He stopped for moment, the smile no longer matching the look in his eyes.

"OK, all right, no problem. I hear ya loud and clear, doll-face."

His hands dropped down toward his belt, and despite her warning, he took another small step closer. He gave her a creepy, slow-motion wink.

"See, you don't really want to kill me, sweetheart. Now, I have an idea. Why don't you give me the gun, and I promise I won't hurt you?"

Sara shook her head. She was angry at her father for being weak. She was angry at the Driver for laughing at her. She was angry at the world for anything and everything, and that anger had now replaced her fear. The girl gritted her teeth and hissed.

"I have a better idea. Why don't I hang on to the gun, and if you take another step forward, or call me sweetheart one more time, I promise that I will kill you where you stand."

The man smirked at the girl, but his once friendly tone was now absolutely gone.

"I see how it is. But promises or not, we both know that you're not going to do a damn thing, sweetheart. All teenage girls do is break promises. Now why don't you shut that pretty mouth of yours for minute, 'cause I'm taking that gun from you whether you like it or not."

The Driver took a final, defiant step forward, but before he could reach out for the gun, the teenage girl proved the man wrong, and with a single pull of the trigger, Sara kept her promise. The sound of the gun going off in her hand shattered the otherwise still morning air, and as the .38 caliber bullet tore through his chest at nearly point-blank range, the Driver was all but dead even before he hit the ground.

The sky went instantly black as hundreds of crows suddenly took to the air, and Sara stared down at the dead man in disbelief at what she had done. Slowly, she set the gun on the ground. She stepped back and looked down at her father, her mouth open, her eyes wide. Startled out of his stupor, Jacob pulled himself to his feet and stared slack-jawed at the dead man lying a few feet away. The words slowly spilled out of his mouth.

"You killed him?"

Sara took a deep breath and looked over at her father.

"He gave me no choice. I couldn't let him just take our things. We would die."

Jacob did not know what to say, and he watched in silence as Sara walked over and stared down at the Driver's body. A dark pool of blood was still spreading in the dirt below him, and as if she were worried that he would somehow come back to life, Sara bent down and quickly took the dead man's silver Beretta pistol from his belt. She stared down at the body for several seconds, but it was not until she stepped back and saw the man's blood on her shoes that the girl was suddenly struck by the fact that she had just killed another human being. Slowly, she backed away and slumped down beside the still idling truck.

Jacob understood her well enough to leave her alone, and he walked over and picked up the revolver and both of their backpacks. He was walking toward the wagon, still in something of a daze, when suddenly Sara screamed and sprang away from the pickup like a startled cat. Jacob instinctively raised the revolver, but he was not sure where to aim or what to do. Sara slid behind him and pointed at the truck with the dead man's 9mm. She was frantic.

"Something moved inside the truck! I heard it and I felt it—someone or something is in there!"

Jacob gave her a skeptical look, but he regretted it immediately as Sara stared daggers back at him. She was in no mood to be second-guessed again, and she made it perfectly clear to her father.

"Really? You don't believe me? Again? I'm not lying, Jacob. Something is definitely inside that truck."

Jacob looked over at the truck and swallowed hard.

"OK, Sara. I believe you. What do you want me to do about it?"

Sara shouted.

"What do I want you to do about it? I want you to find out what it is, that's what I want you to do about it!"

Jacob looked over at the truck again. It was still idling. The air was thick with the strange-smelling exhaust. He looked over at Sara and then back to the truck.

"Are you sure it was not just the engine knocking?"

Sara's frustration with her father had reached a breaking point, and she had to stop herself from pointing the silver pistol straight at his head to make him understand.

"It wasn't the engine! Are you even listening to me? There is something moving inside the truck! I am one-hundred-percent positive. Do I really have to do everything myself? Are you that useless?"

Jacob bowed his head in shame. He knew he had no choice.

"Fine. I will check it out. I am sure it is nothing."

He took the revolver and approached the truck with caution, slowly closing the distance until he was within a single step of the driver's-side window. He pressed his ear to the window and listened for a few seconds. There was no sound coming from the truck. He looked over at Sara and shrugged. She did not shrug back. Instead, she yelled.

"What are you waiting for? Open the door!"

Jacob ignored her, and instead he bent down and peered through the passenger's-side window, cupping his hands to the glass. At first, he saw nothing out-of-the-ordinary, the front seats empty, the steering column cracked, a few exposed wires protruding from the dash. He was about to back away and tell Sara that she was mistaken when he suddenly caught a flash of movement from just behind the driver's seat. For a good three seconds, he stared inside the cab, and then, suddenly, without a word, he turned and walked away. Sara watched in confusion as he picked up his backpack and slipped it over his shoulders, and she stepped over and stood in front of him.

"What are you doing? You saw something, didn't you? What did you see in there?"

Jacob ignored her and cinched up his pack.

"It's nothing. Time to go, Sara. Grab your pack."

He walked over and tucked the tarp into the sides of the wagon. Sara stood motionless as Jacob grabbed the wagon's handle and looked over at his daughter.

"I said to grab your backpack. We have wasted enough time already. We need to go."

Sara looked at him as if he were from another planet.

"Have you lost your mind? I know something is in there! What did you see inside the truck?"

Jacob waved his hand to dismiss her question.

"Nothing. It's empty, just like I thought. Now get your damn backpack on, Sara. We have been here too long already."

Sara walked over and picked up her pack, but she did not put it on. She looked over at the truck and then to her father. He was already starting to walk away, the wagon creaking behind him. Sara could take it no more.

"What are you doing? You want us to walk? Why wouldn't we take the truck if it's empty? What did you see in there?"

Jacob stopped and hung his head. He knew there was nothing more he could say, and for once he made no effort to continue his lie. He looked down at the bright white traffic line beneath his feet and spoke just loud enough for Sara to hear.

"There is a boy in the truck."

Sara was certain that she had not heard him correctly.

"What did you just say?"

He spoke louder this time, his eyes still fastened to the white line on the ground.

"I said that there is a boy inside the truck."

Sara did not have to hear him say it again, and she ran over to the vehicle, her heart racing. She flung the door wide open and looked inside. Staring up at her from the small compartment just behind the front seat was a boy only a few years younger than herself, his mouth curled into a wretched frown, his bright blue eyes the epitome of fear. Sara gasped.

"Oh my god."

Sara looked back at Jacob and then to the boy. He was shaking, with delicate tears leaving pale, white lines down his dirty face. Sara immediately wanted to reach out to the boy, but she somehow knew better than to move too quickly. Instead, she knelt down and whispered softly to him from outside the cab.

"Hi. My name is Sara. What's your name?"

The boy only stared up at her, his eyes the color of ancient blue ice. She repeated herself again; her voice was quiet and warm.

"It's OK. Don't be scared. I'm Sara. What's your name?"

The boy said nothing, and she thought better than to ask again. Instead, she simply smiled and placed her hand gently on his shoulder.

"You don't have to be scared anymore. You're safe now. I promise you that everything is going to be all right from now on. And you can believe it or not, but I never break a promise."

7

For the next several months, Sawyer stayed at the school, rationing his large cache of food and living in relative comfort. Finding water during the warm summer months was still a challenge, but with the ability to purify almost any amount that he discovered, it was rare that he went thirsty. For the first time since the blackout, he felt a real sense of security, and instead of searching for food each day, he divided his time between reading and exploring the foothills surrounding the school.

The virus had played no favorites, wiping out the human race and all other warm-blooded creatures with magnificent efficiency, and although he still saw no signs of human activity, he had begun to notice small changes as he walked the trails. Everywhere around him were signs of renewal, signs of life. He kept track of what he saw and heard, the chirping of a single ground squirrel somewhere in the brush, the prints of mice in the dirt, the droppings from what looked like a coyote or possibly a dog alongside the trail. Sawyer saw these new signs of life as evidence of healing, of re-growth, and despite the crushing loneliness that he often felt, the boy could not help but smile often.

He had put some time into several projects in and around the school, and with winter fast approaching, his first order of business had been to develop a method of collecting water. It was not rocket science, and the boy had simply rigged the rain gutters on the roof to filter directly into a series of fifty-gallon trashcans that he had set up inside the courtyard of the school. Although the rains were often scattered and anemic even during winter, he knew that with just one good storm he could potentially collect more than three hundred fifty gallons of rainwater, all of which he could easily treat with just a few Aquatabs.

His second order of business was simply to keep himself busy, and the boy taught himself a variety of new skills. Not long after finding the school, Sawyer had come across a small public library that he had somehow missed before, and after only a few minutes of wandering the aisles, he began to realize the potentially tremendous value of what he had discovered. He had brought everything he thought he might use back to the school—detailed city maps, building blueprints, reference books of every kind. He sought out any text related to survival and self-reliance, from Peterson's *Edible Plants* to outdated medical handbooks to a ragged copy of the official *US Army Survival Manual*. He devoured them all.

Once he had read a book, Sawyer was quick to put his knowledge into action, searching for edible plants in the foothills, and setting up simple animal traps around the perimeter of the school. In fact, much of the boy's time became absorbed with fashioning traps of every kind, and before long he was catching a variety of birds and reptiles. On extremely rare occasions, he found his traps sprung by something warm-blooded, and although the tiny, gray-brown field mice and their larger cousins did not amount to much of a meal, the simple fact that he was finding mammals in the area gave him a small feeling of hope.

Although he carried the Mossberg with him at all times, he hunted with only a heavy throwing stick made of eucalyptus or an old sling shot, and within a short time, he had become deadly accurate with both weapons. However, with so few warm-blooded animals in the area, game of any kind besides fowl or reptile was scarce, if not completely nonexistent. Early on, the boy had made one trip to the coast to attempt to fish, but he had found that the ocean had been decimated by the unchecked flow of sewage after the blackout, and the water was noxious with contaminants, the beach littered with dead marine mammals and fish. Still, despite the scarce game in the foothills, Sawyer enjoyed the time he spent hunting most of all, his natural instincts taking over as he silently stalked his prey through the tall grass and trees.

He sometimes ate the lizards and snakes that he was able to catch, but while a fat king snake or a dozen blue-bellies could make a decent barbecue lunch, he much preferred to spend his time hunting birds to supplement his diet. Besides the dove and quail, he sometimes bagged duck and coot, and he learned to soak his catch in simmering water before plucking the feathers, taking his time to clean the birds well before gutting them, always saving the livers, hearts, and gizzards for soup.

Of all the animals that he came across, it was only the crow that he hunted for sport, and since arriving at the school, he had killed them by the dozens. The boy had his own deeply felt reasons for killing the crow, and in one of his books he read about an ingenious bird snare that the Native Americans once used. The design was simple and easy to build, and with dark purpose and satisfaction, Sawyer constructed the trap in the center of the courtyard. With a fall-away perch and rock-weighted snare attached to a single pole, once baited and set, it usually did not take long. Alerted by the frantic and shrill cries of the newly snared crow, Sawyer would arrive with a shovel or club, and a single crushing blow was the best ending the bird could hope for. For the sake of revenge alone, Sawyer could not help but take pleasure in each crow that he put to death, leaving the birds' bloody, black feathers to litter the ground before he tossed their broken bodies into the fire at the end of each day.

As his skill in fashioning traps increased, he soon recognized that such devices could be adapted as defensive measures, as well. On several spots along the trails that led to the school, he built spring spear traps, each one with two fire-hardened spikes ready to impale anyone or anything who was unfortunate enough to disturb the trip line. In another spot, he set to work designing a large deadfall trap. It took him over a full week to put all of the necessary elements into place, but after several failed attempts and considerable effort, Sawyer eventually rested a heavy spruce log on top of the trigger stick and moved quickly away. He was not necessarily looking to kill indiscriminately, but he told himself that any person who approached the school was probably not there to make friends in the first place, and that any animal that sprung the trap would sure as hell make a good meal.

With his traps made, the boy had also cleared a patch of ground in the rear of the school for his first attempt at a vegetable garden. Over time, the boy had collected a considerable number of seed packets, but he was no farmer, and with the repeated infestations of pests and the limited water supply he was willing to share with his garden, his initial attempt at agriculture had not gone well. In the end, his harvest could be described as meager at best, producing only a few withered zucchinis, a handful of shriveled, yellowish carrots, and a single row of pale, shrunken heads of broccoli.

On more than one occasion, he had tried to hook up a light to one of the few functioning solar panels he had come across, but for all his skills, the boy was no techie, and the projects always ended in failure. Nevertheless, the boy had grown accustomed to waking and sleeping with the sun, and he had fallen into a routine of running and working out each morning, hunting and searching for water during the day, and reading and relaxing at night. There was no question that he was getting faster, stronger, and smarter with every passing day; still, the boy found that he was not satisfied, he was not happy. He had come across no other living person since his encounter with the Whispering Man several months prior, and his lonesomeness was growing profound.

He tried to remain positive, but he could no longer deny that his life was only fulfilling in the sense that he was still alive when so many others were not. It had been nearly two years since the virus had wiped the slate clean, and the absolute solitude of his existence was suffocating. Quite often, he would fall asleep with a clear conscience, but wake in the dead of the night in a panic, gasping for air in the darkness, praying for someone to help remove the crushing weight of loneliness that was seated on his chest.

As the seasons changed and the weather began to cool, the boy found himself re-checking traps he knew were empty, spending hours cataloging his supplies for the third and fourth time in a single day, doing everything he could to keep his mind occupied. Even though there was no question that the desire to live was still burning white-hot inside of him, deep down the boy understood that a flame that burned alone, could not burn forever. Truth be told, like so many teenagers before him, Sawyer simply wanted something more than the solitary existence that had been thrust upon him. Although the boy had been forced to become a killer to survive, he was not ready to give up on himself or his fellow man quite yet, even if it meant risking his own life in the venture. Sawyer was determined to prove to himself that he was still worth something to the world, and that somewhere out there in the vast wastelands, there had to be someone else who felt the same goddamn way.

8

Jacob's face was bright red, his hands shaking as he screamed at his daughter.

"Don't even think about it, Sara! We are not taking that boy with us one single step!"

Sara looked over at her father and shook her head as she pulled out a bottle of water. The boy looked down at the silver pistol that Sara had tucked into the front of her jeans and then back to the bottle. She smiled and handed the water to him.

"It's OK. The water's good. Take it."

He took it slowly from her, sniffing the mouth of the bottle before he began to drink, the boy nearly draining the entire container before Jacob stormed over and grabbed it out of his hands. Jacob threw the bottle into the middle of the street and turned to Sara.

"You listen to me, Sara. That is the last thing of ours that you give that boy. We are not running a charity. We are leaving right now, and he stays right where he is. I make the decisions around here, and what I say is final! Do you understand me?"

Sara turned around to face her father, the intensity in her eyes forcing Jacob to take a step back.

"So, it's you that makes all the decisions, is that right? Like your decision to ignore the evacuations and let Mom die? Or how about your decision to just lie there on the ground a few minutes ago and do nothing? I had to kill that man because of you! How many other people have to die because of your decisions?"

Jacob was seething, but he could find no words to defend himself, the truth of what she was saying impossible to deny. Sara kept going.

"You can go ahead and do whatever you want, but I am not leaving this boy behind. You say that you make the decisions? Fine. Either he comes along with us, or you can go on without me. The decision is all yours, Jacob."

Jacob could not believe that Sara would dare to speak to him in that manner, and he became enraged, spit flying from his mouth as he screamed.

"You think that you can talk to me like that? I am your father! I don't give a rat's ass how smart the tests say you are, or if you think you know better than me. That boy is not coming with us, and you are going to learn some respect."

He stomped over toward Sara in a rage, a single fist raised. He was only a step away from her when he suddenly came to a stop, his fist unclenching, his jaw falling open. His daughter had turned to face him, the silver Beretta in one hand and the boy's hand in the other. She looked down at the gun but kept it at her side as she spoke quietly to her father.

"This is your last chance to make the right decision, Jacob. I am not leaving this boy."

Jacob stepped back and stared down at his daughter, a look of both defeat and disgust stamped on his face.

"Fine, Sara, just fine. You win. I hope you are happy, but he's your problem from now on. He's your responsibility, and he takes from your share of the supplies, not mine. Do you understand me?"

Sara tried not to show anything.

"Yes. I understand. He is my responsibility now."

Jacob felt as if he were somehow gaining control over the conversation, and he continued.

"Good, as long as you understand what that means. That means that he drinks from your share of the water. That means he eats whatever you have to give him, because I am not sharing one bite with him. Do you understand?"

Sara slipped the pistol back into her jeans. Her answer was curt but civil.

"I said I understood you the first time. And unless you have anything else for us to argue about, we should probably get our stuff loaded in the truck and get moving. Who knows who might be coming down the highway next."

Jacob had known from the very beginning that once Sara saw the boy, she would never leave him behind, and there was really no point trying to persuade her otherwise. He loaded the last of their supplies into the bed of the pickup and climbed into the driver's seat. Sara turned to say something to him, but before she could open her mouth, Jacob put the truck into gear, the roar of the engine drowning out any attempt she might have made to communicate.

They left the highway as soon as they could, slowly winding their way south. The boy sat in the small area behind the seats and silently stared out of the window as they traveled, his hands clasped at his chest. Sara looked back at him every so often and studied his delicate features—his face was pale and flawless like doll's, his eyes a fathomless, crystal blue. He looked to be no more than thirteen, and his blond hair was dirty and cut in a strange fashion, with long, angular bangs covering one side of his face, the back and sides buzzed close to his head. Sara noticed that the fingernails on one hand had been painted a dull black, and on the same wrist he wore a leather band, a series of teeth marks running along the edge. Sara turned to her father. She looked over at the map resting in his lap. She had already calculated the mileage and memorized the highways and routes that would take them south, but as always, she wanted more information.

"So, where are we going now, exactly?"

Jacob looked over at her and sighed.

"Do we have to have this same conversation again? We are going south, Sara."

"I know that. But where exactly? Why can't you pick a destination, make a plan for once?"

"I do not know, Sara. You want a destination? How about Mexico?"

"Mexico? Why Mexico? How do you know that it's safe for us?"

"I don't know, Sara. And when you say 'us,' whom do you think that includes exactly?"

Sara wrinkled her nose.

"I mean all three of us? I thought we had just decided that."

Jacob scowled into the rearview mirror as he looked back at the boy.

"He is not coming with us all the way to the border, Sara."

"What? You said he could come with us. What are you going to do—just drop him off somewhere on the side of the road?"

Jacob nodded.

"Yes. At some point, that is exactly what I intend to do. We will find a good spot and leave him with some food and water, and then he can fend for himself."

"Are you serious? Look at him. Does it look like he can fend for himself?"

Jacob looked back at the boy again and shook his head. Suddenly, he swerved the truck to the side of road and slammed on the brakes. Sara slid as far over from him as she could and remained stone still, the thick exhaust settling all around them as Jacob turned to face her.

"The boy can go with us only as far as the truck takes us. Not a step farther. I am not going to be responsible for carrying two kids all the way to Mexico once the fuel runs out. This is the last and best deal you are going to get from me. I suggest you take it and be quiet. Do you understand?"

Sara looked back at the boy. He was still looking out the window. She nodded her head in agreement.

"Yes. I understand. Only as far as the truck takes us."

Jacob slammed the shifter into gear and punched the gas.

"Good. Now be quiet and let me drive. We have still got a long way to go."

9

They traveled until just before nightfall, Jacob's eyes tired and blurry as he found a suitable spot to pull over and cut the engine. Once stopped, Sara gave the boy a rag and some water to clean himself, and Jacob wasted no time before checking out the items in the bed of the pickup. The small space had been wedged full, and Jacob found several boxes of dried and canned foodstuffs, a large tent, a working propane stove, a few gallons of fresh water, several boxes of 180-grain cartridges, and a Springfield 30.06 bolt-action rifle, which he immediately slung over his shoulder.

While most of the supplies had an obvious utility, Jacob discovered several things he had not expected. Inside one large box, he found some cans of Drano, a few gallons of commercial-grade antifreeze, and a large container full of what smelled like cooking grease. He could not fathom any reason anyone would need such items, and he was about to pull them out and leave them on the side of the road when he suddenly turned and saw the look on Sara's face.

"What's wrong now?"

The color looked as if it had been drained completely out of the girl's face, her skin momentarily as pale as snow.

"It's the boy. You have to come see."

Jacob followed his daughter around the other side of the truck but had to stop short as he finally set eyes on the boy. He was frighteningly thin, that much was certain, and as Jacob stepped closer, the man let out a gasp.

"Jesus Christ."

A line of what looked like fresh burns was tracked up the inside of one arm, and deep, red lashes ran across the top of his back—his entire body was bruised and scarred. Sara walked back over to her father and whispered, keeping her voice down so that the boy could not overhear.

"Why would anyone do that to him? Why would they hurt him like that?"

Jacob knew that he would never win Father of the Year, but even he could only shake his head and put his hand on Sara's shoulder as he spoke.

"I don't know, Sara. I honestly don't know."

They drove for the next few days without incident, staying off the main roads as much as possible, the boy silent the entire time. Despite their best efforts, they had been able to find only a small amount of viable fuel, and they eventually coasted to a stop behind an old strip mall, the tank finally empty. There were still several hours of light left in the day, and they stepped out of the truck and stretched their legs, the boy barely able to open his eyes in the bright sunlight. He had not spoken a single word the entire trip, and Sara was beginning to understand that something was very different about the boy, a peculiar hollowness hiding behind his blue eyes. She wanted so badly to reach out and hug him, to reassure him that everything would be all right, but Jacob took her by the arm and walked her a few yards away from the truck. His voice was well above a whisper.

"We're out of gas. You know what that means, right?"

"Yes. I know. But you don't have to say it so loudly. He doesn't have to know what is going to happen right now. And I still don't see why he can't just come with us."

"A deal is a deal. You agreed. He stays with us only as far as the truck goes. We cannot take him with us from here. I will not sacrifice our lives for that boy. We barely have enough to eat and drink as it is."

"Please. I'll share my food and water with him. It won't cost you a thing."

"No, Sara. Look at him. He is too weak to travel with us. He will slow us down. You know that. We will leave him whatever supplies we cannot carry with us. There should be enough food and water left over to give him some time to figure things out."

Sara knew that she was not going to get her way this time, but the thought of leaving the boy on his own was unacceptable.

"There has to be a way. Can we at least wait until tomorrow morning?"

Jacob stared at his daughter for a long time. He sighed.

"OK, Sara. He can stay with us until we leave in the morning, but that's it. After that, he is on his own."

They camped beside the truck that night, Jacob separating out the items they planned to take with them the next day by the light of a small fire. While Jacob worked, Sara sat down next to the boy and tried to get him to communicate, but he refused to meet her gaze or speak a single word. After nearly an hour, she gave up on asking him questions, and instead she began to tell him about herself, about her favorite foods, the pet snake she once had, the skiing trip to the mountains she would take each year with her best friend's family. For the first time, it seemed that the boy was paying attention, and as the flames from the campfire began to die down, Sara suddenly broke down, fighting back the tears that were welling in her eyes.

"I don't know if you understand me or not, but the truck is out of gas, and tomorrow we have to start walking. I wish you could come with us, but we have a long way to go, and my father says we can't take you along. I'm so sorry."

The boy looked at her blankly, and Sara put her face in her hands and gave up trying to make him understand. She sat there with her face buried for another minute before she finally looked up and noticed that the boy had stood up and walked over to the bed of the pickup. Sara blinked away her tears and watched with curiosity as the boy returned with a large metal bucket and the container of used cooking oil. He set the items down and went back to the truck, this time returning with another smaller bucket, a funnel, a can of crystallized Drano, and a bottle of antifreeze. Jacob had been collecting wood to throw on the fire, but he soon stopped and sat down beside Sara.

"What the hell is that kid doing? What did you say to him?"

Sara put her palms up.

"I don't really know. I just told him that we had to leave tomorrow."

Jacob rubbed at his beard.

"He is up to something, that is for sure."

Together, they watched as the boy quietly went to work arranging and re-arranging the items he had collected from the truck. For more than a minute, he moved the items in different formations until he seemed pleased, finally setting the bucket down in the center of the fire and filling it with the cooking oil. Jacob walked over to the boy, watching with keen interest as he carefully measured out a portion of antifreeze and slowly poured it into the empty, smaller bucket. Next, the boy took the can of Drano and poured in a small amount of the crystals, stirring the mixture quickly as Jacob looked over at Sara and shrugged in confusion. After another few minutes, the oil began to boil, and the boy pulled the bucket off the fire and left it to cool, once again silent as he worked.

Still watching the boy, Jacob walked back over to Sara and sat down beside her, the girl whispering quietly in his ear.

"I wonder what he's doing?"

Jacob smirked and blew air through his nose.

"I have no idea what it is, and I doubt that he does, either. Regardless, it's getting late. We—meaning you and I—have a lot of ground to cover tomorrow."

Sara knew exactly what he meant, and she could not help herself looking over at the boy, his white-blond hair reflecting orange in the firelight. Jacob stepped in front of her and pointed right at her face.

"Remember the deal, Sara."

Sara squinted and flipped her hair.

"I remember the deal just fine. The problem is that the deal sucks."

Jacob allowed himself a small smile, his face smug.

"Either way, a deal is a deal. The boy stays with the truck. I am going to bed; you should get some sleep, too. We'll leave at dawn. Just me and you. Goodnight, Sara."

Sara pursed her lips together, deciding not to tell her father what kind of night she hoped he would have. She walked over to the boy and sat down next to him beside the fire. He was busy stirring the mixture in the smaller bucket, his eyes red and tearing from the fumes. Sara smiled, her voice soft.

"Goodnight, boy. Good luck doing whatever it is that you're doing. I will see you in the morning to say goodbye, OK? Sweet dreams."

The boy did not bother to look up. He added more Drano to

the mixture and just went on stirring. Sara could only shake her head and walk away.

She slept fitfully that night, her dreams of lost boys, gunshots, and snarling dogs. She awoke a few minutes before dawn to find the boy sitting at the end of her bedroll, his blue eyes bloodshot and tired. She sat straight up in surprise and cleared her throat.

"Um, hi there. Good morning."

To her surprise, the boy suddenly smiled. Sara's mouth fell open. She had not seen the boy smile before, and for a moment, she was not sure if she was still dreaming. She smiled back. He reached out for her hand. It was greasy and black with soot. She took it. She could smell the smoke on his clothes. She knew right then that she was definitely not dreaming, but she stood up and followed him as if she were, not sure exactly what he wanted or where they were going.

The boy let her hand go after only a few steps, and he slowly walked over to the truck, waving for her to follow. Sara rubbed her eyes and yawned. She walked over and noticed that the door to the fuel tank was open, a large, plastic funnel stuffed into the hole. Sara reached out to touch the funnel when the boy appeared beside her holding the metal bucket, the smell of chemicals heavy in the air. Sara backed up and stared in confusion as the boy motioned for her to hold the funnel. It took her a moment to understand what he wanted, and she had to ask to make certain.

"You want me to hold the funnel, so you can pour that stuff in the gas tank?"

The boy nodded his head once, pointing to the bucket and then to the funnel. Sara got the message and shrugged.

"OK, I'll help you. The tank's empty anyway. It's not like we really have anything to lose, right?"

Sara steadied the funnel while the boy lifted the bucket and slowly poured the mixture into the tank, the fumes from the concoction making her eyes burn. Within a few minutes, they had emptied the entire bucket, and the boy stepped back and stared at the girl. He smiled again. Sara knew what he wanted, and she shook her head.

"Are you sure it's not going to explode when I turn the key?"

The boy nodded and gave her a thumbs-up. Sara laughed and opened the driver's-side door. She was more than willing to humor the boy as long as he kept smiling.

"Well, the keys are still in the ignition. If it starts, maybe we can take it for a joyride before my father wakes up."

Sara sat down in the driver's seat with a smile, and she was about to turn the key when the boy suddenly stepped away from the open door. Sara leaned out the door and looked up to see her father marching straight at them, his face contorted and red.

"What the hell are you doing, Sara? You are supposed to be getting ready to go. Get the hell out of the truck."

He looked over at the boy and then down at the empty bucket.

"What happened to that crap he was mixing up last night? I can smell it right now."

Sara stepped out of the truck and stood next to the boy.

"We poured it into the gas tank."

Jacob looked at her with unrestrained displeasure.

"Why the hell would you do that? Are you trying to make the damn truck explode?"

"No. I don't really know. He asked me to help, so I did."

"He asked you to help him? He actually spoke to you? I find that very hard to believe, Sara."

"Well, no, not really. He just pointed, and I knew what he wanted me to do."

Jacob stood and looked at the boy as he considered what Sara had told him, finally turning away and lifting the wagon out of the bed of the truck.

"It doesn't matter anyway. Get your things together and say goodbye if you want. We leave in five minutes."

Sara could not bring herself to look into the boy's eyes until she had shoved the last few items into her pack and swung it up and over her shoulders. Her father's voice echoed from somewhere behind her.

"Let's go, Sara. We need to get moving. Say your goodbyes."

The boy was still standing beside the truck, and she approached slowly, reaching her hand out to his shoulder as she spoke.

"I'm so sorry. I wish you could come with us, but my father says no. Please forgive me."

The boy looked up at her with his huge eyes, and she could not help but look away to save herself from crying. Although they had left the boy with several days' worth of supplies, the girl emptied her backpack of nearly all her food and water and set it on ground. She waited for a second to gather her composure before she could speak.

"Please take this. It's not much, but it's something."

The boy nodded, and Sara let out long sigh.

"Goodbye. I will miss you very much. Good luck, and I promise I won't forget you, even though I guess I'll never know your name."

Sara bent down and kissed him on the forehead, but as she turned to walk away, she heard the slightest sound whisper from the boy's lips. Sara's heart seemed to leap inside her chest, and she leaned in and looked into the boy's crystal-blue eyes.

"What did you just say? Was it your name? It's OK. You can tell me. You can tell me anything."

The boy looked down at his feet. She waited another few seconds, and then she asked him again, her voice calm and soft.

"What is your name? Please tell me your name."

Sara put her hand on his shoulder, and finally the boy lifted his chin and leaned into her ear, his voice barely registering as a whisper.

"M-M-Mason. M-my name is Mason."

Sara threw her arms around the boy and yelled out in excitement.

"Oh my god! Your name is Mason?"

The boy smiled and nodded his head. Sara looked over at her father and yelled again.

"His name is Mason! Did you hear that? His name is Mason!"

Jacob walked over with a frown on his face, pacing slowly as

Sara took the boy's hands and jumped up and down.

"I knew you could talk. I just knew it."

The boy nodded, and she was sure that he was about to say something more when Jacob stepped over and grabbed her by the arm.

"I don't care if he can say one word or a thousand. You said your goodbyes. Now it is time to go."

Sara looked up at her father, the anger in her eyes impossible to ignore. She held tightly to the boy's hand as she spoke.

"No. I changed my mind. I'm not leaving him. You can go on your own. I'm not leaving him—I mean, Mason—behind."

Jacob squeezed Sara's arm in anger, and he twisted her around to face him, spit flying out of his mouth as he shouted.

"You are coming with me right now, even if I have to drag you all the way to Mexico! Let go of that boy and come on!"

Sara tried to twist free, but her father only tightened his grip. She screamed up at him.

"Why are you doing this? Let go of me! I hate you!"

Jacob could no longer control his rage, and he grabbed his daughter with both hands and threw her to the cement. He pulled his belt free and doubled it over in his hands.

"It is about time you learned who is the boss around here, Sara. Maybe a few lessons with my belt will finally do the job."

Jacob raised his arm to strike the girl, but before he could follow through with his threat, he was startled as the engine of the truck suddenly came roaring to life directly behind him, a plume of black smoke spewing from the exhaust. Jacob nearly dropped the belt, and he spun around to see Mason staring at him from the driver's seat. The boy revved the engine one time, loudly, and Sara ran over to the truck. She looked down at the fuel gauge.

"Mason, you did it! The tank is a quarter full! I can't believe it. You did it."

Jacob was right behind her, and he pushed his way into the cab and checked the gauge himself, tapping it several times before standing up and shaking his head. Sara turned around and faced Jacob with a huge smile, both unable and unwilling to hide the pleasure written on her face. Jacob looked down at the boy.

"That mixture you made last night, with the cooking oil, the antifreeze, and the Drano. That is what you put in the tank, right?"

Mason nodded.

"And the truck will run on that? Same as diesel?"

Mason nodded again.

"Do you think you can find more of what you need to make it?"

The boy nodded, and Jacob looked over at Sara. He knew exactly what she was going to say, and the girl turned to him and smirked.

"A deal's a deal. The truck is ready to go, and wherever it goes, Mason goes too. Isn't that right, Jacob?"

He was not sure how Sara had been able to twist his first name into nothing less than a patent insult, but Jacob knew that he had been beat, and he had no more stomach for the fight. With a long sigh, he took off his backpack and dropped it in the back of the truck. He looked over at his daughter.

"Yes, that is right, Sara. A deal is a deal. Now help me get this wagon back in the truck, and let's get moving. We have a long way to go, and we have wasted enough fuel standing here already."

Sara stepped over to the boy and kissed him on the cheek.

"Just like I told you, Mason. If we stick together, everything is going to be all right. I promise."

10

For the next few weeks, they continued to travel south in relative quiet, keeping to backroads and scavenging what they needed along the way. Despite Mason's strange behavior and reluctance to speak, as the boy came out of his shell it soon became abundantly clear that he was no liability. Besides his ability to make fuel, he was equally adept at finding whatever they seemed to need when they needed it most: food, water, shelter. More often than not, it was Mason who provided the group with their only meal of the day, and when pressed by Sara, even Jacob could not deny his worth. Nevertheless, the boy seemed to live inside his own world much of the time, lost in daydreams as they traveled, content to quietly sit by and stare into the distance until he was prompted to do something.

However, there were times when he seemed to lose control of himself, sobbing for no apparent reason, sometimes drawing blood as he scratched at his arms or bit down hard on the back of his hand. While Jacob took little interest in Mason except when he wanted something from the boy, Sara felt extremely protective of him, doing her best to calm and soothe him when he became upset. Sara had found that Mason did not usually like to be touched for any length of time, but he would tolerate her holding him while he cried, the girl stroking his fine blond hair until he was finally able to catch his breath.

Still, the boy was no magician, and despite every effort, and after well over a hundred miles of travel, they finally ran out of fuel for the last time. They all three sat quietly in the truck while it died, and Sara looked up at the tall skyscrapers silhouetted against a red-orange sky while the boy rocked slowly back and forth. Finally, Jacob tapped the fuel gauge with his finger and broke the silence.

"Well, that is it. We are officially empty."

No one said a word. Jacob looked over at the boy and scowled.

"Do you understand? We are out of fuel. The free ride is over."

Sara barely let her father finish speaking before she jumped to the boy's defense.

"Free ride? We wouldn't be anywhere near this far south if it weren't for Mason. If anything, he tried harder than anyone to find more fuel. There is no one to blame for this—not Mason, not me, not even you this time."

Jacob sat in the driver's seat and stared out of the windshield. The veins in his forehead were raised and blue, his jaw clenched. Sara knew that he was thinking about the deal they had made, and she wondered if he would actually be rash enough to bring it up. In Sara's mind, there was no longer any deal, because there was no longer any question as to whom she would decide to travel with if the choice were forced upon her. Jacob knew this just as well, and he looked up at Sara and cleared his throat.

"Fine. I agree. No one is to blame. Now get your gear together. We need to get moving. We may have a very long walk ahead of us."

They kept off the highway as they entered the outskirts of the city, walking slowly, keeping to the backstreets and alleys. For four straight days, they traveled through the massive metropolis in the shadow of skyscrapers, Sara leading the way, the stainless steel 9mm carried openly in her belt. Besides the hundreds of screeching crows that seemed to cover each rooftop, they saw few signs of life, but on more than one occasion, Sara stopped and looked behind them, certain that they were at least being watched, if not followed. Each night, they found a new place to rest, and Mason kept watch until early in the morning while the girl and her father slept, the boy needing little rest to function. They covered no more than a few miles each day, and it was not long before Sara noticed that her father was beginning to limp. They were still another day's walk out of the city, and Sara waited for him to catch up and looked down at his right knee. As badly as she wanted to keep moving, she knew that they needed to take a break.

"Are you OK? You're limping badly, and your knee is like twice the size it should be. I think that we're all tired, and maybe we should find a good place to rest up for a day or two. That would give us a chance to search for some food, at least. What do you think?"

Sara waited, and for once Jacob did not argue.

"Fine. A short break, and we will get moving again tomorrow."

That night, they made camp in the lobby of a tower that touched the sky, and Sara and Mason raced up the stairs until their lungs almost burst. They reached the top floor and stood looking out of a broken penthouse window, the streets dark, the city dead. Sara looked over at the boy.

"Do you ever wonder why we are still here, Mason? Like, why we are still alive? I wonder about things like that all the time. Do you?"

Mason only shook his head and stared into the blackness. Sara kicked a broken piece of glass out of the window with her boot and spoke into the wind.

"Sometimes I think that it is just luck, but other times I'm not so sure. Sometimes it feels like something more than that, like we are still alive for a reason, for a purpose."

She followed the boy's gaze out of the window and shook her head.

"I guess it doesn't really matter. We're out of fuel. We're out of food. We only have a few days' worth of water. I don't know about you, but I have this feeling that we're not going to make it out of the city alive. What do you think, Mason? Do you think we are going to be OK?"

Mason turned to Sara and smiled, but she could see in his eyes that it was a lie. A tiny shiver went down her back as she realized that the boy did not believe that everything was going to be all right, but she smiled anyway and took his hand.

"You shouldn't listen to me. I'm just hungry, and I don't know what I'm saying. It doesn't matter what I think. I promised you that we would be OK, and we're going to be OK. Come on—let's get going. We should probably check on my father."

They returned to the lobby to find Jacob fast asleep, and Mason took watch as the girl curled up in one of the many expensive couches in the lobby lounge and closed her eyes. That night, for the first time in more than a year, she dreamt of her mother. She was sitting at the kitchen table. She was drinking and eating, she was laughing. She was so beautiful, so happy. Sara was there, sitting across from her, but no matter how much she tried, the girl could not move, she could not speak. She could make no contact. When Sara finally awoke the next morning, she was upset by the dream, but more worried to find that Mason was gone. Jacob was already awake, rubbing his sore knee, and she walked over to where he was sitting, a deep scowl etched on his face. She could see that he was in obvious pain, but she tried to be positive.

"So, how is your knee? It looks a little better."

Jacob shrugged and grunted. Another non-response. It was getting old. Sara sighed and decided to change the subject.

"Do you have any idea where Mason might be? I hope he went looking for food, although I wish he would have waited for me. I'm so hungry."

Jacob shrugged again and shook his head. Sara threw her hands up in exasperation.

"It would be really nice if at least one other person around here could talk. Is it so hard for you to answer 'Yes' or 'No' every once in a while? It's like living with two mutes. I might as well be alone. Or dead. In fact, I'm completely certain that dead people have better conversations than I do."

Jacob growled.

"You know what, Sara. You are turning into a moody, ungrateful, little—"

Without warning, and before Jacob could finish his sentence, a single gunshot suddenly shattered the morning air with a deafening crack. A second shot followed immediately after, and Sara stood straight up and looked at her father, the sound of the shots echoing between the buildings. Jacob felt for the .38 in his belt, but it was not there.

"My gun. It's missing."

Sara shook her head. The girl could manage only a single word.

"Mason."

In a flash, Sara turned and ran out of the lobby, the silver semi-automatic already in her hand. She burst into the sunlight and screamed the boy's name, her voice cracking with fear.

"Mason! Where are you? Mason!"

She saw him only a moment later. He was running toward her, carrying a bag in one hand, the .38 revolver in the other. The girl ran up to him, but as soon as he came close, she stopped and gasped. The boy's face and shirt were splattered with blood.

"Oh my god, Mason, what happened? Are you hurt?"

The boy shook his head and opened the bag that he was carrying. It was full of canned food. He smiled. Sara was starving, but at that moment food was the last thing on her mind, and she grabbed his hand and pulled him out of the street.

"I don't care what you found! Whose blood is this? Tell me what happened, Mason! You need to tell me what happened right now!"

The boy looked down and stuttered, the tips of his blond bangs stained pink with blood.

"I'm s-sorry I t-took Jacob's gun. There w-was a man f-following us. I k-killed him, and I t-took his f-food."

He handed her the still-warm .38, and Sara stared at the boy in disbelief. Just then, Jacob came limping out of the building with the rifle in hand. He looked at the blood-splattered boy and stopped short.

"What the hell is going on? Is everything all right, Sara?"

Sara turned to her father and gave him the revolver, her voice trembling.

"No, everything is not all right. There was a man following us, and Mason just killed him. There could be others. We need to get away from here right now."

There was no argument from anyone, and they grabbed their gear and left as fast as they could, putting a considerable distance behind them before Jacob was finally forced to stop, the pain in his knee simply too severe to continue. They made camp in a furniture store on the southern edge of the city and ate a meal for the first time in three days. Afterward, Mason kept first watch from the rooftop of the building while Jacob sat down next to Sara and cleared his throat.

"Do you want to talk about what happened this morning, Sara? You seemed pretty shook up when I found you."

Sara shrugged.

"I'm fine. I was in shock, I think. I didn't know Mason was capable of doing something like that, but I guess I shouldn't be so surprised. It's just the way it is now. Anyway, he doesn't seem fazed at all. I just hope that no one else is following us."

In a rare show of affection, Jacob put his arm around his daughter.

"I agree. But even if they are following us, with the two of you kids on our side, we would give them a run for their money. That is a given."

They left the furniture store the next morning and kept moving south for several days, finally leaving the shadows of the skyscrapers behind. For the next few weeks, they traveled slowly through the burned suburbs and small beachside cities, scavenging among the ashes as they went. It seemed as if the entire area had been put to the torch, and finding food and water was difficult. Not only that, Jacob's knee was a constant concern. There were days where he could walk several miles, but there were others when he could not walk at all, and with the arrival of winter and colder temperatures, their pace had slowed to a crawl.

Nevertheless, they continued to press south, until one morning

Sara realized that her father was in serious discomfort and unable to keep down even the small amount of food they had come across. He told her that he was fine, but by midday, he was vomiting a pale-yellow mess, and it was clear that he was seriously ill. There was a storm on the horizon, and with her father barely able to stand, Sara understood that they needed to find some place to make camp as soon as possible. As the first drops of rain began to fall, she pulled out the map and tapped her finger on a spot not far away from where they stood. She squinted and looked up at Mason.

"Come on. I think I know where we are, and I think I know where to go. It should be just over this hill. Help me get him up."

They slipped their arms underneath Jacob's shoulders and got him to his feet, the color drained from his face. It took them almost an hour, but Sara had been right, and as they crested the hill she could see it—a three-story-tall bell tower standing above a screen of trees. The rain was now coming down steadily, the distant rumble of thunder in the background. Jacob struggled to lift his eyes as they finally came to a stop, a single row of black crows lining the whitewashed wall in front of them. He leaned on Sara and grimaced, his voice strained.

"What is this place? Where the hell are we?"

Sara opened the map and pointed to a small cross that was hidden in plain sight among the intersecting lines of streets and off-ramps. She looked over at Mason and then to her father.

"This place is called the Mission. And until we can get you back on your feet, it's where we'll call home."

11

Sawyer looked up at the dark-gray storm clouds gathering in the sky above and tried not to smile. For the first time in months, it appeared certain that rain was inevitable, and more than anything the boy did not want to jinx the prospect. Despite his supply of purification tablets, the dry summer and autumn had made it difficult to collect much water at all, and he was growing anxious for a fresh supply. Thankfully, by early evening a light rain began to fall, and the boy stood in the courtyard of the school with a wide smile, letting the cool rain soak him to the skin.

He fell asleep that night to the sound of raindrops on the roof, and the next morning he awoke to find that he had collected nearly twenty-five gallons of rainwater. The water inside the barrels was tainted with dirt, pollen, and crow droppings from the roof, and although it was not yet drinkable, the boy was ecstatic nonetheless.

As advertised, the Aquatabs worked quickly, and by midday he had filtered and purified every single drop, and for the first time in almost two years, the boy sat down and drank his fill of cool, clean water.

The storm broke the following day, and although Sawyer was happy for the rain, it was obvious that the school's roof was leaking badly. Sawyer was not sure how to go about fixing the leaks, but he had not been on the roof for more than a few minutes before he looked up and noticed something unexpected in the distance. He stared for a long time at the horizon before his jaw slowly fell open, and he quietly whispered to himself.

"It can't be. Can it?"

The boy had to be sure, and he climbed off the roof only to return with the binoculars minutes later. This time, he looked through the glasses for only a few seconds before he pulled them away. Sawyer shook his head in astonishment. There was no longer any question in his mind. The single plume of gray smoke that he saw rising up from somewhere in the city below was real, not some figment of his imagination, and he tried to contain his excitement. The boy had been yearning for any sign of another living human being for much too long, and finally he had something tangible to go on.

He wasted no time gathering his gear, and, with the shotgun in hand, he began walking out of the foothills in the direction of the smoke. The journey took him the better part of the day, and by the time he reached flat land there was no longer any sign of the smoke. It was curious, but Sawyer still had a general idea of where the smoke had come from, and he kept moving in that direction, crossing over the freeway and heading toward the downtown area of what was once a quiet suburb.

It had been many months since he had last visited the area, and Sawyer was surprised at the changes he now saw. There was no other way to put it. Nature was taking over. The blackened frames of the burned-down shops and restaurants were now strangled green with vines, native plants reclaiming the land like an inevitable tide. Sawyer tried not to think about how easy it had been for nature to sweep humankind aside and start over, and instead he focused on looking for the source of the smoke. He spent the next hour searching without any luck, and in frustration he kicked at the ground and tugged at the bill of his cap.

"No signs of fire. No smoke. No footprints. Nothing at all. What the hell?"

Feeling frustrated, Sawyer backtracked and stood at the top of the street, unsure of which direction to go, when the wind suddenly shifted, and the boy took a deep breath. His eyes suddenly grew big. He spun around and tilted his nose to the sky, inhaling deeply a second time. It was faint, but the smell of smoke was now unmistakable, and the boy smiled brightly and whispered to himself.

"Jackpot."

He chased the faint smell of the smoke as he left downtown and headed north, at least now certain that he was moving in the right direction. With each step he took, the scent seemed to grow stronger, and suddenly he knew exactly where he was headed. There was only one major structure in the area that had not only survived the fires but also stood for hundreds of years, and he wondered why he had not thought of it before.

The boy had only to walk for another few minutes before he saw it, and once he arrived he could not help but stop and stare. Rising above him, the old Spanish Mission sat alone among the charred remnants of other, more modern buildings, and the tall adobe structure reminded the boy of a monolithic headstone in a long-abandoned graveyard. In every direction, he was reminded that nature had reclaimed her throne; tangled bougainvillea vines swarmed over the crumbling outer walls of the church, late-blooming wild poppies burst like tiny suns at his feet, and coastal sage and jimson weed grew in scattered patches through cracks in the pavement.

He advanced toward the Mission slowly, his eyes drawn to the belfry standing some three stories above. Like the surrounding walls, the belfry was filled with crows, and Sawyer curled his mouth into a frown. The boy had grown up hearing stories of how the swallows would return to nest at this very Mission each spring, but he could see with his own eyes that this was no longer true. The swallows' once celebrated perches were now claimed by hundreds of rapacious crows, and the pleasing call of the swallow had been replaced by a cacophony of shrill-toned cries and caws.

To Sawyer, the presence of the crows was like a dark stain on the otherwise beautiful landscape, and he gritted his teeth as the image of his mother's body flashed through his mind, her eyes missing, her face pecked clean, bloodstained beaks screeching above her. He could feel his pulse rising, and he took a calming breath. He knew that he needed to remain focused, and he held no illusions about what he might discover on the other side of the wall. Even if he did find the source of the smoke inside, the odds were that whoever was responsible would likely prove to be a threat, but at this point, even a new enemy would be better than no contact at all.

Sawyer approached the main gate with the hope of gaining easy entry, but he saw immediately that it had been barricaded with heavy timbers. There were gaps in the boards, but they were narrow and awkward, and it seemed impossible that the boy's wide shoulders would fit through. He was rubbing his chin and thinking about walking around to the other side when out of nowhere the wall in front of him suddenly exploded in a cloud of brick and plaster, the sound of the single gunshot reaching his ears at nearly the same moment.

Acting on instinct alone, Sawyer immediately threw himself to the ground and buried his face in the dirt just as another shot came smashing into the wall only inches above his head. Plaster rained down on him as he hugged the ground and tried to think. The main entrance was close, but he doubted that he would be able to squeeze through fast enough. The corner of the wall was farther, at least fifty feet away, but he saw no other option, and he kept his head below the grass and started to crawl forward. Almost immediately, another shot buried itself in the earth only a foot short of his position, and the boy froze.

The shooter was obviously no expert, but as a fourth shot whizzed above his head, the boy knew that he had to move, and he had to do it fast. He released the straps on his pack and let it roll off him. It contained nearly everything that he needed to stay alive, but he told himself he would come back for it, and the boy took a deep breath and let the adrenaline hit him full force.

Almost instantaneously, every muscle in his body felt like it had just been doused in rocket fuel, and the boy opened his eyes and counted down from three.

"Three, two, one. Go."

At the word "go," the boy sprang from the ground and sprinted for the corner, his head down, his legs pumping at full speed. He did not think about being shot. He did not think about the shooter. His only focus was on making it to cover. He bobbed just once and stayed low as he made the turn and kept running, vaguely aware that a final shot had hit the corner of the wall only a split second behind him. Within seconds, he came to a section along the top of the east wall that was missing several rows of bricks. Seeing the opportunity, he quickly pulled himself up and over the wall.

Sawyer dropped into the compound and scanned the courtyard ahead of him, the Mossberg back in his hands almost before he hit the ground. He was not surprised to see the remains of a large fire smoldering in one corner of the compound, and with no obvious threats in front of him, he dashed across the courtyard toward the west wall. He had not seen exactly where the shots had come from, but he had a good idea, and he moved quickly as he scaled the wall and dropped back out onto the sidewalk. He sprinted across the street and past the main entrance, sliding to a stop behind the charred frame of a burned-out sedan.

There were only a few spots where the shooter could have possibly been hiding, and Sawyer focused his eyes on a cluster of dead palms and heavy brush no more than sixty yards away. There was ample cover to his right in the form of some dense, low-lying bushes, and he slipped away from the vehicle quietly, the thought of swift and lethal retribution not far from his mind. He took a wide arc as he came in from the west, his looping run leading to the edge of a small, overgrown park. He waited for only a second before he quickly moved through the park, and where there was no trail to follow, he made his own, pushing forward through the brush with clear purpose of mind.

He emerged from the park and stopped for a few seconds in the rear parking area of what was once a burger joint. Unlike many of the adjacent structures, the building had only been half destroyed in the fires, and the familiar red-and-yellow sign was still standing, the logo left twisted and warped by the flames. The crows scattered as Sawyer entered through a scorched doorframe on the west side of the restaurant and weaved through the melted tables and chairs, tiny particles of dust kicking up around his boots. From the front window, he had a clear line of sight to the cluster of dead palm trees and brush, and he crouched down and began to watch. His body was still buzzing with adrenaline, and he whispered in anticipation.

"Come out, come out, wherever you are."

A moment ticked by, and almost as if they had heard his words, the boy was stunned when two figures suddenly emerged from the brush and came running directly toward his position. He could see right away that one of the runners was clearly carrying a rifle, the other a pistol, and Sawyer pulled the shotgun up to his chest and let a dark smile cross his face. He flipped the safety off and did the math. He had six double-zero shells in the shotgun, two targets coming right at him, and no plans to ask any questions.

He stepped away from the window, and he was about to move into position to engage the targets when something in their movements suddenly made him hesitate. Although their faces were obscured by hoods, the two runners coming at him did not move like men, and Sawyer squinted his eyes and shook his head.

"What the hell? Are those—kids?"

There was no time for him to think about it. The runners came to the edge of the street directly in front of him, and Sawyer pushed through the front door of the restaurant, the shotgun leveled straight at them. The two runners came to an abrupt stop in the middle of the road, and he walked toward them, his voice unnecessarily loud.

"Put your weapons down slowly and back away! Do it slowly. Do it now!"

They hesitated for a moment, but Sawyer took a step closer and growled.

"I said now!"

Without argument, they set the weapons on the ground and stepped back, their hands raised. Sawyer could feel the adrenaline pumping through him, and he tried to stay calm.

"Don't move. Just stay right where you are."

Sawyer looked around expectantly.

"Who else is here with you? Where are they?"

There was no answer. Sawyer swung his head left and right, quickly scanning for signs of the ambush that must be coming.

"Look, I know you two can't be alone. Who else is here with you?"

There was silence for only a moment before a soft face emerged from beneath the hood, the voice feminine but confident.

"You don't have to shout at us. We're not deaf. And it's just the two of us. There is nobody else."

Sawyer stepped back and almost dropped the shotgun. His heart was pounding in his chest. He stammered.

"Uh, you're—um, you're a girl?"

She looked up at him with dark, almond-shaped eyes, her small mouth curled into a frown as she replied sarcastically.

"Good guess, smart guy. Nothing gets by you, does it?"

Sawyer did not know what to say, and for a few seconds he just stared at her. She was barely five feet tall, but he could see that she was close to his age, and not only that, she was strikingly beautiful. Sawyer suddenly felt strangely disoriented as he tried to speak.

"You are, uh, out here all alone? That, um, doesn't seem, um, possible."

She gave him a look and mimicked his voice.

"Why, um, not? Because I'm a girl? Who are you to say what's, um, possible or not?"

For another moment, Sawyer had no idea what to say, but as he looked over at the frightened boy standing next to her, he knew that something was off.

"Look, if you just tell me the truth, this will work out better for everyone. I promise."

At the word "promise," the girl took off her hood and slowly brushed her long, dark hair from her face. She looked up at Sawyer.

"OK. The truth is that there are three of us. My father is sick. I think he might be dying."

The genuine worry in her voice seemed impossible to feign, and Sawyer lowered the shotgun a few inches and stepped closer.

"Your father is sick? Where is he?"

"He's nearby."

The girl could not help but glance in the direction of the Mission. Sawyer took notice.

"I saw a column of smoke this morning. I know it came from inside the Mission. Did you start that fire?"

The girl looked over at the boy.

"Well, yes and no. It was an accident."

Sawyer rubbed at his chin.

"An accident, is that right? Sure it wasn't a trap?"

The girl scoffed at him.

"A trap? What, to catch you? Don't flatter yourself."

Sawyer was not sure that he heard her correctly.

"Wait, what? Look, first, I want to know is why you tried to kill me."

"I didn't try to kill you. Those were warning shots. And besides, we thought you were coming to kill us. That's why you're here, isn't it? To kill us?"

Sawyer was confused.

"Kill you? Look, you tried to kill me! I only came here because I saw the smoke this morning. I didn't know what to expect, but I sure as hell didn't come here to kill some girl and her kid brother."

The girl looked over at the boy again.

"Well, I didn't try to kill you either. And he's not my brother."

She looked up and stared into Sawyer's eyes. Sawyer looked away. He was not sure what to say or do, and he asked the only question he could think of at the moment.

"Fine. I believe you. So, what are your names?"

The girl frowned.

"Why do you want to know our names? What does that have to do with anything?"

"Look, it's not a big deal, I was just wondering."

The girl's eyes narrowed ever so slightly.

"Well, wonder about something else, smart guy."

Sawyer could see that he was losing control of the conversation. He was not thinking straight.

"Never mind. Forget that I even asked. Just come with me. We need to get out of the street. I have some other questions I want to ask you, and I don't have time for this back-and-forth right now."

She cocked her head and smirked up at him.

"You don't have time? That's a joke, right? What, are you going to be late to the prom or something?"

Sawyer felt his face turn red, and he took a step toward the girl and pointed his finger straight at her face.

"You're both coming with me right now, and then you're going to answer every question that I have, do you understand?"

The girl's eyes narrowed even more. No one moved. Sawyer was losing his cool.

"Look, we need to get out of the middle of the street right now! Come with me, now. We are going into the restaurant."

The girl scowled and stepped in front of the boy.

"Yeah, right. Do I look like an idiot? We're not going anywhere with you. Just pretend to be a man and murder us right here, if that's what you're going to do."

Sawyer had reached his limit, and he shoved the shotgun in her face.

"Oh yeah, is that what you want me to do? You really want me to blow your goddamn head off right here, right now? You wouldn't be the first girl I killed."

He held the shotgun steady and waited for another sarcastic reply, but this time it did not come. He looked down at her and saw that the girl's bottom lip was quivering, her eyes misting up with tears. Sawyer looked over at the boy, whose face was pale and stricken with fear. Sawyer lowered the shotgun and shook his head.

"Look, I'm sorry. I shouldn't have said that. I didn't mean it. Just don't cry. I promise I don't want to hurt you. I haven't seen anyone in months, and I just want to ask you some questions, that's it. We just need to get out of the street first. Come on. I will carry the guns for you."

The girl wiped her eyes and nodded. Her voice was barely a whisper.

"OK. Thanks."

Sawyer bent down to pick up the two weapons, and just as he reached out to the ground, the girl's arm snapped forward like a whip, the razor-sharp knife she had somehow concealed in her hand slicing through the front of his sweatshirt from navel to neck. The girl stepped to her left and slashed at him again, but he was just as quick, and he smashed the knife from her hand and landed a heavy, backhanded blow across the side of her head. She crumpled to the ground like a ragdoll, and Sawyer kicked the knife away. He felt his chest to make sure the wound was not serious and saw only a faint line of blood on his palm. He looked over at the boy and swung the shotgun straight at him.

"If I were you, I wouldn't move a muscle."

The boy looked as if he were going to pass out. Sawyer aimed the shotgun away from him.

"Do you have a weapon? Another gun? A knife? Throw it away if you do."

The boy nodded and tossed a knife into the grass behind him. One of his eyelids was twitching uncontrollably. Sawyer realized that he did not want to scare the kid any more than he already had.

"It's all right. I'm not going to hurt you. Just don't move until I tell you, understand?"

The boy nodded again. His eyelid stopped twitching. Sawyer wiped away the blood on his palm and pointed down at the boy, whose large blue eyes were as wide as the sky, his thin fingers clasped white at his chest.

"Just come with me. Any games and you won't like how it turns out. Do you understand what I'm telling you?"

The boy nodded.

"Good. Let's go."

Sawyer stuffed the girl's pistol in his waistband and threw the rifle over his shoulder. He quickly checked the girl for any other weapons before he helped her to her feet and shoved her toward the restaurant. The boy followed, and Sawyer motioned for them both to sit down on the floor. He ejected the single round from the rifle and put it in his pocket. He looked down at the girl. She looked dazed. The side of her face was swollen, and there was a trace of blood in the corner of her mouth. He pulled a rag out of his pocket and tossed it over to the girl.

"You're bleeding."

She picked up the rag and threw it back at him. She pointed to his chest.

"So are you."

Sawyer looked down and inspected the rip in his sweatshirt, running his hand along his chest once again. It was no deeper than a scratch, but he had been careless, that was for sure. He could only marvel at how quickly she had moved and how lucky he had been to escape serious injury.

"It's just a scratch. I think I'll be all right. Thanks for your concern."

He looked up to find that she was staring straight at him, her dark brown eyes burning with a cold hatred. She flashed a fake smile.

"Oh, you're so welcome. Hopefully I will get another chance to show you just how concerned I am about you."

Sawyer ignored her taunt and began asking questions.

"Where did you come from? How did you get here?"

They both stared up at him like he was speaking a foreign language. Sawyer tugged at the bill of the baseball cap and asked again.

"Where are you from? How did you find this place?"

Again, he was met with silence.

"Never mind. Look, you're obviously hungry. If you answer my questions, I have some food I can give you. It's in my backpack. I dropped it over by the entrance to the Mission. You might remember that was when you were trying to kill me a short time ago?"

The girl rolled her eyes. Sawyer continued.

"I'm serious. You can have everything I brought with me. I have enough to share. We can go and get it right now, if you want?"

The boy appeared to be in his own world as he rocked backed

and forth, and the girl seemed to be relishing the opportunity to be difficult. Sawyer was getting nowhere, and he shouted in frustration.

"Can one of you please answer me! I'm offering you several days' worth of good food for answering a few questions! Do you want it or not?"

The girl remained silent, but her eyes betrayed the intense emotions festering just below the surface, and Sawyer instinctively took a step back. He knew right then that she was not going to answer a single question that she did not want to, and he looked toward the door.

"Fine. You don't want my help, and you don't want to answer my questions, that's all right with me. But if I were you, I'd get my sick dad and get the hell out of here as soon as you can. If anyone heard those shots, they'll be here before long."

He turned and began to walk away, but as he reached the back door he suddenly stopped, something inexplicably drawing him back. He spun around and walked back within a few feet of the girl, returning her penetrating stare as he spoke.

"I'll only say this once, so listen to me closely, all right? I'm not here to hurt you. I saw the smoke this morning, and I came down to check it out. That's it. I don't want anything that you have, but I'm taking both of your guns whether you like it or not. I can't have some psychotic girl trying to shoot me in the back when I walk away from here."

The girl snorted. Her voice was cold and condescending.

"Psychotic? Really? Now you've reduced yourself to name calling? So very mature. And again, for the last time, I was not trying to kill you. I missed those shots on purpose. If I wanted you dead, I would have killed you already."

Sawyer opened his mouth, but she did not give him a chance to interject.

"And also, thanks so much for planning to leave us unarmed out here. Real heroic of you. Since we are calling each other names, I think from now on I will just call you 'Hero.' How's that sound? Huh, Hero?"

Sawyer just shook his head.

"Call me whatever you want, but the fact is that the sound of those gunshots you fired will have traveled a long, long way. And like I said, anyone who heard them and anyone who saw that smoke this morning will be coming along real soon, do you understand what I'm saying? And my guess is that whoever they are, they won't be quite as easygoing as I am. So, you can take my advice or leave it, but it's not safe to stay here, especially not for some smartass girl, her supposedly sick father, and a scared kid."

The girl looked like she was about to explode, and he turned away from her, his eyes settling on the figure of the boy. He had stopped rocking, and he was now staring straight at Sawyer. There was something in his pale blue eyes that was unnerving, and Sawyer looked back at the girl and shook his head. He figured he would get the last word in, at the very least.

"And by the way, I'm not leaving you unarmed. Your little

knife you slashed me with is still out in the street. If I were you, I would go get it, and then I would get your ass out of here as fast as possible."

He turned his back to her and started to walk out of the rear of the restaurant. He was just about to step through the door when he heard her say something, her voice suddenly quiet and soft. He could not help but take the bait, and he looked back over his shoulder. He did his best to sound annoyed.

"What was that? Can you speak up? I couldn't hear you."

The girl swallowed hard and cleared her throat. She looked straight into his eyes.

"Earlier, you asked me what my name was. I just thought that it was only fair if I told you before you left."

Sawyer tried to tell himself that he did not care what her name was. She was out of her mind. He wanted to walk away, but he felt as if he were not in control of his own body. He could feel his lips moving. He could hear his own voice speaking.

"Well, what is it?"

The girl tucked her long, brown hair behind one ear and tilted her head to the side.

"Sara. My name is Sara. And this is Mason. It's nice to meet you. What's your name?"

She smiled, and time froze. Sawyer stared at the girl named Sara for several seconds without saying a word, his head spinning. He could not deny it. She was the most beautiful girl he had ever seen in his life. But it did not matter; it was too late. He had already made his decision. He was leaving. He looked over at the boy and then back to Sara. He reminded himself that she had tried to kill him. Not once, but twice. He touched the bill of his baseball hat and nodded over to the girl.

"My name is Sawyer. And I can't say that it was nice to meet you, Sara, but take care of that kid, and best of luck. Believe me, you're going to need it."

12

Without another word said, Sawyer walked out of the restaurant and headed straight to the Mission to collect his backpack. Once there, he knew that in good conscience he could not leave the boy and girl without the means to defend themselves, and he leaned the rifle against the wall and set the pistol on the ground. He also took out a few cans of food and a bottle of water and set them down beside the weapons. He could feel Sara watching him the entire time, and as he turned to walk way, he saw her standing in the doorway, her dark eyes following his every move. Still, Sawyer had made the choice to leave, and he nodded at her one last time before he disappeared into the trees.

Mason walked over and stood beside the girl. She turned her head away from the trees and looked over at the boy.

"Keep on walking, Hero. We'll be just fine on our own. Isn't that right, Mason?"

Mason only looked up at her. He did not say a single word. Sara frowned.

"Oh, you disagree. You think he's our savior? You saw what he did to me, right?"

Mason gave her a look and made his hand into a knife. He ran his thumb from his stomach up to his chest and stuttered.

"Y-you tried to s-s-tab him f-first."

"Whatever. How was I supposed to know he wasn't some homicidal maniac? We both thought that he came here to kill us, remember? I was just trying to protect us."

Mason looked down at the ground and shrugged. Sara shook her head.

"Like I said, whatever. None of this would have even happened if you hadn't started that fire in the first place."

Mason hung his head and turned away. His eyelid began to twitch. The boy had accidentally set a large pile of wood ablaze earlier that morning, and the two had been on edge ever since, even going so far as to set up an ambush for anyone who might come to the main gate, just like Sawyer had done. Sara immediately felt bad about what she had said, and she put her arm around Mason and apologized.

"I'm sorry, Mason. That wasn't fair. I know it was only an accident. I'm just upset, I guess."

Her voice softened, and she held Mason's hand.

"Do you think he was right? Do you think it's really too dangerous for us to stay here? Do you think we should leave?"

Mason could only shrug his shoulders again. Sara sighed and took the boy by the hand.

"Come on, Mason. Let's get back to the Mission. We need to check on my father, and besides, it's not like we have anywhere else to go."

By the time they returned to the Mission, Sawyer was already well over a mile away, crossing the freeway and heading toward the foothills. Night had begun to fall, and with it came a light rain, and Sawyer stopped beneath the awning of a gutted café and pulled a plastic poncho out of his pack. He was about to put it on and continue walking when he stopped and looked back toward the Mission. He could not help but wonder about the beautiful, angry girl and the strange, scared boy. Where had they come from? How had they survived this long? Was the girl's father truly sick and dying? Sawyer shook his head and slipped the poncho back into his pack. No matter how badly he wanted to simply walk away from the situation, there were still too many questions left unanswered, and the boy knew that he was not yet prepared to leave.

That night, he made camp inside the café, his mind racing until well after midnight. He awoke at first light the next day, skipping breakfast and following a winding path back toward the Mission. He did not know why he was going back, or even what he would say or do if he saw her again, but nevertheless he kept walking. He was still a quarter-mile away and thinking about the girl's dark eyes when he suddenly heard a single scream pierce the cold morning air, and the boy momentarily froze where he stood and whispered a name.

"Sara."

This time there was no deep breath or drawn-out countdown, and imagining the worst, Sawyer let the adrenaline hit him like a freight train, dropping his backpack and breaking into a full run.

Afterward, he would not remember running, or scaling the wall, or dropping into the compound, but he would remember the screams. They were coming from a small, detached house just across the courtyard, and he ran straight to it, scattering the crows as he sprinted across the open ground and came to a sliding stop just outside the front door. He reached to open the door, but it was locked, and he threw himself against it two or three times before the frame began to split. He heard her scream again, and with one final surge he lowered his shoulder and burst through the door, losing his balance as he crashed to the ground just inside the entryway.

He was still holding the Mossberg and trying to get to his feet when something heavy and hard smashed against the side of his head. Sawyer rolled away from the blow and tried to raise the shotgun to fire, but the weapon was struck from his hands as he pulled the trigger, the errant blast ripping into the clay tiles of the entryway. He dove to retrieve the shotgun, but before he could close his grip on the weapon, he took another vicious hit to the back of his head and collapsed on the floor, barely conscious.

Suddenly, there was loud popping sound, and for what seemed like a long time afterward, Sawyer hovered on the edge of awareness, everything claustrophobic and black. He could hear a voice calling his name, and he groggily forced himself up on one elbow and dragged his other arm across his face and eyes, his vision stained red with blood. Slowly, he became aware that there was something dark and heavy lying across his legs, and as his vision cleared, he looked down in confusion and mumbled.

"What the hell?"

He rubbed his eyes again and said the same thing one more time, only much louder.

"What the hell!"

Lying across his lap was the body of a dead man, a bullet hole in his forehead, a large portion of the back of his skull blown clean off. Chunks of brain matter and skull fragments were all over the boy, and Sawyer had to fight off the urge to puke as he tried to pull his legs free. Somehow, he managed to roll the body off him, but just as he did, he heard someone clear a throat, and he looked up. Standing just inside the hallway was the girl, her eyes flashing, her wrists wrapped in frayed duct tape. The smoking Beretta pistol was held fast in her hands. Her voice was perfectly calm.

"You OK, Hero?"

Sawyer nodded.

"I think I'm all right. What happened?"

Sara pushed the hair away from her eyes. She looked back toward the front door.

"No time for that now. I'm going to go out there and make sure that there is no one else we need to worry about, but after that, we need to talk, OK?"

Sawyer nodded again, his head muddled and pounding, and she turned and walked out of the room. It took him another minute before he could stand on his own, and he picked up the shotgun and looked down at the dead man on the floor. Sawyer felt the bump on the back of his head and saw that there was blood on his hand. He sighed in confusion.

"Seriously. What the hell just happened?"

Sawyer felt like he needed to sit down, but before he could even find a chair he heard the creeping of light footsteps in the open doorway behind him, and he spun around with the Mossberg in hand. Fortunately, it took him only a moment to recognize Mason's silhouette painted jet black against the morning sun, and Sawyer quickly lowered the weapon and smiled.

"Sorry, buddy. I'm still a little cloudy over here. Your name's Mason, right?"

The boy nodded but never looked up, keeping his eyes on the shotgun as he spoke.

"Sara s-says t-t-to tell you t-to f-follow me. OK?"

It seemed as if the sentence had to be torn from the boy's mouth, each word rattled with anxiety, and Sawyer could see that the boy's confidence was as thin as his body.

"No problem, Mason, I'm right behind you."

Mason offered his version of a half-smile and waved for him to follow, Sawyer doing his best to keep up as the boy ran with notable speed across the dusty ground of the compound. The boy led Sawyer across the courtyard and finally stopped at the porch of a large, two-story house located near the east wall of the property. They had not set foot on the creaky boards of the porch for more than a second before the door suddenly swung open, and Sara grabbed Mason and pulled him inside. She looked over at Sawyer with frustration on her face.

"Hey, Hero, are you just going to stand there or what?"

Sawyer was still literally dazed from the blow to his head, and he was not sure exactly what she wanted him to do. She tapped her foot on the ground.

"Hello? Are you coming in or not?"

Sawyer nodded and stepped inside, his finger instinctively sliding down to the trigger of the Mossberg as he entered the dark room. Sara took notice, and she dropped her hand down to the 9mm on her hip and nodded at the shotgun.

"Take it easy. We just need to talk."

Sawyer took his finger off of the trigger of the shotgun and sat down on a wooden chair that was near the door. He noticed that the boy had disappeared entirely, but that the girl's eyes had never left his face, and he swallowed uncomfortably. Finally, Sara spoke. Her tone was not altogether friendly.

"So, Hero. What are you doing here, exactly?"

Sawyer was puzzled.

"I don't understand. The kid told me to follow him here. He said you told him to come get me."

Sara frowned.

"He's not a kid. He's almost fourteen years old. What are you, barely seventeen?"

Sawyer pictured the boy in his head. He could not have been much more than five feet tall and a hundred and ten pounds with his clothes soaking wet. Sawyer was quite literally a foot taller and more than twice the boy's weight, and he could only shrug and apologize.

"All right. Sorry. He looks younger. And yeah, I'm seventeen."

"Well, you shouldn't assume so much. And just shut up for a second. I'm not asking why you're here in this house. I'm asking you why you came back here to the Mission in the first place. You said you were leaving, and we saw you walk away. You said that you didn't want anything from us. So why did you come back?"

Sawyer sat for moment, contemplating how to answer the girl.

"What I told you was true. I don't want anything from you."

"Then why are you here?"

"I don't know why I came back. I really don't. I heard you screaming, and I just couldn't stop myself. That's the only reason I came over the wall."

Sara put her hands on her hips.

"Is that right? And you came rushing over to save me? Sounds like you're trying to live up to your nickname, huh, Hero? Well, you can go ahead and look for someone else to save, because we don't need your help."

Sawyer shook his head.

"No, that's not it at all. Look, I'm not trying to be a hero, so please stop calling me that. All I know is that I heard you scream, I busted through the door, and next thing I know, I come to and I have some guy with the top of his head blown off lying on top of me."

Sara allowed a small smile to cross her lips.

"So, you don't remember what happened at all?"

"Not really. I guess you must have saved my life?"

Sawyer was not exactly sure, but he thought he saw her eyes brighten a little.

"That's right. I did save your life. So now you owe me."

Sawyer laughed.

"I owe you? You tried to kill me twice just yesterday. Once with a rifle and once with your knife."

She gave him a coy look.

"Don't dwell in the past, Sawyer. That was yesterday. Look, I don't know you, and I don't trust you, but I don't really have any other options right now, so just shut up and listen. Here is the situation."

13

Sara spent the next ten minutes telling him their story, the girl checking the windows every few seconds as she explained how her father had fallen ill and that he was now upstairs with excruciating abdominal pain, mostly incoherent or unconscious. Sawyer listened intently as she explained how they had traveled south for many months but were now out of food, and she feared that her father would not survive long without medicine.

He asked about the smoke signal, and she told him in more detail how Mason had set their entire woodpile on fire by accident, and that they had been out looking for something to eat when they saw Sawyer crossing the freeway from a distance. They had honestly believed that he was coming to kill them, and it had been her idea to set up the ambush. Sara left out the fact that she had never actually fired the rifle before, and she let Sawyer guess if she had really missed on purpose or not.

She told him that after he had walked away yesterday, they ate some of the food he left behind, and for first time in several days they had gone to bed with something in their stomachs. However, in the morning, she had awoken to an unnatural silence inside the Mission, and she knew right away that something was wrong. Sawyer listened intently as the girl detailed exactly what had occurred that morning.

"I told Mason to stay with my father, and I took the pistol and went out the back door. The sun wasn't even up yet, but I noticed that the crows were acting really weird. They were all just sitting there, watching me, and I started to get a really bad feeling. I turned around to go back in the house when suddenly I saw a man with a club standing in front of me. I screamed, but he grabbed me and slammed me down on the ground. I guess I dropped the gun. I just remember not being able to breathe. I tried to yell, but he hit me in the stomach, and then I really couldn't breathe."

Sawyer looked over at Mason.

"What was he doing when all this was going on?"

It looked as if Mason was about to answer, but Sara jumped in to defend the boy.

"Mason was doing exactly what I asked him to do, which was stay by my father's side with the rifle in his hands."

Sawyer nodded, and the girl continued.

"Anyway, he dragged me across the courtyard and into that little house. I tried to fight back, and I did bite him one time really hard on the hand, but he hit me again and taped up my wrists. He threw me on the bed and held the club up like he was going to hit me, but I kicked at him and rolled away off the other side of the bed and slid underneath it. I think he was trying to move the bed, but it was too heavy, and I just kept screaming. Then, I heard him say something, and he ran out of the room. I don't know if he heard you at the door, or saw you coming, or what, but I chewed through the tape as fast as I could. I came down the stairs just as you fired the shotgun into the floor, and I saw him hit you in the back of the head. The pistol was just lying there on the floor. Maybe he dropped it, I don't know. I picked it up. I thought that he was going to kill you, and when he turned around and looked at me, I didn't really think about it. I just pulled the trigger. Just like this."

Sara made her hand into a gun and brought her thumb down like a hammer.

"And his head went 'pop.' Then he was dead. Just like that. His brains were everywhere. But I guess you already know that part of the story firsthand, huh?"

Sara looked down at Sawyer's clothing. His shirt and pants were still wet with flecks of blood and gray matter. He smiled despite the gore.

"Yeah, I guess so."

Sara smiled sweetly back at him.

"Well, it was a good thing I came down when I did. Better his brains splattered on the wall than yours, right?"

Sawyer could only stare at her in awkward silence. He was

stunned by her calmness, at her seeming lack of remorse at killing the man. He knew exactly how she felt, but to see that same coldness in such a beautiful girl sent a chill running down his spine. He swallowed the lump in his throat and nodded.

"Definitely. I guess I do owe you one now, huh?"

Sara nodded.

"Yeah, I guess you do."

The two teens stood staring at each other for an awkward moment before Sara continued.

"Well first, we need to do something about the dead man. Maybe you can help me get rid of the body?"

Sawyer felt the bump on the back of his head and nodded.

"Sure, I can do that. And if you want, maybe I can stick around at least tonight in case anyone else shows up again. Always good to have another set of eyes keeping watch."

She narrowed her eyes.

"Right now, I just need your muscle, not your protection, thanks. Be ready to go in two minutes. I saw a wheelbarrow we can use to move the body. I'll be right back."

Sawyer opened his mouth to answer her, but she had already disappeared out the door. He looked over at Mason and shrugged.

"Is she always like that?"

Mason smiled and nodded. Sawyer smiled back. Two minutes later, Sara came back inside. She turned to Sawyer. She was all business.

"What are you waiting for, Hero? Let's go."

Sawyer followed the girl outside, and they walked over to the small house where the man lay dead inside, the screeching of the crows outside the only sound. Sara set the wheelbarrow down outside and looked over at Sawyer.

"There's a rug on the floor inside. Maybe we can just wrap the body up for now and get it out of the house. We can bury it later. I don't want to leave Mason and my father here alone right now, just in case some other psycho shows up."

Sawyer saw no reason to disagree, and together they rolled the dead man's body inside the rug and dragged him out of the house. While Sara did her best to clean up, Sawyer loaded the body in the wheelbarrow and dumped it in the far corner of the compound. As he walked back to meet up with her, he thought about the girl's sick father, and about the small supply of medicine that he had stashed back at the school. He had no idea if any of the random bottles of pills he had come across could help the man, but even so, he was not prepared to offer them up quite yet.

He found Sara on her knees cleaning up what looked like part of the dead man's skull, and he chose to wait outside until she was done. Once they returned to the main house, the girl went upstairs to tend to her father, and Sawyer ran back down the trail to retrieve his backpack. Upon his return, Sara invited him upstairs, and Sawyer looked on as she wiped her father's brow with a cool washcloth. Even in sleep, the man appeared as if he were in pain, and the girl looked up at Sawyer and sighed.

"Can you believe that before this I've never seen my father sick a single day in my whole life? Even when he was smoking two packs a day and drinking whiskey like water, I can't remember him missing one day of work or skipping one round of golf on the weekend. It's so strange to see him like this now. I feel so helpless."

Sawyer thought about his mother, who had died not long after the blackout. She, too, had once been strong, but in the end, she had not been strong enough, and Sawyer nodded in understanding.

"I know exactly what you mean, and it sucks."

The girl looked up at Sawyer, her voice quiet.

"Did your parents ... um?"

Sawyer knew what she meant without her having to say the word, and he nodded.

"Yeah. I watched my mom die. The virus. It was really quick. Too quick. And I don't really know what happened to my Dad, and to be honest, I don't care. All he cared about was his job, and I hadn't seen him for almost a whole year before the blackout. I'm guessing he's dead like everyone else."

Sara sighed again and looked down at her father.

"Everyone's dead except us, huh? Aren't we the lucky ones?"

Feeling as if they were the only two in on a bad joke, the teens left the sick man upstairs and met up with Mason. Sawyer could not help but notice how rail-thin the boy was, and he opened his pack and set the last of his food on the table. He looked over at Mason and Sara.

"It's not much, but it's the last of the food I brought with me. I want you both to have it."

Without so much as a word, Sara dove right in, ravenously consuming as much of the food as she could. Mason was more reluctant, but he had his share and thanked Sawyer with something that looked like a small smile. After eating, the girl went back to looking after her father, and Sawyer walked the perimeter of the compound, the Mossberg in his hands. As he walked, it did not take long for him to realize that the Mission was an ideal place to settle in many ways. Not only was it near one of the only seasonally running creeks in the area, it was also surrounded by hundreds of old-growth trees, as well as a solid, ten-foot-high wall. The multiple buildings, the guest quarters, and the two houses inside the compound were all in decent condition. Even the old stone church was still standing, its white adobe walls rising up to the sky.

He stayed inside the compound keeping watch for the remainder of the day, and as the sun began to dip below the horizon, Sawyer returned to the main house and found the girl waiting for him downstairs. Before she could say a word, he once again offered to keep watch during the night.

"Look, I get that it's hard to trust someone you just met, but I can keep an eye on things while everyone else gets some rest tonight. It's up to you, but I do owe you for saving my life. If there's no problems by tomorrow, I'd say you're in the clear, and I can go on my way—if you want me to."

Sara looked up at Sawyer and studied the boy's face for several seconds before she spoke.

"Thanks, but no thanks. Mason can take first watch. He doesn't sleep much anyway. And besides, trusting people isn't really my thing."

Sawyer nodded at the girl and took a step toward the door.

"I get it. Me neither. Well, good luck. Hope it all works out for you."

Sara stepped over and blocked the door.

"Hold on. You're giving up that easy? Why don't you at least give me one good reason why I should trust you, Sawyer?"

Sawyer was surprised by her directness, but he looked her square in the eyes and answered truthfully and without hesitation.

"Well, just like you, I've lost almost everything, and all I really have left in this world is my word, so, for whatever it's worth, I give you my word that you can trust me. And if that's not enough, you can believe me when I say that you don't seem like the kind of girl I would want to piss off. I already saw what happened to the last guy who did. Parts of his brain are still stuck to my pants."

Sara tried not to smile.

"OK, Hero. Good points. You've sold me. You can stay outside on the porch and keep watch tonight. But just for tonight. And be sure to give a yell if you need me to come save you again."

With a flip of her hair, Sara turned and went back upstairs, leaving Sawyer with a small smile on his lips as he watched her go. He found an old blanket and set himself up in a chair on the porch, staying awake through the night just as he said he would. There was no sign of any danger, and at dawn he stretched his legs and walked a circle around the outside of the Mission compound, happy for a chance to relieve his bladder. The new sun was only minutes old, and Sawyer had barely zipped up his jeans when he saw something out of the corner of his eye that made his heart race. A minute later, he came running back into the main house, and he gently woke Sara from her sleep. He said her name softly and kept a comfortable distance until she opened her eyes. He smiled widely, his excitement evident.

"Come on. Follow me. We have to hurry."

Sara sat up and looked around. Mason was sitting a few feet away, staring blankly out of the window. She whispered to Sawyer.

"What's going on? Why are you smiling like an idiot?"

He faked a frown.

"Is that better? Come on. Hurry up and get ready."

Sara rolled her eyes at him, tossed off her blanket, and stood up. She was still wearing her boots and clothes. She grabbed the 9mm off the table and tucked it into her belt. She put her hands on her hips and stared at him.

"Ready when you are."

Sawyer had expected it to take the girl much longer to get prepared, and he was not unimpressed. Sara noticed.

"What, did you think I needed to put my makeup on or something? Not every girl takes an hour to get ready, Hero, so tell me what's going on."

Sawyer shook his head and jokingly scowled. He whispered through gritted teeth.

"It's a surprise, and please don't call me Hero. It's really annoying and it would be great if you would just follow me and be quiet for like a half-second."

He ran his finger across his lips like a zipper and pretended to throw away the key. Sara tried not to laugh, and instead she whispered quietly.

"OK, Sawyer. I'll be quiet."

The boy waved his hand for her to follow, and he took off in the direction he had just come from, Sara tracking him step by step as they slipped out of the compound and into the trees. The girl moved so swiftly that it seemed as if her feet did not touch the ground, and Sawyer had to move at top speed just to make sure he was still a half-step ahead of her. They ran for about a minute before he stopped them just before a break in the trees, and he handed Sara the binoculars and pointed toward a small patch of grass not more than twenty yards away.

"There. In the grass, straight ahead."

At first, she could see nothing but a blur, but as she twisted the focus on the binoculars, suddenly she could not believe her eyes. For the first time in many months, she was looking at the unmistakable form of a live, wild rabbit. She scanned left and right. Not just one rabbit, but two, actual, real, living, moving rabbits. She looked over at Sawyer and smiled, her brown eyes sparkling, her whisper nearly lost in the light morning breeze.

"I can't believe it."

She tried not to show her excitement as she lowered the binoculars and pulled the pistol from her hip, but Sawyer shook his head and waved his hand for her to put the weapon away. He tapped his finger to his ear, and she understood; then he smiled and pulled the heavy throwing stick from his pack. It was slightly curved and had been sanded smooth. He leaned his head next to hers and whispered into her ear.

"Just watch."

Making as little noise as possible, Sawyer crept slowly on his elbows and knees in the direction of the rabbits, his eyes just above the grass, his breathing a slow and controlled rhythm. He took his time and moved with painstaking deliberateness, the sounds of his movements no louder than the wind through the trees.

It took him nearly three full minutes to get into position, but as soon as he was in range, he sprang to one knee and let the throwing stick fly from his hand in one swift motion. Sara watched awestruck as the weapon toppled end over end for a dozen yards before finally smashing into the side of the nearest rabbit, the animal's fragile spine instantly snapped in two. Within a second, Sawyer was up and moving to collect the still-twitching body with one hand, the knife in his other hand slipping effortlessly beneath the animal's warm fur. He held the rabbit up and looked back at Sara, and at that moment he thought that the smile on her face was quite possibly the best thing that he had ever seen in his life.

They brought the rabbit back to the Mission, and Sawyer skinned and dressed the animal, the girl transfixed as she stood behind and watched every step. He dug a hole and got a small fire going in the bottom of the pit, spearing the rabbit from end to end and letting it roast until the skin was charred and black. He knew from the few rabbits he had killed that the meat inside the skin would still be moist and delicious, and he took the rabbit out of the fire and sliced off a small chunk of steaming-hot meat. He let it cool for a second and offered the first bite to Sara.

Sara blew on the meat, then let it rest on her tongue for a moment before she began to chew. Sawyer waited.

"So, how does it taste?"

Sara kept chewing slowly, and then finally she smiled.

"Indescribable. It's about the best thing I've tasted in months."

Sawyer offered the next bite to Mason, and this time the boy was not shy, the mere smell of the cooked meat intoxicating. After they ate, Sawyer used a tin cup to boil up a rich broth of rabbit meat, and he watched as the girl ladled small sips of broth into the mouth of her semi-conscious father. Sara was relieved that he was able to keep the broth down, but his fever was sky-high, and he was still mostly incoherent with pain. She turned to Sawyer and shook her head.

"He's going to die, isn't he?"

Sawyer shook his head. He had made a decision.

"No. He's not going to die. Look, Sara, I should have told you this sooner, but I have some antibiotics and other medicine back where I stay. I can't promise that it will help, but if you think you are safe here for a day, if I left right now, I can get there before nightfall, and I could be back by midday tomorrow."

Sara stared at him for several seconds, and then she frowned.

"So, you're leaving us?"

Sawyer shook his head in confusion.

"Yes. I mean, no, I am leaving, but I said I could be back by tomorrow."

Sara turned and looked away from him. The tone of her voice was suddenly cold and distant.

"Fine. That sounds like a good idea. Good luck."

Sawyer stood and stared at the back of her head. For once, he understood what she was thinking. She did not believe that he would return.

"I'm not lying to you, Sara. I'm going to come back. I promise."

Sara slowly turned and walked over to him. She stood very close. Her voice was now soft.

"It's OK. I totally understand if you want to walk away. You don't owe us anything, Sawyer. You may promise that you're coming back, and I appreciate that, but the real question is, why would you?"

Sawyer looked into Sara's eyes, and at that moment he realized that there was no longer any reason to hold back. He could feel his heart pounding in his chest as the adrenaline flooded his system, but this time he did not try and slow it down. He reached down and held the girl's hands.

"I know that I don't owe you anything, Sara, but there is one very good reason why I'll come back, and I think you might know what that is."

Sara squeezed his hands and blushed. She came closer to him.

She bit her bottom lip and whispered.

"I have no idea what you are talking about. What very good reason might there be?"

Sawyer was far from experienced with the opposite sex, but he was no fool, and he drew her close, their faces only inches apart. She was breathing hard. He was holding his breath. He smiled and whispered into her ear.

"Maybe this will answer your question?"

He closed his eyes and leaned in, but just as he was about to press his lips to hers, Sara shoved him away and raised one eyebrow.

"Nice try, Hero, but I don't make out with every shotgun-wielding boy that I run into, even if it is the end of the world, and even if I do think he's cute."

Sawyer's pride was briefly wounded, but he looked over at Sara with a sheepish smile on his face.

"So, you think I'm cute?"

Sara smiled coyly and shook her head.

"Did I say that? I don't remember. I think you're maybe hearing things? Anyway, it would be really great of you to do this for my father, and for me. Do you think you will really be back by tomorrow?"

Sawyer nodded.

"Even if it's the last thing I do. I promise."

Sara's eyes lit up, and before the boy knew what was happening, she stood up on her tiptoes and quickly kissed him on the lips. Sara stepped back and smiled. "OK, then. It's settled. I'll see you tomorrow, Hero. Don't be too long. I'll be waiting."

Without saying another word, the girl turned and walked away, and at that exact moment in time Sawyer was certain of only two things. One, his heart might possibly explode out of his chest at any moment, and two, no matter what happened from that kiss onward, he was now in way, way over his head.

14

The school was nearly a full day's hike to the east, and even walking at a brisk pace Sawyer did not reach the campus until just before sundown, arriving tired and hungry. For at least a few minutes while he ate, he tried not to think about the girl, or the sick man, or the strange boy, but it was almost impossible. He told himself that he was not obligated to return if he changed his mind, that they would be fine without him, but he knew that he was telling himself a lie. Like a moth to the flame, he felt irresistibly drawn to the girl, and he pictured the soft curves of her face and body as he found his bed and fell into a deep sleep.

That night, his dreams were connected only in the sense that Sara was in each one, her dark eyes smiling at him as if she knew something that he did not. In one dream, he watched from below as she floated over the whitewashed walls of the Mission like an apparition. In another, they were standing side by side, an open grave at their feet, a crown of black feathers ringing her head. In still another, she was calling for him from a distance, her voice trailing off in a dense fog. When he awoke before dawn, her face was still smoldering in his mind, her hair, her lips, her brown eyes burning with unmatched intensity, and he knew that there was no chance that he would go back on his promise.

As the day broke, he loaded a large cart with supplies, bringing everything that he thought they would need—food, water, tools, camping gear, rope, blankets, seeds, fishing poles, tackle, water-purification tablets, and all the antibiotics and medication that he had. Having managed to pack a surprising number of items into the cart, Sawyer began the long trek back to the Mission, making good time as he traveled downhill. Still, while he walked he could not help but get the feeling that he was somehow being watched, and he often stopped to look behind him, and even up to the sky.

After many hours, he finally returned to the Mission, and Mason met him at the side entrance. The blond-haired boy was smiling widely. Sawyer smiled back.

"Hey, Mason. Good to see you, buddy. I could use some of your muscles over here. This wagon is heavy."

Mason ran over and stood in front of Sawyer. He was beaming.

"Hi, Sawyer. Y-you came back. I knew y-you would."

"A promise is a promise. Where's Sara?"

"She went h-hunting. She made a th-throwing stick, just like yours."

"How is her father? Is he doing any better?"

Mason suddenly frowned. His blue eyes were no longer sparkling. He shook his head and said only one word.

"No."

Sawyer could feel Mason's pain, and he reached out to put his hand on the boy's shoulder. Like a frightened cat, Mason instinctively jumped back and reached for the knife on his hip. Sawyer put his hands up and then took a step back.

"Whoa, buddy. My bad. Everything's cool."

Mason looked ashamed and pulled his hand away from the knife. His voice was barely audible.

"S-sorry, Sawyer."

Sawyer knew what it was like to always be on edge, and he smiled and pointed over at the cart.

"No worries, Mason. I get it. But I could still use some help."

Mason managed his version of an awkward smile, and together they maneuvered the cart inside the compound and loaded the food and other supplies into one of the small rooms running along the west wall. The two worked without a word between them, and for the first time Sawyer noticed the many scars and burn marks on the younger boy's arms. He was not sure what to think about such obvious signs of abuse, and he did his best not to stare. Once they had unloaded the wagon, Sawyer collected all of the medication he had brought and followed the boy to Jacob's room on the second floor of the main house.

Sawyer took one look and could see that Jacob's condition had indeed worsened overnight, his face drawn and pale, his eyes sunken deep in his head. The man's breathing was rapid and shallow, and Sawyer looked over at Mason.

"Did Sara say when she'll be back? I don't want to give him anything without her being here, but I'm not sure he's got much time."

Mason shrugged.

"I-I don't know. She didn't s-say."

Sawyer looked down at Jacob. He could see that the man was literally dying before his eyes.

"Screw it. We can't wait for her. We have to give him these antibiotics now."

Sawyer pulled an orange bottle from the medicine bag and held it up. Inside were at least two dozen fat, white pills. He shook out a pair of the pills, crushed them, and let them dissolve in a cup of water. He grabbed two other bottles of different pills and set them on the nightstand. Sawyer handed Mason the cup.

"See if you can get him to keep this down. If you can, do the same thing with the other pills. I'll be back soon. I'm going to go find Sara."

Sawyer went straight to the spot where they had hunted rabbit the day before and found Sara practicing with her own throwing stick. He knew better than to sneak up on her, and he gave a short whistle and waved. Sara tucked the stick away and came over to Sawyer. He smiled.

"Any luck?"

She shook her head.

"Nope."

"Bummer."

"Yup."

Sawyer looked at the ground.

"So, anyway—I kept my promise. I came back."

Sara looked at her boots.

"Yup, just like you said you would."

Sawyer paused.

"Is that all right with you?"

Sara looked up.

"Yes. I just wasn't sure you really would, you know. Most people break more promises than they keep."

"Well, I think you'll find out that I'm not like most people."

Sara smiled.

"Oh, you're not, huh? Why is that?"

Sawyer smiled back.

"Well, most people are dead, so I have that going for me."

They both laughed, but it was not for very long. Sawyer pointed a thumb back toward the Mission.

"We should get back. I brought the medicine for your father. Mason and I gave him a dose already, hope that's all right. I also brought a whole cart of food and other things that we—I mean you—might need."

Sara held back a smile.

"So, does that mean that you plan to stay with us for a while, Hero?"

"I came back, didn't I?"

"Yes, you did. But are you going to stay?"

Sawyer took her hand.

"Only on one condition."

Sara bit her bottom lip.

"And what might that be?"

The boy grinned.

"That you please stop calling me Hero all of the time. I have a name, you know."

Sara threw her head back and laughed.

"OK, fair enough, Sawyer. I'll only call you Hero for some of the time, but only if that's what you really want?"

"Yes, that is what I really want. But as for me sticking around, that's up to you."

Sara just smiled. She was not ready to have that conversation quite yet, and she quickly changed the subject.

"So, you said you brought some food?"

Sawyer got the message and nodded.

"Yeah, you hungry? I can get a fire going right now if you want. I can heat up a mean can of chicken noodle soup."

Sara was smiling, but something about her face changed.

"How much food did you bring? I mean, how long will it last?"

Sawyer shrugged.

"It's hard to say. It depends on a lot of things. I would guess maybe a month or two."

"So, is that how long you plan to stay here? A month or two? Then what—you go back to wherever it is you came from?"

Sawyer stared at Sara and thought about what he should say.

"I really don't know. It depends on a lot of things."

"Name one thing it depends on."

Sawyer finally pulled his gaze from the ground and looked straight into her eyes.

"Fine. It all depends on you. Is that what you want me to say?"

Sara walked over to Sawyer and looked deep into his eyes. She whispered.

"Yes, that is what I wanted you to say. And I want to say thanks for coming back, Sawyer. Thanks for everything so far."

Sawyer smiled.

"You're welcome."

Before he could say anything more, the girl pulled him close and kissed him softly on the lips. Then, just as quickly, she pushed him away and smiled.

"Now, will you please go and cook me some soup? I'm absolutely starving."

15

Sawyer and Sara returned to the Mission walking side by side, but within seconds of entering the compound, Sara looked over at Sawyer and wrinkled her nose.

"What is that smell? And what's up with the crows?"

The putrid smell of death was heavy in the air, and Sawyer took one look at the mass of crows hovering in the corner of the compound and suddenly remembered the corpse he had dumped two days before. He looked over at the girl.

"Why don't you go check on your father, and I'll see what's going on?"

He left Sara and took off running toward the far corner, the sickening smell and the shrieking of the crows growing stronger with each step. He rounded the corner of the last structure blocking his view and stopped cold, the scene unfolding before him like something straight out of a horror film. The crows had somehow managed to expose the man's dead body, and the hovering swarm above it looked like a single, malevolent organism, the birds lost in a feeding frenzy as they tore at the flesh of the mutilated corpse.

The boy had seen it all before, on the day of his mother's death, and he could picture it as if it were yesterday. Her body left unguarded for only a few minutes. The sound of the crows' screeching. The sight of her face. Her eyes gone. Her lips missing. The crows taunting him from the trees above, beaks still wet with blood. To Sawyer, it was as if it were happening all over again, and in a rage, he took hold of the barrel of the shotgun and let the adrenaline hit him full force.

All Sawyer could see was red and death and destruction, and he rushed into the mass of feathered bodies as if possessed. He swung the shotgun with deadly accuracy, the heavy stock crushing the life out of any crow within range of his swing, his boots kicking and smashing until the ground was littered with the bloody feathers of dead crow. It was all over in less than a minute, and the surviving crows took to the air and hovered above him, their cries echoing across the compound. Sawyer bared his teeth and shouted back at the birds, the crows going mad as he slammed his heel down and smashed the head of one of their wounded comrades.

Still glaring upward, he crushed the life out of several other injured birds before he finally wiped the blood off the Mossberg and slipped it over his shoulder. He looked down at the dead man and shook his head. The body was in a horrific state: the eyes, nose, lips, and ears torn from what was left of the head, the stomach cavity ripped open, the man's entrails pulled in every direction like strings of wet confetti on the ground. Several small, pink, unidentifiable body parts lay spread around the man, and Sawyer grimaced as he noticed a strip of hair-covered scalp still stuck in the beak of a dead crow near the body. He kicked the dead crow as hard as he could and yelled into the sky.

"Goddamn it! Goddamn it all!"

Sawyer suddenly felt eyes watching him, and he turned to see that Sara and Mason were standing only a few feet behind him. Sawyer's face and hands were splattered with blood, and there was a mixture of anger and embarrassment on his face. He looked over at Sara.

"How long have you been standing there?"

Sara shrugged.

"Long enough, I guess. Are you OK?"

Sawyer shook his head.

"No. I'm not OK. But it's a long story, and I really don't want to talk about it."

Sawyer walked past them and headed back toward the main house. He sat down on the porch and looked down at his feet, a few bloody feathers still pasted to his boots. Sara walked over and sat down beside him. They rested in uncomfortable silence for a few moments before she finally spoke, a hint of sarcasm in her voice.

"So, I take it that you don't like crows very much, huh?"

Sawyer gave her a look that said he was not in the mood to talk, and Sara took the hint. She smiled sweetly.

"It's OK. I don't like them much, either. I mean, of all the animals, it had to be the crows that take over the world? I guess now we know that we have at least one more thing in common."

Sawyer smiled weakly, and he turned and faced her. He was not yet prepared to talk about his mother's death, or what the crows had done to her, and he wanted to change the subject.

"So, how is your father? Was he able to keep those pills down?"

"Yes. Hopefully they will do him some good. Thanks so much again."

Sawyer sighed and pulled a bloody feather from the sole of his boot.

"You're welcome. Look, I didn't know that you were both watching. I kind of lost control for a minute there. Will that upset Mason?"

Sara shrugged.

"You never know with him. He never talks about it, but I think he came from a pretty messed up situation. I'm guessing he's seen a lot worse. To be honest, it seemed like he kind of liked it."

Sawyer raised his eyebrows.

"He liked it?"

Sara shook her head.

"I think so. And you know what is even more strange?"

"What's that?"

The girl pulled a second bloody feather from the bottom of Sawyer's boot and held it up in the sunlight.

"In a weird way, I think I kind of liked it, too."

There was a long pause. Sawyer was at a loss for words. Sara was not.

"Anyway, I think we should probably bury that body soon, don't you think?"

Sawyer nodded.

"Yeah, I can take care of it."

Sara shook her head.

"I can help. I know where a few shovels are."

Sawyer looked surprised.

"Are you sure? You saw the body, right? He's not a pretty sight. You may want to sit this one out."

Sara laughed.

"Thanks for the advice, but he wasn't a pretty sight even before I blew his brains out; I think I'll be just fine."

The few crows that were bold enough to remain near the body quickly scattered into the sky as soon as Sawyer came near, their high-pitched alarm calls spreading the word of his return. He knew from experience that crows had the rare ability not only to identify individual people on sight but also to communicate if that individual was a known threat or not, and he could only assume that he was now number one on their enemies list.

Sara sent Mason off to retrieve the shovels, and together, Sawyer and the girl picked up the body—and the pieces surrounding it—and dropped it all into the wheelbarrow. Mason stayed behind to watch over Jacob, and once outside the walls it was not long before

Sawyer and Sara found a suitable patch of earth to dig a grave. Sawyer had barely lowered the body to the ground and picked up a shovel when he heard the crows cawing overhead, and he could not help but scowl. Sara looked up at the circling birds and shook her head.

"Crows are one of the most intelligent birds. Have they really gone so insane to come after the body with us right here?"

Sawyer shrugged.

"I think that the taste of meat has made them lose their minds. Let's see what they do if we walk a few feet away."

A small cluster of crows had followed them from the Mission, and almost as soon as Sawyer and Sara stepped back, the birds descended upon the body like a black cloud. Sawyer was ready with the shovel, and he leaned in and crushed the first bird to come within his reach, the spade swinging freely as he sent several more of the black birds to their deaths. Sawyer waited until the remaining crows gave up and flew off before he turned to Sara and smiled. He pointed to a wounded crow that was fluttering weakly on the ground only a few steps away from her.

"I think I've reached my crow-killing limit for the day. Maybe you can take care of that last one for us."

She looked down at the crow and then up to Sawyer.

"My pleasure."

Sara lifted the shovel above the wounded crow, and with a look of serenity on her face, she brought the blade straight down with surprising force, severing the crow's head from its body in one clean cut. She kicked the bird's head into the bushes and looked over at Sawyer. His mouth was hanging open. She laughed.

"What? You told me to take care of it, so I did. Didn't I?"

Sawyer shook his head and smiled.

"Yes, you did take care of it. And with obvious pleasure, too."

Sara cocked her head to one side.

"Why should you get to have all the fun?"

Sawyer just smiled and shook his head.

"Remind me to stay on your good side. Now come on. You came here to help me dig, not murder crows. So, let's start digging."

It took them an hour before they were satisfied with the depth of the hole, and Sara watched intently as Sawyer dumped the mutilated corpse into the freshly dug grave, the body hitting the bottom with a stomach-turning thud. Sawyer picked up his shovel, looked at Sara, and motioned toward the grave.

"You took this guy out; I guess it's only fitting if you throw the first dirt in his grave."

Sara dug her shovel into the dirt and looked over at Sawyer.

"Look, I know your hands aren't clean. Do you ever think about the people you've killed? About who they were before all of this? Or even what their names might have been?"

Sawyer leaned on his shovel and shook his head.

"No, not really, and neither should you. If you ask me, this scumbag deserved to die, no matter what his name was. All I know is that there's one less 'Cult of the Crow' psycho left walking the planet, and that's a good thing."

Sara pinched her mouth to the side and grabbed Sawyer's arm.

"Wait, what did you say about a cult? What are you talking about?"

Sawyer pointed down to the crudely drawn tattoo of a ragged-feathered crow on the dead man's arm.

"That tattoo there. That's the mark of the Cult of the Crow on his arm. Do you know it?"

Sara nodded, her face suddenly turning dark as she recognized the symbol.

"Yeah, I've seen it before—more than once, actually, but I never knew what it stood for. I saw it at this checkpoint we passed through, and the man who we saved Mason from had that same tattoo. What do you know about it?"

Sawyer scowled.

"Not much, really. Only what I've heard. Apparently, the Crows were one of the doomsday cults that banded together in the last days. They were death-worshipers or something. They sacrificed crows, tortured other survivors, and worse. For whatever reason, they lasted a lot longer than most groups. I haven't seen any sign of them for a long time, but I did have a run-in with them once. It didn't go well."

Sara raised her eyebrows.

"Really? What happened?"

Sawyer looked away from her. He sighed.

"I was out raiding houses one day a few months after the blackout when I came across one of the places they stayed. The virus had already killed pretty much everyone else, but some of the Crows were still alive somehow. I knew it was their pad because that same symbol of the crow was spray-painted all over the outside of the building, and the words 'Cult of the Crow' were written on one wall. I won't get into details of what else I saw in there, but it was messed up. Anyway, a few of them came back while I was still inside the building. I killed two of them with the Mossberg and left another half-dead, but the truth is I was lucky to get out alive."

Sawyer pulled his shirt off to show her a thick, purple scar on his upper back.

"I took a hatchet in the back. Hurt like all hell, but like I said, I was just lucky to get out of there with my life."

Sawyer turned back around and saw that Sara was staring at him, her lips lightly parted. The girl had long ago noticed that the boy was handsome, but it was her first look at his heavily-muscled chest and arms, and she could not help but stare. It was not until Sawyer pulled his shirt back on that the girl finally looked away, her cheeks blushing, her voice quiet.

"Well, hopefully this guy was the last of his kind."

Sawyer could only shake his head and sigh.

"Yeah, well, I hope you're right, and if I never see that symbol again for the rest of my life, it won't be a day too soon."

Sara nodded, and Sawyer watched with fascination as the girl tossed a shovelful of fresh dirt into the hole, painting the first layer of eternity over the dead man's body. If anything, the girl seemed completely at ease with the grim task, never even covering her nose to block the overpowering smell of death that wafted out of the grave. Sawyer was about to start tossing dirt in as well when Sara unexpectedly stopped and reached into the pocket of her jeans. She pulled out a brass, 9mm shell and held it up for Sawyer to see.

"You are probably going to think this is weird, but this is the cartridge from the bullet that killed this guy. I don't know why I kept it, but it has been in my pocket for two days now, and I was thinking that I should bury it here, with him, right now. What do you think? Is that not normal?"

Sawyer shrugged.

"To be honest, I don't have the slightest idea what's normal or not anymore, so I'm definitely not the best person to ask that question. But I don't see how that shell can do any more harm than it already has, if you know what I mean?"

Sara flashed a quick smile. Then she closed her eyes for a moment, the smile fading from her lips. She whispered something and then dropped the shell into the dirt just above the dead man's chest. She reached down and tossed a handful of earth into the grave before she looked up at Sawyer and bit her bottom lip.

"Come on, Sawyer. Let's get this body covered up and get back to the Mission. I think we've both had enough death for one day, and you still owe me a can of soup."

16

For the next few days, Sara spent most of her time by her father's side while Sawyer placed a few traps, hunted, and started setting up a way to collect rainwater. On the morning of the fifth day after his return from the school, he entered the house and called Sara's name, somewhat disappointed when only Mason came to the top of the stairs. Still, the younger boy had a strange little smile on his face, and Sawyer looked up at him and smiled back.

"Hey, Mason, what's going on? Everything OK, buddy?"

Mason nodded and motioned with his hand for Sawyer to follow him up the stairs. Sawyer was slow to climb the stairs, but as soon as he entered the small room where Sara's father lay, he understood why the boy was smiling—the sick man was finally awake. Jacob was sitting up in his bed, and he looked over at Sawyer with bloodshot eyes, his voice low and hoarse.

"So, you must be Sawyer?"

"Yes, sir. Nice to meet you."

Sawyer reached out to shake hands with the man, but Jacob ignored the gesture.

"Mason has spent the last half hour telling me about what you did for us. Commendable. Depending on the motive, of course."

Sawyer was not sure how to respond, and he said nothing as Jacob hacked up a mass of phlegm and cleared his throat.

"Mason said that you left and then came back. Why is that?"

The man's tone was not altogether friendly, and Sawyer answered slowly, measuring his words carefully.

"Well, I had medicine that I thought might help, and I made a promise to your daughter that I would come back. So, I did."

Jacob coughed until Sawyer was sure that he was going to pass out, but the man eventually found his breath, and he looked up at Sawyer with suspicious eyes, his tone now openly antagonistic.

"And is that why you are truly here, Sawyer? Because of my daughter?"

Sawyer was caught completely off guard. He had not expected their first meeting to be so confrontational, but he was not one to back down easily.

"Not exactly. I figured I should come back for the kid, too. With you lying down on the job, somebody needed to look out for them, don't you think?"

Jacob did not find the comment amusing, and he immediately cut to the chase.

"What I think is that you need not concern yourself with us any longer, Sawyer. I am sure that I will be up and around in no time. Until then, we can get along without your help. You can be on your way."

Sawyer smiled and shook his head.

"Thanks for the suggestion, but I think I'll stick around for a while."

The veins on Jacob's forehead began to bulge, and his face burned red.

"What I am saying is that you are no longer welcome here, Sawyer. You can go on back to wherever you came from. I will tell Sara you said goodbye."

Sawyer swallowed hard and tried to stop himself from losing his cool. He looked over at Mason. The boy was staring straight at him, one eyelid twitching, his hands clasped at his chest. Sawyer smiled at the boy, and then he stepped forward and stood directly over Jacob's bed. His voice was quiet and calm.

"You may as well save your breath, Jacob. I'm not going anywhere, because, unlike you, this is 'where I am from.' I've been walking these trails long before you showed up—you're the tourist here, not me. And besides, if there is anything that I need to tell Sara, I will tell her myself."

Sawyer nodded to Mason, and then he walked out of the house without another word, leaving Jacob speechless and fuming.

Sara arrived only a few minutes later with an armload of wood and a rabbit over her shoulder. She smiled when she saw Sawyer on the porch, but he did not smile back. She dropped the wood and hung the rabbit over the railing. Sawyer looked over at the cottontail and nodded.

"Got your first kill, huh? Good job."

Sara patted the dead rabbit on its head.

"Well, not exactly my first kill, but my first rabbit kill, that's for sure. What's the matter with you?"

Sawyer gave a half-smile.

"So, I have good news and bad news. The good news is that your father is awake and talking."

Sara's eyes grew big.

"Seriously, he's awake? Did you talk to him?"

"Yes. That's the bad news. It didn't go well. He told me to take off, that my help wasn't needed."

Sara sighed.

"Well, I can't say that I'm surprised, but don't let it bother you. My father can be hard to get along with, but don't feel too special. He's like that with everyone. He'll come around."

Sawyer shrugged.

"I won't hold my breath."

The next two weeks went by quickly, and with no surprise visitors, or subsequent bodies to bury, Sawyer and Sara spent much of their time together—hunting and scavenging for food, collecting water, and making improvements to the Mission compound. Mason appeared content to look after Jacob as he recuperated, even though the man showed little appreciation of any kind. In truth, Jacob was not accustomed to needing help, and although it was obvious that the antibiotics and around-the-clock care had been essential to his recovery, he gave no credit to anyone else and offered no thanks.

By the end of the next week, Jacob had regained much of his strength, but as he watched Sawyer and his daughter walking side by side each day, he felt weak with rage. Nonetheless, the man held his tongue. Jacob knew he could do little to influence Sara at this point, and although he would not admit it, it was obvious that his daughter was as happy as he had seen her in a very long time. Even Mason appeared to be growing more confident, and, taking their cue from Sawyer, Sara and the boy also began to broaden their approach to finding food—hunting for duck and quail, scaling trees to raid birds' nests, turning over dead logs and stones to scavenge for fat grubs and reptiles that they might have previously overlooked.

At the end of their first full month together, Sawyer checked the supplies and realized that nearly three-quarters of the food he had brought with him was still securely packed away. Somehow, they were beginning to scratch out something more than just day-to-day survival, and for the first time both Sawyer and Sara were cautiously hopeful, and more than just that—they were quickly falling in love.

For her part, Sara was no longer worried that Sawyer was going to leave one day; she could tell by the way that he looked at her that he was not going anywhere soon. For his part, Sawyer felt as if he had met his equal in Sara, and besides her physical beauty, he was enchanted by her intelligence and sharp wit. In fact, the more time they spent together, the more he realized how similar they were. They both had no brothers or sisters. They had both lost their mothers. They both had complicated relationships with their fathers. And, most amazingly of all, they had both somehow survived this long.

Even though Sara had none of his training, the girl was exceptionally quick to learn, and Sawyer happily spent time showing her how to properly set traps, tie knots, and hunt for small game with the throwing stick and slingshot. She took to the hunt like it was second nature, her movements quiet and lithe, her stalking skills instinctual and deadly. After only a few weeks of practice with the stick, she was nearly as good as Sawyer, and the girl was able to take out a crow on the ground, or in the air, from ten yards away without making a sound. Almost as if she were collecting enemy scalps, Sara kept a single memento from each kill, and by the end of her training she had more than a dozen jet-black tail feathers hanging from her belt.

On most days, as the sun began to set, Jacob and Mason would retire to the main house, while Sawyer and Sara would sit alone by the fire, talking until late into the night. Typically, it was Sara who shared the most, but on one such evening, as the girl twirled a single tail feather in her hand, she asked the one question she had been dying to know the answer to.

"So, what is it with you and the crows? Why do you hate them so much? I know you said it was a long story, but really, all we've got is time."

Sawyer stiffened at her question, but Sara stared into his green eyes and smiled. She was not going to let him off the hook.

"Tell me. Why do you hate them so?"

Finally, Sawyer took a deep breath and stared off into the distance. His voice was full of emotion.

"In the last year before the blackout, my mother was not well. She was still kind and beautiful like before, but she was not the same person I remembered as a kid. Mostly, she was afraid all the time—afraid of a knock at the door, afraid to answer her phone, afraid to go outside. My father was a high-ranking officer in the military, and he expected everyone to be perfect all the time. He simply could not understand that she was sick and needed help. I guess at some point he just gave up on us. He took a post in D.C. and left my mom and me without even saying goodbye."

Sara shook her head.

"I'm sorry. That must have been hard."

Sawyer nodded and met eyes with the girl.

"Yeah, it was. And by the time the soldiers came to enforce the mandatory evacuations, she refused to go, and I wouldn't leave her. For some reason, they let us stay behind. When the power finally went out, almost everyone else was gone, and my mother and I waited for the end to come. It wasn't long before we knew the virus had arrived, and my mother began to show symptoms. I assumed the virus would kill me, too, just like everyone else who stayed behind, but it didn't. It only took two days for her to die, and when she was gone, I carried her body outside, so I could bury her in our backyard."

Suddenly, Sawyer's voice began to waver, and he looked down at the ground, his eyes welling with tears.

"I left her lying outside for only a few minutes to grab a shovel, but I couldn't find it at first, and I took too long."

Sawyer squeezed his fists together and closed his eyes.

"When I came back outside, the crows had already found her. I killed as many as I could, but it was too late; the damage was done. Her beautiful eyes, her beautiful face—it was all gone, and I know it doesn't make sense, and that it doesn't change anything, but I vowed that day to kill every crow that I could. To avenge what they did to my mother."

Sara reached out and took Sawyer's hand.

"I'm sorry, Sawyer. I shouldn't have asked."

Sawyer opened his eyes and shook his head.

"No, it's all right. You know what it's like to lose your mom. It was terrible, but maybe someday I'll be able to put it all behind me."

Sara smiled and squeezed his hand.

"Yeah, I know what you mean. Maybe someday both of us will be able to put it behind us."

As spring approached, they planted a vegetable garden inside the compound and spent hours walking the trails near the Mission, hunting, and scavenging for food and water. Since the day they had taken that first rabbit together, they had noticed signs that other small mammals were returning to the area, and after weeks of stalking, Sara finally bagged her first squirrel. The rodent had been nearly invisible against the mottled brown and gray background of the brush, but her keen eyes had detected a minute movement of the tail, and her throw had crushed the skull of the unsuspecting creature with deadly accuracy. Sawyer could not hide his own pride in her obvious skill, and he smiled as she skinned and gutted the animal on her own.

However, the land was not the only place returning to health, and the ocean that had suffered from unprecedented contamination immediately after the blackout was now slowly coming back to life. With no power to run the wastewater treatment pumps, millions of gallons of raw sewage and human waste had leached into the ocean, and nearly every living creature along the coast was soon dead. However, Sawyer and Sara had found time to make a daytrip to the coast, and they found that the water was no longer a sickly brown, and a few seabirds could even be seen flying above. In the end, they caught no fish, but they raided an abandoned boat that had washed up on shore, and they returned with their packs filled with canned goods and other useful supplies.

For the most part, Mason appeared content to spend his time alone, but it was clear to Sawyer that the boy could fend for himself. He continued to speak little, but Sawyer noticed that the stutter was becoming less noticeable when he did, and Mason seemed happy to quietly follow behind him as they walked the trails or worked inside the compound. Despite his frail appearance, the boy was wiry and surprisingly strong, carrying heavy buckets of water and large pieces of firewood without struggle or complaint. He was also still growing, and in just the short time that Sawyer had known him, the boy had gained several pounds and at least an inch in height. On more than one occasion, Sawyer did catch a smile slipping out of the boy, and whether he knew why Mason was smiling or not, it seemed to be a pleasant glitch in the boy's often odd, robot-like demeanor. Still, Sawyer could sense that Mason had a dark side as well, and he was careful not to spook the boy, or even look him in the eyes for too long of time.

While there was little question that Sawyer was growing closer to both Sara and Mason, his relationship with Jacob remained cool and distant. Sawyer found Jacob to be obviously intelligent, but equally egotistical and bombastic. On the rare occasions that he found himself near the man, Sawyer would listen without comment as Jacob regularly detailed his many accomplishments. Jacob was fond of recalling the foreign sports cars, the staggering bank accounts, the power suits, and the country clubs, but none of it impressed Sawyer. Money and social status meant very little to the boy who had been forced to kill with his bare hands, and who had kept himself alive on garbage, rainwater, and luck for nearly two full years. Nevertheless, despite Jacob's arrogance, the man made no further mention of wanting Sawyer to leave the compound. Jacob had quickly come to realize the value of keeping the teenager at the Mission, and he was content to tacitly accept the benefits of

Sawyer's hard work while he gradually regained his strength.

While Sawyer kept his opinion of Jacob to himself, he could also not help but notice an unmistakable distance between Sara and her father. The daughter who had appeared so diligent and caring during her father's illness was no longer present, and now that Jacob was conscious, they spent almost no time together. The few conversations that Sawyer had witnessed between them had been awkward and passive-aggressive at best, neither father nor daughter willing to give ground or compromise on any issue. Worst of all, Mason seemed to be caught in the middle, his feelings pulled and torn between them, their contentious relationship all that he knew. Sawyer sometimes wondered why Mason seemed to be so attached to Jacob in the first place, as the man appeared to ignore the boy most of the time. Still, he tried not to judge the boy; Sawyer's own relationship with his father had been complex at best, and he knew what it was like to crave acceptance from a person who would likely never reciprocate.

As much as both Sawyer and Sara kept clear of Jacob, they sought each other's company at every free moment. They had still not moved beyond the few innocent kisses that they had shared, but Sara was beginning to grow impatient, and Sawyer could sense the question on her lips as they sat alone by the fire one evening. It was not long before Sara looked away from the flames and broke the silence.

"So, what is going on with us, Sawyer?"

Sawyer chose to play dumb to give himself a moment to think.

"I don't know. What do you mean?"

Sara smiled, but her tone let him know that she was serious.

"You know exactly what I mean. I want to know what is going on with us."

Sawyer stared at the fire and let her question hover in the air for another moment before he finally responded.

"I guess it's like I said before, Sara. It all depends on what you want."

Sara looked up at him, her eyes sparkling in the light of the fire.

"Don't you already know what I want, Sawyer? I want you."

Sawyer smiled, and he knew that neither one of them had to say another word. He turned and looked at her for what seemed like the very first time: her beautiful face and delicate neck flushed red, her lips slightly parted, her dark eyes closing slowly as he leaned in and kissed her passionately on the mouth. They pulled back for only a moment before they embraced again, both lost in the immense and absurd feeling that they were quite possibly the last two lovers left on the planet Earth.

17

Although there was no one keeping track on any calendar, it was not long before spring quickly turned to summer, and the days inside the compound were soon hot and dry. Just as he had done at the school, Sawyer had gone to considerable effort collecting as much water as he could during the sporadic rains, and the Mission was now relatively well stocked with clean water. The group's supply of food was also in fair condition, and along with the garden and a rebounding population of small mammals, they were in little danger of going hungry. Even Mason's wiry frame was beginning to fill out, and the boy continued to put on pounds almost as fast as he was growing in inches.

Jacob appeared to be fully recovered from his illness, and he too was growing stronger. Nevertheless, the man's gruff demeanor kept him isolated, and he seemed to wear a permanent scowl much of the time. While he did not outwardly disapprove of his daughter's relationship with Sawyer, he was envious of the boy and of the respect that both Sara and Mason had for him. Most of all, Jacob feared the sway and influence that Sawyer now held over the group, and he was focused on finding a way to tilt the balance of power back into his own favor.

One night not long into the summer, Jacob was eating dinner with Sara in the kitchen of the main house when he looked over at the girl and offered a rare smile.

"You know, Sara, I had an idea the other day. Instead of continuing south, what would you think about staying here at the Mission and possibly adding to our group? It would be easy to accomplish; we could just build a big fire and see who shows up."

Sara continued eating her rabbit soup, collecting the last slice of carrot with her spoon before tilting the bowl to her mouth and drinking the last of the warm broth. Jacob waited for her to answer, but after a few seconds he realized that she was ignoring him, and the smile quickly faded from his face. He used her name to clear his throat loudly.

"Sara. I asked you a question. What do you think?"

Sara looked up at her father and scowled.

"Oh, you're being serious? I thought you were joking. What happened to your plan to head south to Mexico or wherever?"

"I have changed my mind and I'm one-hundred percent serious. It would be an opportunity to rebuild. Think of the possibilities."

Sara made a face and shook her head.

"Think of the possibilities? What are you talking about? Last time we lit a big fire, I was nearly raped and murdered, and, oh yeah, I also had to kill a man. The only possibility is that it would put us all in danger. It's reckless at best and suicidal at worst."

Jacob smirked.

"What about Sawyer? You would have never met him if Mason hadn't started that fire, am I wrong?"

Sara shook her head and frowned.

"No, you're not wrong, you're just transparent. I know that the only reason you want to risk bringing more people here is so you can try and play king or whatever. Really, it's just sad."

Jacob stood up in anger and left his half-empty bowl of soup on the table.

"I am sorry I even said anything to you, Sara, but now I remember why I rarely ever do."

Sara shrugged.

"Fine by me. You can go ahead and keep your stupid ideas to yourself from now on; I don't really care to hear them."

Jacob slammed his fist down on the table and sent the bowl of soup tumbling over and onto his boots. His face was bright red.

"Jesus Christ, Sara! Now look what you have made me do!"

Sara could not help but laugh. Her father's words seemed to carry less and less weight with every sentence that he spoke, and now she openly mocked him.

"Wait, let me get this straight. Is it my fault that your boots are soaked with soup, or is it Jesus's fault? Is it also our fault that you come up with such terrible ideas?"

Jacob pointed at her face and took a step toward her. His voice echoed in the small area.

"That's enough, Sara! I am tired of your smartass remarks, and I don't want to hear another word out of your mouth!"

Sara stood up and looked straight at her father. She had seen him at his weakest, and she was no longer afraid of him like she once was. She pointed her finger straight back at his face and yelled even louder.

"That's perfect, because I have nothing else to say to you except leave me alone from now on!"

Sara understood that it was all just a game between them—the arguments, the silent treatments, the power struggle—but she was growing tired of it, and she kicked her chair away and stormed out of the front door, leaving her father to clean up his own mess.

As was their routine, Sara did not speak to her father for several days, and when they did begin talking again, Jacob was certain to make no further mention of his idea. For her part, Sara had all but forgotten why they had begun to argue in the first place. The demands of daily life at the Mission kept her busy, and as a rule she spent as little time thinking about her father as possible. Not only had the small garden they planted nearly doubled in size, but they had also been able to catch four half-wild chickens, and their care was now her responsibility.

Mason sometimes helped her when he was free from his duties of collecting firewood and fresh water from the creek, but even then, Sara spent the bulk of each day inside the compound. She killed pests and pulled weeds, she cared for the chickens, collected eggs, prepared and preserved food, purified water, and basically ran the essential functions of the Mission. It was not fun work, but it needed to be done, and Sara did not complain. When she did have a few moments of free time, she would try to walk the interior perimeter of the compound, keeping a written ledger of anything in need of repair.

She was doing exactly that one mid-summer afternoon, checking on a new crack in the wall near the main entrance, when she suddenly stopped writing and lifted her nose to the sky. It was not uncommon to smell smoke at different times during the day, depending on their needs, but Sawyer was off at the coast, and she had not seen either Mason or her father inside the compound the entire day. She scented the air again. It was so familiar, but the smoke did not smell like wood. She took another breath, and suddenly she could taste it in the back of her throat. It reminded her of hot asphalt, of traffic jams, and of honking horns. She was right. It was not wood that was burning. It was rubber. She thought out loud.

"Rubber? Who is burning rubber?"

Then she looked up. Just beyond the tree line, not far from the south wall, a thick column of black smoke was suddenly rising into the cloudless sky. Sara stared at the smoke for several seconds before she finally dropped the pencil and pad and started to run.

Within a minute, she was standing before her father, the man grinning from ear to ear as an enormous stack of burning tires spewed black smoke into the sky behind him. Mason was standing beside him with his back turned, the boy oblivious to her presence, his eyes locked on the flames. Sara could barely control herself, and she screamed at her father above the roar of the fire.

"What the hell are you doing, Jacob? Have you lost your mind?"

Jacob threw his head back and laughed out loud as he rolled another tire into the fire. Sara reached over and grabbed Mason by the arm. The boy spun around quickly and tore his arm free.

"Mason, you come with me right now! I can't believe you would make him do this with you!"

Jacob laughed out loud again and smacked Mason on the back.

"Did you hear that, kid? She thinks that I made you do it! Hell, once he heard my idea, he insisted that he help."

Sara spun the boy around to face her.

"Tell me what he said isn't true, Mason. Tell me that you didn't go along with this. Don't you remember what happened last time? I could've been killed!"

Sara looked at Mason, but the boy only lowered his head, and she knew that her father was telling the truth. She looked at the fire. The flames were already at least twenty feet tall, the smoke another one hundred feet above that. There was nothing she could do. She glared at Jacob as she grabbed Mason and dragged him away, her father ignoring her as he smiled and sent another tire into the burning heap of rubber.

At that exact same moment, more than five miles away, Sawyer was headed back from the coast, a huge smile plastered across his face. For the first time since before the blackout, he had managed to catch a few fish, and he was thinking about just how delicious the three halibut were going to be when he casually glanced into the sky and saw a dark plume of smoke rising from the northeast. He stopped in the middle of the trail and stared at the smoke.

"What in the hell is that?"

The smoke was too far way to know for certain, but he could tell that the plume had to be coming from somewhere very close to the Mission, and by the time the adrenaline rush caught up to him, he was already running toward the compound at full speed.

As he came near, the smell of burnt rubber was as unmistakable as it was inexplicable, and even when he saw Jacob standing beside the pile of burning tires he still did not understand.

"What the hell is going on, Jacob? What is this?"

Jacob was covered in black soot, with his revolver on his hip and the 30.06 rifle slung across his back. He saw Sawyer and waved him over. He had wrapped a shirt around his face and head, and only his eyes were visible, his disembodied words coming from behind the mask.

"What does it look like? It's a damn signal fire, boy! Help me throw another tire on!"

Jacob rolled another radial in the direction of the fire, but Sawyer intercepted it midway and kicked it to the ground. Jacob pulled the shirt from his face and laughed out loud. Sawyer had to stop himself from going after Jacob with his fists, and instead he spun around, looking for some way to douse the flames. Jacob laughed again.

"Good luck putting this fire out. It will burn as long as I want it to."

Jacob reached for another tire to roll into the flames, but Sawyer stepped over and grabbed him by the shoulder.

"No. You're through here, Jacob. I'm ending this right now."

Jacob turned and slapped Sawyer's hand off his shoulder, the veins on his forehead bulging.

"Get your hands off me, boy. Now get the hell out of here, or else."

Sawyer took a step closer to Jacob. The boy was half a head taller and heavily muscled in comparison to the older, weaker man, and he stared straight into Jacob's eyes.

"Or else what, Jacob? What are you going to do?"

Jacob's face was now crimson, his jaw clenched tight. He said nothing. Sawyer tilted his chin back and laughed.

"That's what I thought, Jacob. You're all talk. Now, unless you want me to drag your ass back to the Mission, it's you that needs to get the hell out of here."

Jacob spit on the ground and turned as if he were going to walk away, but then, without warning, he suddenly spun around and threw a right cross straight at Sawyer's face. Sawyer was caught almost completely off guard, and the blow hit him hard just below the eye. He stumbled back, but before Jacob could land another punch, Sawyer stepped to the side and dropped his shoulder, sending an uppercut squarely into Jacob's chin.

The man saw a flash of white light as the punch connected, and when Jacob awoke a minute later, he was on his back, and his face and shirt were soaking wet. Both the rifle and the revolver were gone. Jacob sat up in confusion and looked to see Sawyer standing over him with an empty bottle of water in his hand. Sawyer tossed the bottle at Jacob and touched the newly-bruised skin around his eye.

"How was your nap, Jacob? I've got to say, not a bad sucker punch. If you didn't have such a soft chin, you might have been a decent fighter."

Jacob slapped the bottle away and stood up on wobbly legs. He rubbed at his sore chin. Then he looked up at Sawyer and let his hand slide toward the knife in his waistband.

"You little bastard. I'll kill you for this."

Sawyer shook his head and scowled.

"You know if you pull that knife out then it's all over, right, Jacob? I promise, you won't walk away. But right now, I'm giving you a chance. I suggest you take it."

Jacob looked down at the knife and then back to Sawyer. He pulled his hand away and spit on the ground again.

"Go to hell, Sawyer. You're not going to do a damn thing to me. Sara would never forgive you, and you know it. Now get the hell out of here like I told you before."

Sawyer took a step closer to him and balled his hands into two fists. The fire was raging only a few yards away.

"No, you're the one who needs to get the hell out of here. Walk away while you still can. Do you understand what I'm saying to you, Jacob?"

Jacob stepped forward, raised his arm, and extended his middle finger only a few inches from Sawyer's face. He smirked.

"Do you understand what I am saying to you, Sawyer?"

Sawyer sighed and stared off into the distance.

"I do, Jacob. I hear you loud and clear. Now let me reply."

Without another word, Sawyer suddenly lunged forward and grabbed Jacob by his collar, lifting the man off his feet and throwing him to the ground like a ragdoll. Jacob tried to stand up, but the air had been knocked from his lungs, and he could only gasp as Sawyer grabbed him by the leg and began to drag him toward the fire. The smoke was swirling around them, and Jacob could feel the heat from the fire bearing down on him. When they were only a few feet from the flames, Sawyer finally released his grasp, and Jacob rolled to his back and tried to sit up, his lungs stinging from the toxic smoke. He screamed up at Sawyer.

"I hope you know that you are finished with my daughter. When she hears all about this, she will never forgive you."

Sawyer's face reflected red in the flames as he looked down at Jacob and spoke, his face calm, his voice quiet.

"That's where you're wrong, Jacob. Sara is not going to hear anything about this."

Jacob scoffed.

"And why is that?"

Sawyer smiled.

"Because Sara doesn't even know that I'm here, Jacob. She thinks I'm miles away, fishing on the coast. No one knows that I'm here right now. Just you and me. And the fire."

Sawyer looked up at the stack of tires burning overhead.

"Be a hell of thing for Sara to have to find her father's dead body underneath a pile of burning tires tomorrow morning, don't you think, Jacob? But accidents do happen sometimes. I'm sure she would get over it eventually, but even if she didn't, she would have no reason to blame me in the first place. Like I said, I'm not even here right now."

He leaned down and whispered just above the roaring of the flames.

"Do you get what I'm saying to you now, Jacob? I've killed better men than you and haven't lost a minute of sleep. Do you really want to try me?"

Jacob stared up at Sawyer, and for the first time, he truly did understand. The boy was not bluffing. Utterly defeated, Jacob finally held up his palms and nodded once. Sawyer looked down at the miserable, soot-covered figure cowering below him, and he shook his head in disgust.

"Good. Now stay away from me, and don't come asking for help when all of this blows up in your face. And if you tell Sara one single word about what went on here today, you'll regret it. I'll hold onto your gun and the rifle for now. In the meantime, get the hell out of here, Jacob. I won't ask again."

Jacob struggled to his feet and wiped the dirt and soot from his face. He kept his eyes on the ground as he walked past Sawyer, but as soon as he was a few feet away, he turned and yelled.

"You really think that you have won here today, Sawyer? The smoke is already in the air! You are too late. Things are going to change around here, and you will see that you haven't won a goddamn thing."

Jacob knew better than to say any more, and he turned and walked away, limping back toward the Mission with his tail between his legs, both of his weapons and much of his pride left in the toxic smoke behind him.

18

The next day went by without incident, yet the tension among those living inside the Mission was palpable. Sara was still livid with Jacob for starting the signal fire in the first place, and Sawyer spent the day walking the compound on high alert, the Mossberg locked and loaded. He had not been able to extinguish the fire, but it had eventually died out, and now they could do little but wait. More than anything, Sawyer feared that the smoke would bring some form of danger to their doorstep, and on the evening of the second day, he noticed a thin plume of white smoke rising a short distance away. At that moment, he knew that someone had indeed answered Jacob's call, and he ran straight back to find Sara inside the main house.

Jacob was already standing beside his daughter when Sawyer arrived, and by the wide, smug smile on the man's face, Sawyer could see that he had already told her the news. Jacob looked over at Sawyer and smirked.

"Ah, Sawyer. I am sure that you have seen that we will soon have a guest, or possibly guests."

Sawyer walked over and stared into Jacob's face. Mason was standing beside Jacob, and he stepped away.

"Guests? For all we know, whoever is out there came here to kill all of us. They're sure as hell not guests. You've risked all of our lives, Jacob, and for what reason?"

Sara could see the vein on her father's forehead beginning to pulse, and she jumped in before he could reply.

"Sawyer is right. We don't know anything about who is out there yet; we need to be careful until we know what they want."

Jacob snorted.

"I know exactly what they want. They want to make contact, and I am going to be the one to give it to them. Come on, Mason. It is time to go."

Sara and Sawyer stood shoulder to shoulder, Sawyer's mouth clenched shut, Sara's open and moving fast.

"What are you talking about? Mason is not going out there. Neither should you."

Sara reached out and took Mason by the hand. The boy stepped next to her and hung his head. Jacob raised his voice and pointed to the column of smoke.

"If they wanted to kill us, why would they let us know they are here? Why would they set another signal fire?"

Sara opened her mouth to answer, but Jacob would not listen.

"Now come with me, Mason. We are going out there right now."

Jacob reached out to grab Mason by the arm, but Sawyer quickly stepped in between them and gently pushed the boy back toward Sara.

"Mason isn't going anywhere, Jacob. If you want to risk your own life, then go ahead and do it, but you aren't taking him outside of this compound."

Jacob glared at Sawyer for a moment before he spoke. His teeth were clenched tight.

"So, is that how it is? You speak for everyone now, Sawyer? Well, we will see how long that lasts. Get out of my way. You don't speak for me, and I am going out there—alone, if I have to."

Jacob brushed past them and headed outside of the compound without saying another word. Mason stood watching him go in silence, one eyelid twitching, his hands clasped tightly. Sawyer could see that the boy was upset, but he turned his attention to Sara, who was also trying hard to control her emotions. Still, Sawyer knew exactly what was on her mind. He put his hand on her shoulder.

"You think that your father is going to get himself killed out there. Don't you?"

Sara nodded her head.

"Yes, but he won't listen to me. He won't listen to anyone."

Sawyer sighed.

"Do you want me to go with him?"

Sara thought for a moment, then shook her head.

"No. If he wants to risk his life, that's his choice."

She wrapped her arms around Sawyer and buried her head in his chest. Her voice was soft and quiet.

"I just hope he comes back."

Sawyer squeezed her tight.

"He will. Your father's a tough bastard; I'm sure he'll be back sooner than you think."

A half hour later, Sawyer was proven correct; Jacob returned to the Mission unharmed and smiling. Sara tried not to seem relieved, but she ran over to her father and began to ask questions.

"So, what happened? How many were there? What did they say?"

Jacob looked at Sara and raised one eyebrow.

"I thought that you weren't interested in our guests? Or has Sawyer changed both of your minds so quickly?"

Sara ignored his taunt.

"I haven't changed my mind about anything. We just want to know what happened."

"Well, in that case, I can only tell you that there are three of them, two men and a woman, and they are unarmed and hungry. Starving, even. I only spoke to the woman. Her name was Rebekah. We made plans to speak again tomorrow morning."

Sara raised an eyebrow.

"That's it? They didn't tell you where they're from or why they came here?"

"No, Sara. I am sure we will find all of that out in due time. Now, if you are done with the questions, there are preparations that must be addressed."

Sara sighed and smiled over at her father.

"To be honest, I'm just really glad that you're OK."

Jacob raised both eyebrows.

"Is that right? I wish I could believe you, Sara, but most of the time, it seems quite obvious that you couldn't care less about what happens to me. I am not sure why today would be any different."

Jacob turned and walked away, leaving Sara speechless as he disappeared up the stairs. Mason followed the man, and Sawyer stepped over to Sara and shook his head.

"It sucks that your father treats you like that, Sara. Let me know if you want me to adjust his attitude, if you know what I mean."

Sara shrugged.

"No. I'm over it. Besides, we need to talk about what's going on, not how much of an ass my father is."

Sawyer rubbed his chin and thought for a moment.

"Well, if those people really are starving, then we can't just turn them away. We have to do something to help them, but I need to talk to your father first. I'll come find you afterwards."

He kissed her goodbye and found Jacob carrying a box of bedding out of the main house. Sawyer stood and watched him without a word, waiting for him to say something first. Finally, Jacob stopped and looked over at him.

"What do you want? I am busy here."

Sawyer stepped in front of him, blocking his path.

"Tell me that you are not actually planning to bring those people inside here, Jacob. This is something we all need to talk about. Whether they're hungry or not, we can't take that risk."

Jacob set the box on the ground.

"I am simply planning for all potential contingencies, Sawyer. I would think that a mind like yours would appreciate that. Obviously, I will know more after I speak with them again tomorrow."

"You mean after 'we' speak with them again tomorrow. I've changed my mind. I'm going with you."

Jacob stared at Sawyer for several seconds. He was thinking. He smiled.

"Good. I am glad to see that you are finally coming around. Now, if you will step aside."

Sawyer did not move.

"I'm not done talking to you, Jacob. You need to understand that you don't make the decisions around here alone. Even if they are starving, if you think that you can just bring those people inside here without any discussion, then you've lost your mind."

Jacob set the box down on the ground.

"Oh, my mind is just fine, boy. It's like a steel trap."

Sawyer thought for a long moment about what he should say next. He swallowed hard.

"Look, I agree they may deserve help, but we don't have enough food and supplies to support three strangers for any length of time. I say we give them what we can spare and send them on their way.

Anything more than that is a mistake."

Jacob laughed out loud.

"What do you know about mistakes, boy? Nothing! Is it such a mistake to want to start over, Sawyer? To begin a new chapter, to make up for the mistakes that we made in the past? You don't know a thing about mistakes, or you would have never fallen in love with my daughter. I don't care that you grew up here. I was here at the Mission first, this is my family, and I never asked for your help. This is not a democracy, and as long as I am alive, this is my Mission, not yours. If I want to bring these people inside, I will bring them inside. This is just the beginning, Sawyer. You can be a part of it, or you can simply walk away. That is up to you."

They stood facing each other for another few seconds before Sawyer realized that there was no use negotiating with Jacob, and there was no chance he was going to walk away.

"All right. But if these people do even one thing to hurt a single hair on either Sara's or Mason's head, I'm holding you personally responsible. Do you understand me, Jacob? One goddamn hair, and you'll see what I'm really capable of."

Jacob opened his mouth to respond, but Sawyer's posture reminded him of a viper coiled before the strike, and the man thought better of it. Instead, he simply nodded and picked up the box.

"Are we done, Sawyer?"

Sawyer shook his head.

"No, Jacob. We both know that we're not done, not by a long shot. Just remember what I said, and I'll see you in the morning."

19

The next morning, Jacob and Sawyer left the Mission to meet the newcomers, their backpacks filled to the seams with food and water. Despite Jacob's insistence that they go unarmed, Sawyer refused to leave the Mossberg behind, and he kept the shotgun in hand as they announced their presence and stepped into the newcomers' camp. The three newcomers stood in unison as they entered the small clearing, and Jacob wasted no time before he began to speak.

"Hello, my friends. I trust that you slept well. We have brought you some breakfast as a show of goodwill."

Sawyer stood silently behind as Jacob began removing the food from his pack, naming the items as he pulled out each one, setting everything on a small piece of fabric he had placed on the ground. Sawyer followed suit and set the contents of his backpack on the cloth. Jacob turned and smiled at the newcomers.

"All of this is for you to keep, no strings attached. You can take it and go, if you like, or you can stay and be our guests for dinner this evening. Either way, I do feel that now would be an opportune time to get to know each other. As I told you before, my name is Jacob, and this young man is named Sawyer."

Sawyer nodded, and the woman stepped forward and smiled at him. She looked to be in her twenties, and despite the thinness of her face, she was clearly quite attractive. She pushed her long black hair away from her eyes and spoke quietly, her voice clear and steady.

"It's a pleasure to meet you both. My name is Rebekah."

She looked back at her two companions.

"This is my dear friend, Edward, and my younger brother, Benjamin."

The two men nodded, and Sawyer took a long look at them. Edward was close to Jacob's age, tall and thin, with a salt-and-pepper goatee. Benjamin, on the other hand, was only a few years older than Sawyer, his jet-black hair hanging down to his shoulders. Sawyer nodded back at the men and allowed Jacob to take center stage again, the man motioning to the food at his feet.

"It is a pleasure to meet you all. Now, please, enjoy some food. We can talk while we eat."

The newcomers wasted no time as they began eating, barely taking the time to chew while Jacob continued speaking.

"Obviously, we are curious about many things, but first, where did you come from?"

Rebekah answered.

"We came from the base."

Jacob shook his head as if he did not understand. Rebekah pointed south.

"From Camp Pendleton."

Jacob wrinkled his brow. The name sounded only vaguely familiar.

"Camp Pendleton, eh? About how far is that from here?"

Rebekah smiled.

"You don't know about Camp Pendleton? About what happened there?"

Jacob shrugged and looked over at Sawyer. Sawyer was reluctant to speak, but he cleared his throat and met eyes with the woman.

"I know something about Pendleton. It's just south of the old nuclear generating station. I know that there was once a special quarantine zone there. I heard that they were working on a vaccine at one point. I think they called the place 'Paradise' for some reason. Is that what you're talking about?"

Rebekah looked over at the two men by her side and nodded. Taking his cue, Edward smiled and spoke, his voice deep.

"Well, you're not far off, son, but I can tell you that if anyone ever called it 'Paradise,' they had one hell of a sarcastic sense of humor."

Sawyer nodded, and Edward extended his hand.

"Nice to meet you, Sawyer. I take it that you are from around these parts?"

Sawyer shook the man's hand. His grip was firm. His back was straight. Sawyer had seen the same mannerisms in his own father, and he knew that the man had to have a military background.

"My father was an officer in the Army, so we moved around a lot when I was younger, but yeah, I'm from around here. And you? What branch were you in—Marines?"

Edward looked surprised for a split second, and then he saluted crisply and snapped to attention.

"You've got a good eye, son. Before everything went FUBAR, I was the newly retired Battalion Sergeant Major for the 1st Marine Raider Battalion, at—you guessed it—Camp Pendleton. But that's all in the past now. The future is going to be about young men like you, not old has-beens like some of us here."

Edward glanced over at Jacob, and Sawyer could not help but smile. Jacob took notice as well, and he did not like the fact that Sawyer was commanding so much attention from the newcomers. He stepped forward, and again he motioned to the food at his feet.

"Please, Edward. Eat and drink."

Edward understood, and he nodded.

"Yes, of course. Thank you very much for the chow and drink. We are very much obliged."

Jacob took a small bow and smiled, happy to have the attention removed from Sawyer.

"Of course, my friends. The pleasure is all mine." He looked up at the sun and tapped his wrist. "Unfortunately, we must take our leave now. Nevertheless, I did want to invite you all to dine with us this evening—that is, if you are so inclined?"

Edward looked over at Rebekah, but this time he let her answer.

"Of course, Jacob. By the grace of God, we have been delivered to your doorstep, and we would be honored to accept your invitation."

Jacob smiled and clasped his hands together.

"Excellent. Now enjoy the food and the rest of your day. Tonight, you will dine inside the Mission. Tonight, you will all be my guests."

20

The three newcomers arrived at the Mission gate just before dusk, each one conspicuously carrying a small package wrapped in newsprint. Jacob escorted them into the main house, and although the one table was too small to allow everyone to sit comfortably, Mason sat off to the side, happy enough to listen passively as the others exchanged greetings. Jacob waited until everyone was settled before he spoke.

"Thank you all for coming, and welcome to the Mission, my friends. No doubt you are all as curious about us as we are about you, so let me tell you something about myself and how we all came to be here."

Having everyone's attention, Jacob commanded the table for the next quarter hour, introducing Sara and Mason and detailing the events that had brought them to the Mission. The visitors asked only a few questions, and when he was finally finished, Jacob allowed Rebekah to share their own tale.

According to the young woman, it was during the first voluntary evacuations that she and Benjamin were initially routed through Camp Pendleton, and it was there that they were first identified as carrying a potential immunity to the virus. Along with a small group of others, including Edward, they were forcibly quarantined in hopes of developing a vaccine from the antibodies in their blood. However, in the end, time was not on their side. Within days of the blackout, and without any warning, the military evacuated all personnel, abandoning the remaining survivors with nothing more than a few weeks' worth of supplies. Rebekah shook her head as she finished her story.

"With most of the other immune survivors choosing to leave the base, it was just the three of us left at Pendleton. We did our best to scavenge what we could, but we never had enough food or water. We had talked about leaving the base many times, but then we saw the plume of smoke rising into the air, and, with God as our guide, we decided unanimously to follow the smoke signal wherever it might lead. And, praise the Lord, here we are."

Rebekah's eyes welled with tears as she continued, but her voice remained clear.

"It was by God's hand that we came here. Thank the Lord for you, Jacob. And for your family as well."

Rebekah reached out and put her palm over the top of Jacob's hand. Her black hair was pulled back in a single braid, her full lips slightly parted. Jacob could feel Sara watching his face, and he pulled his hand away.

"Thank you so much, Rebekah. As I have said, the pleasure is all mine. Now if you will excuse me for one moment, dinner is nearly ready to be served."

Jacob motioned for Mason to help him bring out the food while Sara and Sawyer sat staring at each other, neither one sure what to say. Sara knew her father well enough to see that he was trying not to show how much he enjoyed Rebekah's flattery, but even she could see that the young woman possessed a certain presence that was difficult to ignore. When he returned, Jacob stood at the end of the table and addressed the group once again.

"It appears that we have all been through remarkably trying times, but from here on out, I see blue skies ahead. And now, before we enjoy this meal, let us give thanks."

Jacob lowered his head and closed his eyes.

"First and foremost, let us give thanks to the Lord above for giving us the precious gift of life. Thank you also for the food on our plates, and for those that share our table with us tonight. May you guide us and forgive us of our sins. In the name of the Lord, Jesus Christ, Amen."

At the word "Amen," Sara's jaw nearly fell to the floor. She was dumbstruck. The words pouring out of her father's mouth were unlike any she had ever heard him say before. Not only had she rarely heard him thank anyone for anything in the sixteen years she had been alive, she had always known him to be an outspoken critic and unabashed disbeliever of Christianity, using the Lord's name in vain almost as often as he breathed. She was speechless, and she sat stunned as Rebekah took her cue from Jacob and continued giving thanks.

"Lord above, thank you for this bounty before us, and thank you for delivering us to this Mission, for delivering us to Jacob. We are eternally grateful and forever in your debt. Amen."

Jacob opened his eyes and smiled broadly, clasping his hands together as he spoke.

"Wonderful. Thank you, Rebekah. Now let us enjoy this fantastic meal that my daughter and Sawyer have provided for us."

Everyone besides Sara began eating. The girl looked at her father with bewilderment, knowing his newfound faith was absolutely counterfeit, his gratitude hollow and empty. She looked over at Sawyer, and she saw in one look from him that he knew exactly what she was thinking: her father was a fake, and he always had been. She was deep in thought when Rebekah suddenly spoke, her words snapping Sara back to the dinner table.

"Sara, this soup is delicious. Did you prepare this? What is in it?"

Sara was caught off guard.

"Oh, uh, nothing much. Just some rabbit and squirrel, a few vegetables, and some herbs from the garden."

"Well, it is quite good. We never had much luck catching the few skinny rabbits on the base. I don't recall even seeing a squirrel."

Rebekah turned to Sawyer.

"And the roasted duck is excellent as well, Sawyer. Thank you."

The boy had recently killed a pair of mallards, and he looked up from his plate and nodded, dipping his spoon back into the soup without saying a word. She ignored his somewhat rude response and continued speaking.

"So, Jacob told us all about his life and how he came to be here, but what about you, Sawyer? Have you been on your own all this time? I can only imagine that must have been difficult for you. How did you survive?"

Sawyer pushed out his bottom lip and set his fork and knife down on the table.

"I guess on luck, mostly."

Rebekah smiled knowingly.

"Oh, somehow I doubt that, considering that there is no such thing as 'luck.' The Lord was clearly looking out for you, Sawyer. It was only by the grace of God that you have survived. Don't you agree?"

Sawyer was not one to wear his beliefs like a badge, and he shrugged.

"Luck, the grace of God, a good shotgun—whatever you want to call it, I guess I'm still here."

The young woman sighed.

"Well, I consider it nothing less than a miracle that we are all alive, and I for one am thankful for that. Without God, not a single one of us would be here at this table. What do you think, Sara? Do you think it was just 'luck' that brought us all together today?

Would you call it 'luck' that brought you and Sawyer together?"

Sara stared over at the young woman and frowned. Jacob had raised her to question everything, especially religion, and if anything at all, her experiences had only confirmed her belief that there was no omnipotent architect guiding the world. In her mind, even if one such entity did exist, he was far from the benevolent miracle-maker that Rebekah seemed to hold in mind, and Sara did not sugarcoat her reply.

"I don't know what I would call it, but as far as I'm concerned, God hasn't had a single thing to do with it."

Rebekah looked shocked, but before she could say a single word, Sara looked over at Jacob. She smiled.

"Isn't that right, father? Or do you think it was God that brought us here to the Mission?"

Jacob tried not to overreact, a fake smile drawn across his mouth, his face instantly flushed with embarrassment by Sara's question.

"What Sara means to say is that we have all survived with a lot of hard work, self-sacrifice, and perseverance, but I think we would all agree that nothing short of a miracle has brought us all together this evening."

Rebekah did not reply and slowly raised another spoonful of soup to her lips, an uneasy silence falling over the table, the clinking of silverware and quiet chewing the only noises in the room. Jacob broke the silence again with small talk, engaging both Benjamin and Edward in superficial chatter, but the conversations were awkward at best. Sawyer ate quickly, and as he rose to leave the table, Rebekah looked over at Jacob, the woman obviously expecting him to say something. Jacob fumbled for the right words, trying not to provoke either Sawyer or Rebekah.

"Excusing yourself from the table so soon, Sawyer? It looks like our guests have come bearing gifts. Maybe now is a good time, Rebekah?"

Rebekah smiled.

"Of course. I think we are all nearly finished. We have one gift for each of you. Please excuse the wrapping paper; newsprint was the best we could offer."

Sawyer set his plate on the counter and returned to the table, choosing to stand rather than sit. Rebekah leaned over and slid a small package in his direction. Benjamin and Edward did the same for Jacob, Sara, and Mason. Sawyer stared down at the gift. He could feel Rebekah watching him.

"Please, Sawyer, take it. It's but a small token of our appreciation."

Sawyer slowly picked up the package, immediately struck by the sheer weight of the item. Slowly, he peeled back the newsprint, the edges tearing easily as he let the paper fall away. When it was finally unwrapped, he held the gift up above the table and frowned in confusion.

"A gold bar?"

Rebekah's eyes fastened on Sawyer's face as she answered.

"Yes. One-thousand grams and 99.9 percent pure. So beautiful, almost perfect. A bar that size was once worth tens of thousands of dollars. We have carried it with us for many miles, and now we give it to you as a gift. What do you think?"

Sawyer ran his finger along the smooth, yellow metal.

"I don't know what to think. Where did you find this?"

Rebekah looked over at Edward.

"I didn't find them. Edward found them."

All eyes drifted to Edward, his weathered face and deep-set eyes betraying nothing. He smiled and gave a wink.

"Just came across them, that's all. Not much good they can do for anyone now, but they are nice to look at, and they are yours to keep. Maybe someday they will be worth something. Doubt it, but who knows?"

Sawyer set the gold back down on the table and slid it over toward Rebekah.

"Thanks for the thought, but I don't really have a need for a gold bar around here. Maybe it would be better if you kept it."

The dining room was dead quiet. Sawyer looked over at Sara and then to the door. He tilted his hat to the table and waved goodbye.

"I hope you enjoyed the food. You all have a good night."

Sawyer left the house and walked into the warm evening air, the door barely shutting behind him before Sara followed him out. She was not sure what to say, so Sawyer said it for her.

"That went well, huh? Since when did your father become such a good Christian soldier?"

Sara frowned.

"I know. He is so full of it. But you didn't have to give the gold back—I think that made everyone pretty upset. Rebekah looked like she was about to explode."

"Well, you lit the fuse in the first place. And honestly, what the hell do I want with a bar of gold? And why would a group of starving people carry around gold bars in the first place? It makes no sense, if you ask me. Nothing about them makes any sense. Where are their weapons? They were on a military base, and they couldn't find a single gun? That guy Edward is a professional soldier—there's no chance he walks in here unarmed. I know my father wouldn't. I know I wouldn't."

"I thought the same thing. But now what? My father is going to be really pissed off."

"Who cares? He's always pissed off. What's the difference? Come on—let's go. I'm not sure I trust a single person here."

Sara grabbed him by the waist and pulled him close. The moonlight was reflecting in her eyes, and she pressed her body against his.

"What? You don't even trust me, Sawyer?"

Sawyer was not necessarily in the mood for romance, but he was still nearly helpless against her charms. He playfully pushed her away.

"All right, you're right. I trust you—and the Mossberg, but that's about it."

Sara shoved him backward and put her hands on her hips.

"So, what you're saying is that I'm running neck and neck with your shotgun for who you trust most in the world? Thanks so much for the vote of confidence, Hero."

Sawyer's eyes went wide, and he bit his lip, trying not to smile.

"Hey, you promised not to call me that anymore. Now you're in trouble."

Sawyer reached out to grab her, but the door to the house suddenly opened, and the three newcomers came filing out. Rebekah said goodbye to Jacob and walked past the two teens without a word, Benjamin trailing silently behind her. Edward was the last to leave, and unlike the others, he stopped for a moment and shook both of their hands.

"It was nice to meet you both. Thanks again for the chow. Have a good night."

Edward quickly caught up to Rebekah and Benjamin, and Jacob waited until they had left the compound before he turned to his daughter.

"I hope the next time we meet with our guests that they are treated in a friendlier manner. I expected this from Sawyer, but not from you, Sara."

Sara laughed.

"Oh really? You didn't expect this from me? What about you? Next time you have a complete religious conversion before dinner, please feel free to let me know, Pastor Jacob."

"You don't know what you are talking about, Sara."

"Neither do you. You're nothing but a fake, and they'll see through you just like we do. And just so you know, you don't have to worry about what I am going to say or do anymore; Sawyer and I will keep to ourselves from now on. Feel free to pretend to be whoever you want with your new friends, Jacob. Just be sure to leave us out of it."

21

In the days following the dinner, as she promised, Sara and Sawyer isolated themselves from the newcomers, and they disappeared outside the walls while Jacob played the role of mediator. Somewhat surprisingly, he was exceptionally adept at the task, finding the opportunity to meet separately with Sawyer and Rebekah, asking both what they thought might ease the initial hostility festering among the group. Rebekah offered no particulars, saying only that she was open to any solution and that she was confident that God would take care of everything. For his part, Sawyer was hesitant to even talk to Jacob, but he understood that the man intended to integrate the newcomers no matter how he felt, and his argument was brief and to-the-point.

"Look, I don't know them well enough to trust them, and I'm not sure I believe their story in the first place. Besides that, they've been here for several days now, and what have they done but eat our food and drink our water? Sara and I are busting our asses trying to keep everyone fed, and if they are going to stay, then it seems to me that if they have the time and energy to lug gold bars around, they have the time and energy to work. Get them pulling their own weight around here, and we can see where it goes from there."

Jacob agreed.

"Yes. I can do that. But what about their beliefs? Can you and Sara coexist with a person like Rebekah? A true believer?"

Sawyer did not hesitate to answer.

"I have no problem with it at all, but I can't say the same for Sara. But who knows? It seems like it was pretty easy for you to change your mind. Aren't you a true believer now, too, Jacob?"

Jacob smirked back.

"To be honest with you, Sawyer, I don't see the problem with pretending to be a believer if it is for the greater good. You think every person who walked around with a cross hanging from their neck truly believed in Jesus Christ? It was all a show. All a lie, and even now, nothing has changed. You know that. I know that, and all I am asking is for you to suck it up and get Sara on board. Can you do that for me, son?"

Sawyer's eyes narrowed at the last word, and he took a step toward Jacob.

"Just get them pulling their share around here, Jacob, and we'll go from there. And don't ever call me 'son' again. You're not my father, and you never will be."

Jacob stared over at the boy, his blood boiling but for once, the man weighed his words before speaking.

"Fine, Sawyer. I understand. I will see what I can do."

Much to the boy's astonishment, Jacob took his advice, and by the next day, a full work schedule had been drafted for the newcomers. At first, the two teens were skeptical, but after only a few days it was clear that the new schedule was everything that they had wanted. Not only did the newcomers seem willing to work, but they effectively took over all of Sara's duties inside the compound, leaving the young couple free to hunt and scavenge together full time.

For the next few weeks, they spent every minute together, happily stalking the trails surrounding the Mission and making frequent trips to the coast. Inside the Mission, the newcomers were also hard at work, and by the end of the first month, no one could deny that their combined efforts were benefiting everyone. Even Sara appeared to accept that the newcomers were likely staying for good, and the once measurable tension inside the Mission was now barely recognizable.

The fact was that under Jacob's mediation the group had quickly settled into familiar routines that kept everyone both busy and tired at the end of each day, and Sawyer could not deny that the results had been impressive. With everyone working diligently inside, and with Sawyer and Sara collecting food full time, there was no question that the Mission was beginning to prosper. For the first time since they had arrived at the compound, the entire group was now consuming far less than they were producing, and as summer turned to fall, it seemed that even Jacob and Sawyer had little to disagree about.

If anything, Sawyer and Sara had become much closer since the newcomers' arrival, the intensity of their relationship magnified by their self-imposed isolation. Nevertheless, despite their youth and the almost unbearable magnetic attraction between them, they showed little sign of outward affection in the presence of others. The hard truth was that they had both grown accustomed to a life that rewarded controlled emotions, but away from prying eyes, they existed in a state of unbridled excitement that only new love could understand.

For his part, Sawyer was willingly powerless against Sara's charms, and he had allowed her full control. They had discovered many secret hiding places along the trails and inside abandoned buildings, and the nights that they snuck outside the walls of the Mission were passionate and intense, with more time spent awake than asleep. Not unlike so many teenagers before them, they were consumed in each other's love, and for the first time in as long as they could remember, they were both unequivocally happy.

Autumn came quickly, and one cool evening while out checking his traps, Sawyer watched as Benjamin left the compound and headed downtown. Although they were relatively close in age, Sawyer had spent almost no time with Benjamin since he had arrived, and he knew little about the young man. For the most part, Benjamin rarely left his sister's side, and when he did, it was mostly to pray on his own. Sawyer had no issue with his devotion to God, but he did not particularly like the way that Benjamin sometimes looked at Sara with a strange mixture of both interest and disdain. Nevertheless, and without much forethought, Sawyer began to follow him downtown, the trail ending when Benjamin ducked into the doorway of a cinderblock building resting behind the frame of an old movie theater.

Sawyer stopped and wrinkled his brow. The building itself was small, with one weather-stripped wooden door leading inside. The roof appeared to be completely missing, and a dim light floated weakly out of the ivy-covered structure. Sawyer crept within a few feet of the building and listened. He could hear Benjamin's voice coming from inside, and he was somewhat surprised when it was followed by a shrill response from Rebekah.

"Shut up and sit down, Benjamin. No one is asking you to think."

Sawyer had not seen Rebekah leave the compound and he crept closer, his curiosity piqued. Still, as he drew near they seemed to lower their voices, and the few words he did understand made little sense to him. He waited outside the building for only another minute before slipping away, deciding that there was little to gain by eavesdropping on a conversation that he could not hear. Although he thought it peculiar that they would meet in such a seemingly random place, he assumed they must be praying, and he had all but put it out of his mind by the time he had returned to the Mission.

As the temperature began to fall, Sawyer and Sara were cordial with the newcomers, but they did their best to remain solitary and aloof as much as possible. Sara was especially aware of the influence that Rebekah held over her own father, and she could not help but cringe upon seeing Jacob praying alongside the younger woman. Sawyer did his best to steer clear of Rebekah altogether, but the woman continued to seek out interactions with him whenever she could. He noticed that she made it a point to make physical contact with him each time: a light touch on the hand, a brush against the shoulder. While she clearly sought to cultivate some type of relationship with the teenage boy, she made no such effort with Sara, offering her little more than a nod of the head on the rare occasion that they passed each other during the day.

Of the three newcomers, Sawyer interacted mostly with Edward, and with time the boy found that he had much in common with the former Marine. Not only had they both been raised in military families, they were also of a similar mindset, finding that they agreed on most any topic they discussed. Not unsurprisingly, Sawyer noticed that Edward also appeared to keep his distance from Jacob, and despite the fact that the two men were of similar age, they had clearly been cast from two very different molds.

Sawyer would not say that he completely trusted Edward—in his world, trust was something earned, not given—but he could not deny that some part of the man rang true to him. Sawyer had nothing but respect for Edward's military credentials, but it was also the way that he carried himself; he had a certain dignity that Jacob sorely lacked.

More than just that, Sawyer also noticed the man showing kindness to Mason, offering the boy words of encouragement here and there and even teaching him to whittle. He was also friendly and engaging with Sara, regularly helping the girl without needing to be asked. And, much like Sawyer, Edward was not prone to argument, and he also felt no need to wear his beliefs on his sleeve. Mainly, Edward reminded Sawyer of the best parts of his father, and in some ways, the boy could not help but look up to him.

It was also no secret that Edward and Rebekah often did not see eye to eye, and on more than one occasion, Sawyer had overhead them sharing unmistakably contentious words. Sawyer did not know her well, but he had the impression that Rebekah simply liked to be in control at all times, and he was not surprised that Edward kept away from her as well. Still, not everyone felt that same way about the young woman, and it was no secret that Rebekah and Jacob had begun to spend a great deal of time together, both during the day and at night.

Most evenings, Rebekah would read from the Scriptures by candlelight while Jacob listened intently, the man entranced by her voice as she invoked God's words with unwavering conviction. Rebekah believed without question that each one of them had been specifically chosen to survive the apocalypse, and that such a gift did not come without obligation. She felt that it was her duty to carry God's message out of the ashes of civilization, and that one day in the future she would be rewarded for doing so.

Jacob found himself intrigued by the younger woman and

her message. He was captivated by the idea that they had been chosen to survive, and something about Rebekah's unwavering belief was also compelling to him. Although it was true that he held no confidence of his own in any higher power, he had no qualms about feigning his commitment to God. When Rebekah quoted Scripture, he appeared completely absorbed in her words, nodding in agreement with prayers that he did not truly believe in his heart. In Jacob's mind, the threat of his own eternal damnation was already something of a foregone conclusion and pretending to be a true believer would make little difference when the day of judgment finally came.

One evening, while they were sitting alone by the fire, Jacob noticed that Rebekah was unusually quiet, and as they sat staring into the flames, he turned and faced the young woman.

"I feel like you have something you want to talk about, Rebekah. What is it?"

Rebekah smiled. Despite their age difference, Jacob could not help but think that she looked especially beautiful in the firelight.

"You are a very perceptive man, Jacob. But you've done so much for me already. I'm not sure that I should burden you with any more of my problems."

"It is no burden, Rebekah. Any problem you have is a problem of mine. Maybe I can help."

Rebekah looked over at him and put her hand on his shoulder.

"I'm just not sure. Can I trust you to keep everything I say in strict confidence, Jacob? What I have to tell you cannot be shared with anyone. Not with my brother, not with Edward, not with your daughter, not with anyone."

Jacob was intrigued.

"Of course, Rebekah. You can trust me. I will not say a word to anyone."

"That is very good, Jacob. For many sleepless nights, I have been waiting for the Lord to give me a sign to share this with you, and once again, he has delivered."

Jacob was now very much intrigued.

"Well, I am happy to listen. What is it?"

Rebekah turned and took Jacob's hands in her own. She stared deeply into his eyes.

"It's about Pendleton. And about Edward's gold. There's much more to the story then what he told you."

Jacob listened in disbelief as she told her tale, wondering if she could possibly be telling him the truth. He let her finish without asking any questions, and they sat in silence for several seconds as she waited patiently for a response. Jacob was at a loss for words.

"I don't know what to say, Rebekah. What does this all mean? How can I help you?"

"What it means is that I need to ask a favor of you, Jacob, for the good of your family, for the good of the Mission, for the good of us all."

The young woman's hands were soft and warm, and Jacob nodded.

"Yes, Rebekah. What would you like me to do?"

"There is something I want you to look after for me. Something to keep safe."

"Keep safe? I don't know. What is it?"

Rebekah squeezed his hands and leaned in close, her voice barely a whisper.

"I promise to tell you when the time is right. Will you do me this one favor? Will you help me? I have no one else to turn to—only you, Jacob."

Rebekah put her hand on Jacob's knee, and to his surprise, she kissed him softly on the lips.

Jacob was stunned. Rebekah pulled away and smiled.

"Will you help me, Jacob?"

The man nodded slowly. His faced was bright red.

"Of course; I will help you, Rebekah. Anything you need. Just let me know."

"Thank you so much. I cannot tell you how much this means to me. The Lord has truly sent you as my savior. God bless you, Jacob. Stay right where you are. I will come for you soon."

Without another word, Rebekah kissed Jacob again and quickly left the fire, unaware that a pair of jealous, spying eyes were watching as she disappeared into the night.

22

R ebekah returned a short time later to find Jacob waiting beside the dying fire. She crouched down and whispered in his ear, her voice breathy and soft.

"Everything is ready. I need you to meet me outside the east gate in ten minutes. Can you do that for me, Jacob?"

Jacob smiled. He liked the idea of being needed by Rebekah.

"Of course. Shall I bring Mason along? Would he be of any help?"

Rebekah shook her head and frowned. The soft tone of her voice was suddenly gone.

"No. I told you that this must be kept between us, Jacob. You must tell no one of this."

Jacob nodded.

"Very well, Rebekah. I will meet you outside in ten minutes."

Jacob had enough time to put out the fire, and he found Rebekah waiting for him just outside the east gate, a wheelbarrow and shovel resting beside her. Jacob looked down at the tools and then back to Rebekah. He half-joked.

"Please tell me that we are not burying any dead bodies tonight, Rebekah."

Rebekah did not laugh.

"No, Jacob, no dead bodies. But please, follow me."

By the light of a single candle, Rebekah took the wheelbarrow and led Jacob south until they came to the same clearing in the brush where Jacob had first met the newcomers. Jacob recognized it immediately, and he looked over at Rebekah in confusion.

"What exactly are we doing here, Rebekah?"

Rebekah ignored his question and walked over to a small tree and began to dig. After only a few minutes, she motioned for Jacob to come over. In the flickering light of the candle, the man could barely see inside the hole, but as he bent down he saw a leather satchel with a small lock clasped around the buckle.

"What is that? A bag? What is inside?"

Rebekah shook her head.

"Please, Jacob, no questions now. All will be answered soon. Help me get it into the wheelbarrow; it's much too heavy for me to lift on my own."

Jacob hesitated and gave her a questioning look.

"Look, Rebekah, I agreed to help you, and I will, but I expect some sort of explanation. I don't like being kept in the dark."

Rebekah reached out and took Jacob's hand as she kissed him softly on the lips once again.

"Please. All your questions will be answered in due time, I promise. We've been gone long enough already."

Jacob nodded and reached down for the bag. Even with two hands, he struggled to lift it out of the hole, the veins on his neck bulging as he finally heaved it into the wheelbarrow. He gave Rebekah a profoundly confused look.

"This feels like it weighs a hundred pounds. What in the hell is this, Rebekah?"

Rebekah pressed one finger to Jacob's lips.

"Please, don't curse, Jacob. I need you to take this satchel with you and to keep it safe until I come for it. Do you understand? Just do this one favor for me. I will explain everything when the time is right."

Jacob nodded as if in a trance, and they headed back to the Mission. No one was there to see them, and when they reached the porch of the main house, Jacob lifted the satchel free and set it down. He looked over at Rebekah.

"I don't like all of this sneaking around, Rebekah. I will expect an explanation for all of this very soon."

Rebekah stepped close and placed her cheek against his.

"Patience, my dearest Jacob. All in due time."

She kissed him one last time and quickly turned away, Jacob watching her go before he finally lugged the heavy satchel into the house. Based on what she had told him by the fire, the man had a good suspicion of what might be inside the bag, but it seemed too incredible to be true. He quickly lit a candle and looked down at the lock. He saw that it would be easy to pry it open, but Rebekah would know that he had broken her trust. He thought of Mason—he had seen the boy pick a lock before. He went over to the couch and shook Mason awake.

"Mason, my boy. I need you to do something for me, and I need it done right now."

Jacob pointed to the satchel. The boy rubbed his eyes and looked down at the dirty bag, a blank look on his face.

"I need you to open this lock for me. Can you do it?'

Mason still did not seem to understand, until Jacob pointed to the small lock attached to the buckle. The boy's eyes grew wide.

"Y-you want me to pick the lock?"

"Yes, that is exactly what I need you to do. But I need it done with no damage. Can you do it?"

Without a word, Mason stood up and walked away. He returned moments later with an improvised pick and tension wrench he had fashioned out of scrap wire, the sleepy look on his face replaced with inimitable intensity. Jacob held the flame of the candle near the boy's hands as he went to work, Mason's ethereal skin glowing white as he quickly opened the lock and looked up at Jacob. The man pushed Mason aside and opened the buckle, his eyes growing wide as he peered inside. He picked up a single gold bar and held it up in the candlelight.

"Well, I'll be damned."

The bag was full of gold bars, fifty in total, and for the first time, Jacob realized that what Rebekah had told him about Pendleton might be true. He spent another minute looking inside the satchel, and from a hidden pocket he pulled out an envelope. He opened it and looked at the documents inside. Slowly, he returned the envelope to the satchel and looked over at Mason.

"If anyone ever asks you, this never happened. You don't know a thing about any of this, understand?"

Mason nodded.

"W-where did all of this gold come from?"

Jacob could only shake his head.

"I don't know, Mason. But I am sure as hell going to find out."

23

That night, Jacob dreamt of black-haired angels and gilded thrones, and by the time he awoke the next morning, the sun was already peeking well above the horizon. He dressed and made his way outside, his mind still fixated on the events of the night before when he noticed Benjamin working in the garden. Jacob had paid Rebekah's brother little attention in the short time he had been at the Mission, but he waved courteously and walked over to the young man.

"Hello, Benjamin. How are you this morning?"

Benjamin looked up at Jacob but said nothing. Instead, he pulled a fat caterpillar off a leaf and clenched his fist, the creature's green and yellow guts squeezing out between his fingers. Jacob stepped closer and repeated himself.

"I said hello, Benjamin. How are you doing this morning?"

221

Benjamin wiped the caterpillar's guts on his pants and muttered a barely audible reply.

"Go screw yourself, Jacob."

Jacob was not sure that he had heard him correctly, and a scowl formed across his brow.

"What was that, Benjamin? I didn't understand what you just said."

Benjamin stood up and pushed his long black bangs out of his eyes.

"You heard what I said, Jacob. I said to go screw yourself. I saw you by the fire with my sister last night. I saw everything. And so did God."

Benjamin reached down and picked another caterpillar off the plant, but this time he only pinched off the creature's head. Benjamin let the caterpillar's squirming body fall to the ground, and he pointed at Jacob.

"You may have fooled my sister, Jacob, but not me. You're no believer. I could see it from day one. Now you're trying to deceive my sister. To take her away from me, but your day of reckoning will come. And it will come sooner than you think."

Jacob balled his hands into fists.

"Is that supposed to be a threat, Benjamin?"

Benjamin's eyes grew big, and he took a step back. Jacob repeated himself.

"I asked you a question, Benjamin. Are you threatening me?"

Benjamin took another step back, his voice shaky with anger and jealousy.

"The Lord doesn't make threats, Jacob; he only makes promises. I know that you're nothing but a liar and a heathen, and I think it's time we find out what my sister thinks about that right now."

Benjamin had barely marched halfway across the compound when he looked up to see Sara standing just inside the main gate. From the very first moment that he had laid eyes on her, Benjamin had been gripped by guilt over his lust for the girl, and he stopped and stared over at her, his emotions running unchecked.

Despite the cool air, the girl was wearing only a t-shirt and jeans, and Benjamin licked his lips at the way the fabric pulled tightly against her skin. He could see that she was looking at something out past the gate, and he approached her slowly from behind, his eyes traveling up and down her body. When he was only steps away, Sara finally heard his heavy breathing behind her, and she turned around in surprise.

"Whoa! Benjamin. I didn't hear you walk up."

Benjamin's lips curled into an awkward half-smile.

"Hello, Sara."

Sara looked up at him, slightly confused. It was not normal for Benjamin to speak to her unless he had a good reason to, and she saw no good reason now.

"Uh, hello, Benjamin. Can I help you?"

Benjamin's eyebrows went up. He was breathing hard.

"I don't know, Sara. Can you?"

Sara frowned. It was not the first time Benjamin had given her the creeps.

"Huh? Look, I'm kind of busy here, so what do you want?"

Benjamin licked at his lips again as he stared directly at Sara's chest. Sara followed his eyes and scowled.

"Seriously, what do you want, Benjamin?"

Benjamin smiled and let his eyes drop lower, down past her chest, down below her navel, the words spewing out of his mouth before he could choke them back.

"I can think of at least one thing that I want from you, Sara. Or is that just for Sawyer to enjoy?"

For a moment, time seemed to stand still as Sara stared up at Benjamin in disbelief, her mind trying to process what had just been said. Then, very slowly, Sara's hand drifted toward the knife on her hip. Benjamin's perverted smile quickly faded from his face. Sara took a step closer to him, her words coming slow and measured.

"I'm going to give you one chance to take that back, Benjamin. Just one chance."

Benjamin's face turned white as the girl slipped the knife out of its sheath, the sun catching the razor-sharp blade in a flash of light. Sara's deep brown eyes were as cold and fierce as any he had ever seen, and he put his hands up and backed away, stumbling and stammering.

"I was just joking. Please, you don't have to tell anyone what I said."

Sara looked down at the knife in her hand and then back to Benjamin.

"It doesn't matter if I tell someone or not, because right now this is just between me, you, and this knife in my hand. Now, take it back."

Benjamin looked down at the knife. Genuine fear rested behind his eyes. His voice was shaking.

"Please, I take it back. I'm sorry."

Sara reached out and pointed the knife straight at Benjamin's forehead, each word spilling from her lips like pure venom.

"Good choice, Benjamin. Now listen very closely. From now on, stay away from me. Don't look at me, don't think about me, and if you so much as say one thing like that to me ever again, I won't hesitate to gut you right where you stand. Do you get where I'm coming from, Benjamin? Because unlike you, I'm not joking."

Benjamin nodded and wiped the sweat from his upper lip.

"Yes, I get it. It won't happen again."

Sara slowly returned the knife to her hip.

"Good. Now get the hell away from me, creep, and go pray to your God that I don't change my mind."

Like a scolded child, Benjamin went straight to his sister, his chin trembling as he told her about his encounters with both Jacob and Sara. The woman listened without a saying a word. When he was finished speaking, Rebekah pulled Benjamin close and stroked his hair.

"This is troubling news, but do not worry, dear brother. As said the prophet John, 'Whoever believes in him is not condemned, but whoever does not believe is condemned already.' As for the girl, she is already lost. Pay her no mind. I will speak with Jacob myself, and we will know the truth soon enough. Until that time, find refuge in the stone church and wait for me to come for you."

Rebekah left Benjamin alone and found Jacob in the main house. She sat down beside him, her hands clasped in her lap.

"I just finished speaking with Benjamin, Jacob. He told me what happened between you two and also how Sara threatened his life. Is what he told me true?"

Jacob stiffened.

"I have no idea if something happened between your brother and Sara, or what Benjamin told you about what happened this morning."

"He told me that he accused you of being a non-believer, and that you did not deny it. Is this true?"

Jacob did his best to act offended, but his true feelings were festering just below the surface.

"Benjamin needs to learn some respect, Rebekah. He's lucky I restrained myself. And as far as his claims against me, I don't have to defend myself to the likes of your brother. You said yourself that we were chosen to survive the end of days, why would God keep me alive if I was a not a true believer? Isn't that enough?"

Rebekah frowned.

"I do not pretend to know how God chooses who will live and who will die, but you have not answered the question, Jacob. My brother is a young man of many flaws, but he sees the world through God's eyes. The question is, do you?"

Up until that moment, Rebekah had truly believed that Jacob was a man of faith, but now she could see the truth behind his eyes. For several long seconds, there was nothing but quiet as they stared at each other, and finally it was Jacob who broke the silence.

"No, Rebekah. I see the world through my own two eyes."

Jacob looked down at the ground and Rebekah offered a sad smile. Her voice was very quiet.

"I can't tell you how sorry I am to learn of this now, Jacob. I had high hopes for you, and for us."

Jacob looked up. He tried to salvage what he could.

"Nothing has to change between us, Rebekah. This changes nothing."

The young woman slowly shook her head and looked to the heavens.

"No, Jacob. Unfortunately, you are wrong. This changes everything."

Jacob opened his mouth to speak, but Rebekah placed a single finger on his lips.

"Shhh. Say no more. I see that it was wrong to trust you, but it is all in God's hands now."

Rebekah kissed Jacob on the cheek, but without so much as another word she turned and walked away to find her brother, leaving Jacob standing alone and confused.

That night, the first true rainstorm of the fall season swept in from the sea, and for the next two days, Sawyer and Sara were forced to remain inside the walls as the storm raged outside. After the second full day of being cooped up inside with the girl, Sawyer could tell that something was wrong. He sat down and put his arm around her.

"What's up, Sara? I know it sucks being stuck inside like this, but something else is bothering you. What is it?"

Sara looked over at Sawyer and let out a long sigh.

"If I tell you, do you promise not to do anything stupid?"

Sawyer rubbed the thin stubble growing on his chin and shook his head.

"No. Maybe I like doing stupid things. Besides, I have no idea what you're going to tell me, and I only make promises I know I can keep. I'll do my best, how about that? Now, what is it, Sara? Just tell me."

Sara met eyes with Sawyer.

"I had this very random interaction with Benjamin the other day, and he said something that you really wouldn't like. Something really creepy. I handled it on my own, but I don't like keeping things from you, so I thought you should know."

A scowl formed on the boy's face.

"What did he say?"

Sara took a deep breath and repeated Benjamin's exact words. For a long moment, Sawyer said nothing. Then he gave Sara a questioning look.

"You said you handled it? I'm curious. What happened after that?"

Sara allowed a small smile.

"Nothing much. I pulled my knife and told him that I would gut him where he stood if he ever talked to me like that again."

Sawyer tried not to smile back.

"And how did Benjamin take that advice?"

Sara laughed.

"He took it well. I think he pissed himself, but no tears, at least."

Sawyer laughed out loud.

"I figured as much. Well, it sounds like you took care of it, but as soon as this storm breaks, I'm going to go talk to him myself. Don't worry. I promise not to do anything stupid. Maybe I'll just see if I can get him to piss his pants again."

Sawyer left the main house a few hours later and walked across the compound to the smaller house where Rebekah and Benjamin stayed. The rain had finally stopped, and he knocked on the door and waited for someone to answer. After a moment, Rebekah opened the door. She smiled.

"How can I help you, Sawyer?"

The boy looked past her into the house.

"Is Benjamin here? There is something I need to talk to him about."

Rebekah shook her head, the smile fading from her face.

"Benjamin has been in bed the last two days. He is not feeling well. What do you need to speak to him about?"

Sawyer hesitated. Part of him wanted to tell Rebekah exactly what her supposedly devout brother had said, but he thought better of it.

"Just tell him to come find me the first chance he gets. He'll know why."

Sawyer turned to walk away, but it was Rebekah who was not finished.

"I will be sure to tell him, but before you go, I have something to ask you, Sawyer."

The boy looked back at her.

"Sure, Rebekah. What is it?"

The young woman left the doorway and leaned in so close to Sawyer that the boy could feel her warm breath on his cheek. She whispered.

"You are quite the enigma, Sawyer. You know that, don't you?"

The boy raised his eyebrows.

"I am?"

Rebekah smiled warmly.

"Yes. Since the day I first arrived, I've sensed something special about you. But the question is the same now as it was that first night at dinner. When the Lord returns to this Earth, whose side will you be on? That of the righteous, or that of the damned? Will you follow the soldiers of God or the Cult of the Crow?"

Sawyer's eyes narrowed at the mention of the cult.

"What? The Cult of the Crow? I would never align myself with those scumbags, but they're all dead anyway. They don't exist anymore."

Rebekah sighed.

"Evil will always exist, Sawyer, and I fear that if we don't come together under God's banner soon, we risk losing everything."

Before Sawyer could say a word, she stepped even closer to the boy, pressing her lithe body against him. She smiled coyly and ran her fingers through his hair.

"Those who choose wisely will be rewarded, but those who choose to follow the path of darkness will never see the light. We both know what path Sara has chosen, but tell me, Sawyer, do you want me to help you see the light? Do you want to believe? Or have you chosen darkness as well?"

For a split second, even Sawyer was powerless against Rebekah's charms, but despite the warmth of her body and the softness of her curves he finally pushed her away. He stepped down off the porch and shook his head.

"I know what you're trying to do, Rebekah, and it might work with Jacob, but not with me. I've got no love for any death-worshippers like the Crows, but I do love Sara with all of my heart, and nothing will change that. And to be honest, even if I did want to be a true believer like you, my path was chosen for me the moment I picked up the shotgun. And whether it was God or the devil who decided that path for me, the fact is that I never really had a choice."

24

Sawyer left Rebekah standing speechless on the porch and returned to the main house to find Jacob and Mason sitting downstairs, eating in silence. Sawyer looked over at Mason and smiled. While the boy was still thin and wiry, he seemed to grow taller by the day, and Sawyer could not help but take notice that he was not the same scrawny kid that he had first met. Sawyer slapped him on the back and smiled.

"How's it going, buddy? You're getting tall. Pretty soon Jacob will be looking up to you."

The boy allowed a small smile, and Sawyer continued.

"It looks like the sun's finally out to stay—you think you can do me a favor and go check the traps for me? I'll owe you one. I need to talk to Jacob about something."

Mason looked over at Jacob. The man nodded.

"Go ahead, Mason. But I will need your help once you are finished."

Mason gave Sawyer a small smile and jumped off his chair, throwing on his unlaced boots and heading out the door. Jacob turned to Sawyer and frowned.

"What is it, Sawyer? I don't have all day."

Sawyer rubbed his chin and sighed.

"Fine. I'll make it quick. Benjamin crossed the line and said some exceptionally rude things to Sara the other day. I just went over to talk to him, but Rebekah says he's been sick for a couple days, and I didn't get a chance. I thought you might care, as her father, but I guess I'm probably wrong."

Jacob stood up from his chair. He had a perplexed look on his face.

"No, I do care. Rebekah did mention something about it to me, but I haven't spoken to her for several days. I also had a rather rude interaction with Benjamin, but are you certain that he is sick? I am almost positive that I saw him out by the east gate just yesterday morning."

Sawyer shrugged.

"I don't know. That's just what she told me. I didn't see him lying in bed with a fever or anything if that's what you mean."

Jacob shook his head with doubt.

"Whether he is sick or not, I would like to know exactly what he said to my daughter."

Sawyer had no interest in rehashing Sara's unpleasant exchange with Benjamin.

"It doesn't matter what he said. All you need to know is that it was way out of line, and I plan to have a talk with him about it. Maybe you should do the same."

Sawyer had said all that he needed, and he left Jacob to go find Edward. As usual, the man was in the workshop, and he put down his tools when he saw Sawyer.

"Good day, Sawyer. How are things going?"

The boy nodded.

"Things are going, that's for sure."

Edward nodded as if he understood.

"I see. What's on your mind?"

Sawyer sighed.

"Look, you know that Sara and I like you, and don't take this the wrong way, but I just had a bizarre conversation with Rebekah, and I can't shake the feeling that you all aren't telling us something."

Edward shook his head.

"I can't say that I know what you're talking about, Sawyer. What do you mean?"

Sawyer thought for a moment as he stared across the workbench. His voice was quiet.

"I want to know two things. Why did you really come to the Mission? And what do you know about the Cult of the Crow?"

The man looked up at the boy and stared into his green eyes.

"You're a smart young man, Sawyer, and you deserve as straight of an answer as I can give you. The truth is that we all came here for different reasons, besides finding something to eat. For me, it was about finding good people and making up for past choices that I've made. But for Rebekah and Benjamin, it's always about faith, and about fulfilling what they think is a mandate from God."

Sawyer raised one eyebrow.

"What kind of mandate?"

Edward shook his head.

"That I cannot tell you for sure, but it does have something to do with the Crows. Or at least Rebekah thinks it does. You see, Rebekah believes that there is a war coming, a war between good and evil."

Sawyer nearly laughed out loud.

"A war? With the Crows? There is no Cult of the Crow anymore. Hell, there is only a handful of people left on the goddamn planet. How can she think there is going to be a war?"

Edward shrugged.

"I don't rightly know, Sawyer, but that's what she's preparing for. The truth is that Rebekah may tolerate my existence, but we rarely see eye to eye, and I'm not so certain that I fit into her long-term plans. If you ask me, there's two notions of how to get along with a woman like her, and neither one is worth a damn."

Sawyer nodded.

"Well, just do me a favor and tell her to back off. Like I've said before, I have no problem with whatever anyone wants to believe, but Sara and I don't like being judged every time we step out the goddamn door."

Edward looked up at Sawyer. For a moment, it seemed like he wanted to say something more to the boy, but in the end, he simply nodded and agreed.

"I understand, Sawyer, and I'll make sure she gets the message."

Sawyer was not necessarily satisfied with their conversation and he returned to the main house with more questions than answers. Jacob was gone but he found Sara sitting at the kitchen table, sharpening her knife. He leaned in to kiss her, but as soon as he came close, the girl pulled away. Sawyer took a step back.

"What's wrong with you?"

Sara's mouth was pinched tight, and it took her a moment to speak.

"I saw you talking to Rebekah from the upstairs window. I thought you went over to talk to Benjamin, not his sister."

"I did. She said he was in bed sick for the last few days. What was I supposed to do?"

"Sick? I saw him skulking around yesterday morning, and he looked perfectly fine."

"Your father said the same thing, but that's what she told me."

Sara ran the edge of her knife along the sharpening stone and frowned.

"And did she have to run her fingers through your hair to tell you that?"

Sawyer shook his head and sighed.

"Are you being serious right now? You know I don't want anything to do with Rebekah."

Sara slowly set the knife down on the table and walked to the foot of the stairs.

"Sorry, that's not what it looked like to me. And it's not the first time I've seen her flirting with you."

Sawyer shook his head and laughed out loud.

"You're acting insane right now, you know that?"

Sara clearly did not find any humor in being called insane, and her eyes narrowed.

"Is that right? Well, if you think that, why don't you go hunting by yourself today? And maybe you can find somewhere else to sleep tonight, too. Have a good day, Sawyer. Goodbye."

Sara stormed up the stairs and slammed a door behind her, leaving the confused boy with his mouth hanging wide open. He stood there for a moment, debating whether to follow her up the stairs or not, but in the end, he decided against it. Instead, he grabbed his backpack and the Mossberg and walked out the door, muttering sarcastically under his breath.

"What a fun day so far. Wonder who I can piss off next?"

Just as Sara had so kindly suggested, Sawyer spent the day hunting by himself, traversing the muddy trails north of the Mission. Game was scarce that day, and although he was excited to come across the clearly outlined paw prints of a dog or coyote in the mud alongside one trail, his traps were empty, and he was only able to bag one rabbit before dark. Having decided to sleep under the stars for the night rather than return to the Mission, he found a mostly dry patch of ground beneath a massive oak not far from the compound and set up camp. He sparked a fire, and after roasting the rabbit over the open flames, he stretched out on his bedroll with a full stomach. For the first time in several days, the night was clear, and the moon was full, and the boy fell asleep thinking of Sara, the not-so-distant howl of an unknown canine echoing in the dark.

25

By midnight, the boy had already been asleep for several hours, but only a stone's throw away, inside the main house, Sara was tossing and turning in her bed, her eyes wide open. The girl had felt badly about what she had said to Sawyer earlier in the day, but she had expected him to return at some point so that she could apologize. However, as the sun set and the boy did not return, Sara found that she could not fall asleep. Instead, she had done nothing but lie awake in her bed, worried and wondering where he was. Finally, she gave up trying to sleep, lit a candle, and reached for her latest journal.

She went downstairs and sat at the kitchen table, setting the candle down and opening the book. She flipped through the pages until she came to the entry from the day that she had first met Sawyer. She smiled as she read what she had written about him.

How he had left them food and water. How he had looked back at her before walking away. How his impossibly green eyes had sparkled in the sunlight. However, before she could turn the page to read more, she suddenly heard footsteps creaking on the porch. She looked up and smiled brightly, a wave of relief washing over her. She let out a sigh and whispered quietly.

"Oh, Sawyer. I'm so glad you're back."

The girl closed her journal and walked over to the door, but as she reached for the handle she noticed that the footsteps on the porch had abruptly stopped, and she took a step back and wrinkled her brow. She spoke his name again, but this time more loudly.

"Sawyer?"

Sara held her breath as she waited for an answer, but the night remained eerily silent, and a cold chill slowly trickled down the length of her spine. At that very moment, the girl somehow knew that it was not Sawyer outside on the porch, and as she took a step back from the door, a single gunshot suddenly shattered the silent night.

The girl was given no time to react as the bullet came straight through the door with tremendous force, splintering the wood and exploding against the far wall only inches away from her head. Sara screamed in surprise and ran for the stairs, grabbing her 9mm before bursting through the door of her father's room. At the sound of the gunshot, Jacob had nearly jumped out of his bed, but before he could say a word, Sara placed one finger on her lips and whispered, keeping one eye on the doorway behind her as she spoke.

"Someone just tried to kill me. They shot through the door. Get the rifle and the .38 and wait here with Mason. I'm going out on the roof to check it out."

Jacob rubbed his eyes and picked up the rifle from beside his bed. He handed the .38 to Mason. He looked over at Sara.

"You're going on the roof? Wait—where the hell is Sawyer?"

Sara shook her head.

"I don't know where he is. Somewhere outside the walls. Just get Mason and do what I said."

With her father too stunned to argue, Sara climbed out of the window and into the cool night air. In the moonlight, she could make out the silhouettes of at least two people running along the side of the house, but before she could take aim, she suddenly heard the sound of glass shattering directly below her. For a moment, she assumed someone was trying to break in, but within seconds, the ground below was painted in a flickering orange and red light, and even before the smoke hit her nose, she realized that the bottom floor of the house had just been set on fire.

In a panic, Sara jumped up and started running back to the open window. Before she could reach the window, a double round of gunshots suddenly rang out in the darkness, and this time the girl stopped and froze. She had only heard the sound of the Mossberg discharging once before, but when she saw a familiar form running toward the house, holding a shotgun, she lifted her head and yelled as loud as she could.

"Sawyer, watch out! They're right below me!"

At the sound of her voice, several gunshots rang out again, and Sara dove back as a bullet tore through the shingles near her feet. A split second later, she heard the Mossberg go off a third time, but she could no longer see where Sawyer was, and she ran back toward the window. She had barely put a foot inside when several more shots ricocheted inside the house, followed by the unmistakable crack of the 30.06 rifle from somewhere downstairs. Jacob was no longer in the room, and Mason was sitting in the corner with the .38 revolver in his hand. The boy was shaking and muttering to himself. Sara grabbed him and shook him by the shoulders.

"Where's my father?"

Mason pointed to the closed door.

"H-he took the rifle. H-he told me to stay here."

Sara went to the door, slowly twisting the knob and peeking into the hallway. A thin cloud of smoke rose from the stairway. She could see the warm glow of the fire below her. She yelled down the stairs.

"Jacob! Where are you?"

She called out again and waited breathlessly just inside the doorway, looking back at Mason as the sound of footsteps began to echo in the stairwell. She whispered to the boy.

"Someone's coming up the stairs."

Sara slipped her finger over the trigger of the Beretta and swallowed hard, the approaching footsteps barely audible over the heavy pulsing of her heart.

Just outside the main house, Sawyer's heart was also racing full tilt as he watched the flames spreading throughout the ground floor. Only minutes before, he had been sound asleep on his bedroll outside the wall, but at the sound of the first gunshot he had sprung to his feet, dashing through the east gate with the Mossberg in hand. Almost immediately, he had seen the silhouette of a man he did not recognize holding a pistol and looking for a way into Edward's quarters, and the boy knew there would be no need to ask any questions.

He closed the distance between them quickly and fired as soon as he was in range, the buckshot tearing through the man's back and blowing out the other side of his chest. Although the man was dead before he hit the ground, Sawyer was not taking any chances, and he pumped another round into the body and took off running toward the main house, a massive dose of adrenaline propelling him forward like a runaway train.

He could see the flames leaping out of the downstairs windows, and he was almost across the courtyard when he heard Sara call out to him. He looked up to see her standing on the roof, but as he came near, a series of gunshots pierced the air. Sawyer dove to the ground, not certain if the shots were coming in his direction.

Sara was no longer visible on the roof, but his eyes caught a glimpse of single figure moving swiftly away from the house, and he fired the Mossberg once in the runner's direction. Whoever it was disappeared into darkness, but Sawyer did not give chase. He had only one thought on his mind, and he ran to the base of the burning house and shouted the girl's name.

"Sara! Where are you?"

There was no reply from the girl, but several more gunshots erupted from the opposite side of the house, including one the boy recognized as coming from Jacob's rifle. Fearing the worst, the boy ran around the building with the Mossberg raised and peered into the darkness. There were no signs of any movement, but he noticed there was something on the ground a dozen or so yards ahead of him. Sawyer cautiously took a few steps forward and crouched down, his jaw dropping as he drew close.

On the ground just below the window was the dead body of a young man, the dirt beneath his head soaked dark with blood, a still-smoking pistol held fast in one hand. Half of his face and part of his skull had been all but obliterated from his head, but despite the horrific wounds, Sawyer recognized the body, and he shook his head in disbelief.

"What the hell? Benjamin?"

Sawyer was too confused to understand exactly what had happened, but there was no time to waste, and he took the still-warm pistol out of Benjamin's dead hand and tucked it into his belt. The entire bottom floor was now engulfed in flames, and

Sawyer stepped back and once again yelled above the crackling of the fire.

"Sara! Where are you?"

Sara could hear Sawyer calling her, but she dared not answer. She was still waiting inside the doorway with the gun in hand, her heart racing. The footsteps coming up the stairway were slowly getting closer, and she looked back toward Mason. The boy was shaking and mumbling. She looked back down the hall. Finally, she could wait no more.

"Who's there? I have a gun!"

A low moan answered her from the top of the stairs.

"Sara, it's me—your father."

Sara could hear in his voice that he was hurt, and she ran from the doorway and reached out to Jacob, helping him up the last few stairs and into the bedroom. She looked down at the blood on his hands and clothes.

"Oh my god, you're bleeding! What happened?"

"I will be fine. That son-of-a-bitch shot me, but I got him back. I shot him right in his face!"

Sara stood motionless and stared at him, her eyes locked on the dark, circular stain spreading across his shirt and hip.

"Who shot you? What just happened down there?"

Jacob shook his head and leaned against the wall.

"Sara, just go. There is no time. The house is on fire. Get out the window. I will be right behind you. There is something I need to get before I go. Just take the rifle, get Mason, and get the hell out of here! Go!"

Sara grabbed the rifle by the stock and the boy by the hand, and together they climbed out of the window and onto the rooftop. The flames were now licking up above the edge of the roof, and Sara had the sickening feeling that the old house would not stand for much longer. Mason was staring back at the open window, looking for Jacob, but Sara grabbed his arm and dragged the boy to the edge of the roof. She looked down to the ground below her and saw Sawyer standing at the edge of the darkness, frantically motioning for them to jump. Parts of the roof were already beginning to collapse and catch fire, and she grabbed Mason by the shoulders and screamed in his face.

"Mason, you have to jump! Roll when you hit the ground and get away from the house as fast as you can! Go now!"

Mason took one last look at the empty window, and, with a push from Sara, he ran and jumped off the roof, his feet clearing the flames by mere inches. He rolled as he hit the ground, but instead of moving away from the house, he limped back toward the burning structure and stared up at Sara. The girl could literally feel part of the roof beginning to give way beneath her feet, and she screamed down at him.

"Mason! Get away! The house is going to collapse any minute! Sawyer, pull him back!"

Sawyer was already reaching for the boy, and he grabbed Mason by the collar and pulled him backward out of harm's way, at the same time yelling up at Sara.

"What are you waiting for? Jump, Sara! Jump!"

Sara stood at the edge of the roof, ready to jump, but just like the boy she looked back at the window and knew that she could not leave her father inside. She tossed the rifle to the ground and looked down at Sawyer. She shook her head.

"I'm sorry, I can't do it! My father's still inside! I have to go back for him!"

As Sawyer watched helplessly, Sara turned and ran back toward the open window, shouting her father's name as she climbed back inside, the hot smoke stinging her eyes and lungs.

"Jacob! Where are you?"

She could barely see inside the room, but she pushed through the door and saw her father stumbling toward her, his eyebrows and hair singed and smoking, his hands and forearms badly burned. She saw that he was carrying a smoldering leather satchel in his hands, and he let the bag fall to the floor as he collapsed in front of her. Sara looked down at him in shock.

"Your hands! Your arms! What have you done?"

Jacob was still conscious, but the heat from the fire had seared his throat, and each breath was excruciating. Sara pounded on his back with both fists before she rolled him over and saw the two gunshot wounds up close, a single dime-sized bullet hole only inches below his navel, another just beneath his ribs. Blood was pumping out of both holes like an open faucet, and Sara instinctively shoved her fingers into the wounds to try and slow the bleeding. She looked up at Jacob.

"We have to get you out of here right now."

Flames were now raging in the hallway just outside the room, and Sara knew that they needed to get out of the house right away. She grabbed Jacob by the shoulders, and with all her strength she pulled him into a sitting position and screamed in his face.

"Jacob! We need to get out of here or we're both going to die! You need to stand up!"

Jacob raised his head and looked up at his daughter. There were tears welling in his eyes. He opened his mouth, and Sara leaned in, holding her head next to his as he struggled to get the words out.

"Sara. This is all my fault. I should have listened to you. Take this satchel and go before it's too late."

Sara was growing frantic.

"What are you talking about? Just get up!"

"No, Sara. It's too late for me. Take the satchel. There is a map inside. A map that leads to something amazing."

"I don't care about any map! Just get up right now!"

Jacob began to cough violently, a fine spray of red mist settling on his chin. He looked at her again, and Sara could see in his eyes that there was nothing more she could do. Jacob wiped the blood from his mouth.

"Take the damn bag, Sara."

Sara pounded her fists on the floor and screamed at him.

"No! We have to get out of here together!"

With every ounce of strength left in her body, Sara tried to lift Jacob to his feet, but she could not get him up, the heat from the flames almost unbearable. She looked down at her father. His eyes were rolling back in his head, his clothing soaked in blood and sweat, his face and arms raw with burns. The fire was now in the doorway, hot flames reaching out for her, and Sara leaned down and rested her head on her father's chest.

"I can't leave you."

Jacob said something she could not understand, and Sara lifted her head. His eyes were now looking straight into hers, hot tears running in thin, white lines down his soot-covered face. It was the first time that Sara had ever seen her father cry. His voice was quiet, and she leaned in and pressed her cheek to his as he spoke.

"I am so sorry, Sara. For everything. I should have listened to you and Sawyer. I should have never sent up that damn smoke signal."

Sara shook her head in confusion.

"What are you talking about? I don't understand."

Jacob looked up at his daughter, his eyes growing dim.

"It was Benjamin and Rebekah who did this to us, Sara. I don't know why, but I am so sorry, Sara. Please forgive me. I love you, my daughter. Now, please, go."

Jacob dropped his head and closed his eyes, his breathing

shallow and raspy, a thin line of blood running from the corner of his open mouth. Sara could feel the waves of heat on her back, and she knew it was time to go. She leaned down and kissed her father on the forehead, her own tears falling to the floor as she whispered to him one last time.

"I'm so sorry too, Daddy. I love you, and I forgive you. Goodbye. Goodbye forever."

A gust of flames and superheated air rushed into the room, and although Sara looked back at the leather satchel that her father so desperately wanted her to take, she knew that she was out of time. Instead, she left the bag behind and launched herself out of the window, dodging pockets of flames as she rolled out onto the roof. Smoke and flame were swirling all around her, and although she could not see, she heard Sawyer calling her name, and she knew what she had to do. With no other choice and Sawyer's voice echoing in her ears, Sara closed her eyes and flung herself off the roof, her hair and clothing singed as she burst through a wall of fire and landed hard on the ground below.

Sawyer was beside Sara almost as soon as she hit the ground, and he picked her up and carried her away from the raging flames. Her ankle was twisted in an unnatural position, and she moaned in pain as he set her down on the ground. She was fighting to breathe, and she coughed up a small pool of blackened phlegm before she could speak, tears rolling down her face.

"My father. I couldn't lift him. I tried."

Sawyer stood up and ran toward the burning house, looking in vain for any way that he could safely get inside. The flames were now rising well above the rooftop, and he turned and looked back at Sara.

"I'm sorry, Sara. There's no way in. There's nothing we can do now."

Out of the darkness, Mason came running over to them, screaming as he pointed up to the rooftop.

"L-look! Jacob's alive! Jacob's alive!"

Sara and Sawyer looked up in astonishment as a human form suddenly emerged from the window of Jacob's bedroom, the flames rising around him like an aura of amber and scarlet. Mason screamed his name again.

"Jacob!"

For a moment, a gust of wind cleared the roof of smoke, and they all three watched in silence as Jacob stood just outside the window, the fire surrounding him in every direction, the leather satchel in his hands. Suddenly, Mason gripped Sawyer's arm with surprising strength, his voice piercing as he screamed at the top of his lungs.

"S-save him, Sawyer! S-save Jacob!"

Sawyer wrenched his arm free and shoved Mason away, the smoke-laden wind flipping burning shingles off the roof, a shower of sparks and embers raining down on his head. Sawyer ignored the pain and ran toward the burning house, yelling up at Jacob.

"Do it! Jump, Jacob, jump!"

Suddenly, there was a loud cracking sound, and a huge plume

of fire and smoke billowed out from the ground floor. Sawyer was forced back, but even through the smoke he could see Jacob standing at the edge of the roof, and as they met eyes for a split second, Sawyer suddenly knew that Jacob was not going to jump. Instead, the man swung his arms forward with all his might, and Sawyer watched in confusion as the satchel came flying through the flames and crashed to the ground only inches away from his feet.

Sawyer instinctively grabbed the bag and backpedaled away as fast as he could, running to safety as the entire west side of the house came crashing to the ground in an explosion of flames and splintered wood that no man could possibly survive. Sawyer barely had time to stand up before Mason was on him again, shrieking and clawing at his chest, his words coming out in stuttered screams.

"S-save him, Sawyer! P-please save Jacob! Please!"

Sawyer grabbed the boy by his shoulder and pointed at the collapsed structure.

"Can't you see it's too late, Mason? He's gone. There's nothing we can do."

"No! Y-you have to save him! S-save him!"

Mason ran toward the inferno, staring up at the place where Jacob last stood, the spot now consumed by smoke and flames. Sawyer tried to pull the boy away, but Mason broke free and wailed uncontrollably, his terrifying cries echoing into the night. Sawyer looked over at Sara. He did not know what to do. Sara looked as if she was in shock, but she slowly reached up with her hand.

"Help me stand."

Sawyer pulled Sara to her feet, and she limped over to Mason. The girl's face was streaked with tears, but she gathered her composure and bent down beside the boy.

"Mason, it's OK. You need to take a deep breath and get control. There was nothing we could do. Jacob is gone now, but it's not safe here. We need to be quiet. OK, Mason? Quiet and calm."

She lifted Mason's chin and looked at his face. Tears were rolling out of his eyes, but when she reached her hand out to wipe his face, he suddenly lashed out and slapped her hand away, shoving her back as he sprang to his feet and howled into her face.

"Y-you let him die! How could you let him die?"

Sawyer was standing only a yard away, and he quickly stepped in between them and pushed Mason back.

"You need to calm down and stop yelling right now, Mason. We don't know who is still out there, and you're going to get us all killed."

Sara put her hand on Sawyer's shoulder to steady herself, but she did not want his help.

"That's enough, Sawyer. Let me handle Mason on my own."

She turned to speak to Mason, but before she could say a single word, he suddenly lunged forward, his long nails scratching Sawyer across the neck. Sara tried to reach for Mason, but he was too quick, and a bolt of searing pain exploded in her ankle as he shoved her backward. Sawyer had been completely caught off guard by the boy, but he was practically twice Mason's size and just as fast. As

Mason came close a second time, Sawyer grabbed him by the neck and flipped him over backward, slamming him hard to the ground. Sawyer let go of the boy and stepped back as Mason tried to catch his breath, the wind knocked clean out of his lungs.

"Just stay down, Mason. I don't want to hurt you."

Sawyer helped Sara to her feet. She was trying to remain calm, but she was losing the battle.

"Please, Mason. Just listen to Sawyer. He's trying to help you, and we have to go now."

Suddenly, Mason was on his feet again, his wiry frame silhouetted against the burning wreckage of the house. For a moment, no one moved, and then very slowly Mason pulled Jacob's .38 revolver from the back of his pants. He looked straight past Sara and leveled the gun at Sawyer.

"This is all your f-fault."

Sara struggled to her feet and quickly stepped in front of Sawyer. She held up her hands and spoke calmly.

"Please, Mason. Put the gun down. You're wrong. There was nothing any of us could do. You can't blame Sawyer for this."

Mason reached up to his scalp and ripped out a chunk of blond hair as he shrieked like a banshee and glared at Sara.

"S-shut up, Sara! Y-you don't know anything! Sawyer hated him, y-you both hated him, and y-you let him burn to death!"

Sawyer stepped out from behind Sara. The boy was becoming even more frenzied, snot running out of his nose, his arms flapping at his side. Sawyer raised his hands and spoke calmly.

"Mason, just calm down. Take a deep breath."

Mason looked up at Sawyer, spit flying from his mouth. He pointed the gun straight at Sawyer's face.

"You shut up, Sawyer! Y-you let him burn! I hate you! I'll kill you!"

Just as Sawyer had hoped, the boy took a final step forward, and with Mason now only an arm's length away, Sawyer moved in and smashed the revolver from his hand. The boy was caught by surprise and Sawyer slapped him across the face and sent him crashing to the ground. Mason stayed where he fell and buried his face in his hands as he began to wail. Sara stepped around Sawyer to reach out to the boy one last time, but as she came near him, she could see that it was not safe, and she stopped and spoke softly.

"Mason, please. Let us help you. We're your family."

Mason stopped crying and slowly stood up, challenging Sara with his eyes. His voice was now eerily calm.

"F-family? What do either of you know about family?"

Sara opened her mouth to speak, but Mason would not allow it. His eyes glowed red in the firelight, and he looked straight at Sara.

"Y-you don't know anything about family. The Cult you *saved* me from was more of a family than this. You only care about Sawyer. You never l-loved Jacob. And you never loved me."

Again, Sara tried to speak, but Mason cut her off and pointed a long, dirty finger in Sawyer's direction.

"It's all his f-fault. He t-took you away from me, and now he's let Jacob die."

Mason looked straight into Sawyer's eyes, white foam spraying from his lips, his words laced with poison.

"Because of y-you, I don't have a family. Because of you, I have n-nothing."

Suddenly, and without another word, Mason turned and ran, his legs digging frantically into the dry ground as he bolted away from them. Sara tried to limp after him, but Sawyer grabbed her and held her tight as the boy ran toward the main gate, the girl crying out in vain as Mason disappeared into the night.

26

Sawyer held onto Sara and tried to calm her as she dropped to her knees and put her face in her hands.

"Please let him go, Sara. He'll come back. Just let him go."

Sara pushed him away.

"There are killers out there, Sawyer! You have to go after him. They'll kill him if they catch him. Please, Sawyer, you have to do something."

Sawyer shook his head.

"No, Sara. Mason made his choice. Right now, we need to get you somewhere safe. Come on. I know where to go."

The girl finally nodded, and Sawyer picked up the satchel, the revolver, and the rifle and helped Sara hobble away from the fire. When they were tucked safely inside a small storage shed near the northeast corner of the compound, Sawyer pulled a rag from his pocket and wiped the soot and tears from her face. The girl struck a single match, and even in the low light he was again reminded of how strikingly beautiful she truly was, and for a moment, he stared at her face as if it were something only conjured in the most wonderful of dreams. He knew what she wanted him to do, but for once, he could not do it.

"I'm sorry. I know you want me to go after Mason, but I just can't right now. I need answers, Sara. I just killed a man who was trying to break into Edward's quarters, at least one other ran off, and for some reason Benjamin is lying dead on the ground back behind the main house. Nothing makes sense to me. Like, why the hell did your father trade his life for this bag? What is going on, Sara? Who did this to us? Someone has to pay."

The girl looked over at the burning wreckage of her home and shook her head.

"I don't know anything about what's in the bag, the man you killed, or anything else, but I do know that Benjamin shot my father, and that my father killed Benjamin."

Sara paused and looked up at Sawyer. She could see that he did not yet understand.

"Don't you see who is responsible for all of this, Sawyer? Deep down, don't you already know?"

Sawyer stared at Sara, and as if the question itself had keyed the answer, it all finally fell into place. The boy's eyes grew wide, and he whispered a single name as if it were a curse.

"Rebekah."

Sara reached out and took his hand.

"Yes, and she's still somewhere out there, Sawyer. If she can't control us, she wants to destroy us. And she's not done yet. I can feel it. We can't let her get away with this."

Sawyer's eyes suddenly narrowed, and he squeezed the girl's hand.

"Don't ask me how, but I think I might know where to find her."

Sara raised her eyebrows.

"Are you sure?"

Sawyer leaned close and sighed.

"No, but what other option do we have? Look, Sara, I swear to you that I will do everything I can to find Mason, but right now, Rebekah and the people that killed your father are still out there, and if I don't go after them now, we might never get a chance to end this for good."

Sara knew that he was right, but she turned her gaze to the satchel.

"I understand, but my father gave his life for that bag. Before we do anything else, I have to know what's in it."

Sawyer picked up the satchel and set it beside Sara.

"Whatever's inside, it's heavy as hell."

The leather bag was scorched and blackened, but the lock was still secure, and Sawyer pulled out his knife and sliced through the buckle. He flipped the satchel open and reached inside. Slowly, he lifted a solid gold bar into the moonlight and looked over at Sara.

"More gold bars? I don't get it. Why would your father risk so much for this? They're worthless."

Sara was dumbfounded.

"I don't know. He was burned and bleeding. He wasn't making sense. He kept just telling me to take the bag, and he said something about a map."

Sara spent a moment searching inside the satchel before she pulled out a worn envelope and handed it to Sawyer. He pulled out a folded document, his eyes barely making out the markings of a hand-drawn map and what looked like a list of numbers. He handed the paper back to Sara.

"It looks like a map of the military base, I think, and some codes or something. I still don't get it, but it doesn't matter right now. I need to go. Keep the Beretta and the rifle ready. Shoot anyone that comes near. If I'm not back in an hour, get yourself somewhere safe, and I'll find you."

Sara nodded.

"Are you sure you know what you're doing?"

Sawyer took a moment to reload the Mossberg, and then he looked down at Sara.

"Yeah. One way or another, I'm going to find Rebekah. And when I do, I'm going make her pay."

He bent down and kissed the girl softly, but as he turned to leave Sara reached out and took hold of his hand one last time.

"Sawyer, I want you to promise that you will do two things for me before you go."

"Of course, Sara. Anything. What is it?"

"First, promise that you'll come back. I've already lost my father and maybe even Mason tonight. I can't bear to lose you, too."

Sawyer smiled and squeezed her hand.

"Don't worry, Sara. I will come back to you. I promise."

Sara smiled back at him, but only for a moment as she let go of his hand.

"I'm going to hold you to that, Sawyer, but there is still one more promise that I need you to make before you go."

"Of course. What is it, Sara?"

Sara reached out and ran her finger down the length of the Mossberg.

"When you find Rebekah, and whoever else is responsible for my father's death, promise me that you will kill every last one of them for me, Sawyer. I want them all to die. Can you promise me that, Sawyer? Can you do that for me, Hero?"

At that moment in time, Sawyer would have killed every last person on Earth if it made the girl happy, and he leaned in close and kissed her one last time, whispering softly into her ear before he turned to go.

"I promise, my love. I promise, I will kill them all."

27

With nothing more to be said, Sawyer left Sara concealed in the shed and sprinted out of the compound, confident that Rebekah would have done the same. There was only one possible location that stood out in the boy's mind, and as soon as he approached the small, roofless building behind the theater, he knew that he was on the right track. Sawyer bent down and looked at the fresh footprints in the wet grass surrounding the structure. It was obvious that someone had been there not long before and he whispered under his breath.

"Jackpot. We may have another winner."

Sawyer held his breath as he crept up and pressed his back against the ivy-covered cinderblock, the shotgun held tightly in his hands. He listened. A few crickets chirped softly in the distance, but there were no other sounds. He moved silently toward the front of the structure. The door was partially open. He peeked inside. There was no one there. He cursed under his breath and pushed through the door.

"Goddamn it. Where the hell could they be?"

He bent down and looked at the ground. It was hard to make out in the moonlight, but the floor was scattered with dusty footprints, and not all from the same boots. Sawyer was about to step back outside when suddenly he heard a low whisper and footsteps approaching the building. With nowhere to go, he quickly crouched in the corner behind a stack of old pallets and held his breath as the door swung open and two unknown men stepped inside.

Sawyer sat motionless, his heart thumping, his finger on the trigger of the Mossberg. In the tight confines of the room, Sawyer knew it would be easy for him to kill the two men with the shotgun, but he remained patient. More than anything, he wanted to know where Rebekah was, and he kept perfectly still as the shorter of the two men spoke first, his voice betraying a faint Southern drawl.

"What are we going to do now? Just sit here? Where is she? She should be here by now."

His partner, who was at least a foot taller, replied quietly.

"How should I know? We just need to wait here."

The Short Man was not satisfied.

"Benjamin said that she would be here. I knew we shouldn't have listened to him. He screwed it all up. She's going to be pissed."

The Tall Man seemed cool and collected.

"Just calm down, man. Benjamin is dead, and we'll just tell her that it was his idea to light the house on fire in the first place. That's not our fault."

The Short Man did not sound relieved.

"Sure, whatever you say. But where do you think she is? She should be here by now."

The Tall Man sighed.

"Like I keep telling you, how should I know? She told us to meet here, and now we're here. Just keep your voice down, and let's wait outside. This place gives me the creeps."

Sawyer remained frozen as the two men stepped back through the doorway and continued their conversation just outside. The boy looked down at the 12-gauge in his hands. The Mossberg had been the difference between life and death on so many occasions that he had lost count, but Sawyer understood that if he wanted any chance at Rebekah, he could not use the weapon now. If these men were going to die, it would have to be done quietly, and Sawyer strapped the shotgun tightly to his back and reached for the top of the wall.

The wall of the roofless structure was ten feet high, but, using the pallets as a boost, Sawyer quietly pulled himself up to the top and slipped his knife from its sheath. Below him, the two men were deep in conversation, and neither took notice as he silently crouched above them, his breath held. He had no idea how he expected to disarm and interrogate two armed men with only his knife, but he noticed a broken piece of cinderblock resting on top of the wall beside him, and he suddenly had an idea. As quietly as he could, he picked up the block, and with one swift motion he heaved the brick into the darkness, the heavy concrete crashing noisily through the brush several dozen yards away.

As soon as they heard the block hitting the brush, the two men spun around and raised their weapons. Sawyer remained motionless atop the wall, but he heard them whispering, and then the Short Man quickly disappeared into the darkness. Just as Sawyer had hoped, one of them had taken the bait, and he edged his way into position directly above the Tall Man. The boy knew that he only had seconds to act, and he did not bother counting down as he swung his legs off the wall and dropped silently through the darkness. The sheer weight of the boy smashed the man to the ground, and Sawyer buried the blade of his knife deep in the soft flesh of the Tall Man's neck. Once on the ground, the stricken man tried to stand, but Sawyer pulled the knife loose and drove it home one more time, the sickening sound of the metal blade grating on cartilage as he severed the man's trachea in one violent slash.

The boy knew that he needed to act quickly if he wanted to catch the Short Man off guard, and he left the Tall Man where he fell and headed into the darkness. A light fog was beginning to appear at his feet, and he crept quietly forward, the knife held straight in front of him. The moon was newly shrouded in clouds, and Sawyer could not yet see the Short Man, but the sound of his heavy breathing was not difficult to track, and Sawyer circled around to his left as he silently closed the distance between them. Sawyer was within ten feet when the Short Man suddenly stopped and spun around a full 180 degrees, his pistol swinging erratically in Sawyer's direction. The man was beginning to panic, and the distinct pitch of terror had crept into his voice.

"Who's there? Jeb?"

Sawyer quietly slipped the knife back into his belt and swung the shotgun off his shoulder. He crouched down low as he waited for the right moment, a new round of adrenaline seeping into his veins. Again, the Short Man repeated himself.

"Who's there? Jeb? That you?"

Inexplicably, the man lowered his gun for a split second, and Sawyer saw his chance. Without a sound, the boy materialized out of the darkness and smashed the heavy stock of the shotgun across the Short Man's face, pieces of teeth splintering in the moonlight as the man collapsed at Sawyer's feet.

Sawyer threw the Mossberg over his shoulder and pulled his knife free. He dropped down and pressed it against the Short Man's neck, the edge of the blade biting into the skin just below the man's Adam's apple. Sawyer's voice was chillingly calm.

"You so much as make a noise and I'll cut your throat. Understand?"

The Short Man nodded, and Sawyer continued.

"I'm going to ask you some questions, and I don't have time for games. How many are in your group? I want a number. And I want names."

The Short Man coughed up a piece of broken tooth and answered without hesitation.

"There were five of us. Dawson, Jeb, me, Benjamin, and Rebekah."

Sawyer pushed the blade harder against his throat.

"What about Edward? Wasn't he part of this? Wasn't he with you?"

The Short Man shook his head and spit out another mouthful of blood.

"Edward was always part of this, but he was never one of us. He can rot in hell, for all I care."

Sawyer could not be sure if the man was telling the truth or exactly what he meant, but there was no time to dig deeper.

"Where are the others now? Where's Rebekah?"

"I don't know. We were all supposed to meet behind the theater if anything went wrong. That's the truth, so help me God."

Sawyer lifted his head and looked back toward the roofless building for only a split second, but that was all the distraction that the Short Man needed. Without warning, the man swung his arm across his body, the rock he had grabbed off the ground smashing into the side of Sawyer's head with tremendous force. The Short Man rolled out from under Sawyer and attempted to stand, but his equilibrium was still off, and he stumbled forward, falling to the ground only a few feet away. Sawyer was still conscious, but he was also dazed and bleeding heavily from a large gash above his ear. He staggered to his feet, both his knife and the shotgun lost somewhere in the darkness.

By the time Sawyer looked up, the Short Man was on his feet as well, and he was now wielding a knife of his own. The man spit out a thick batch of blood and snarled at Sawyer through his nearly toothless mouth.

"You better make your peace with the Lord, boy, because you are about to meet him right quick!"

The Short Man lunged toward the boy, but Sawyer dodged to his left and drove his knee into the man's ribs, the knife missing its mark by mere inches as the two of them fell to the ground. Sawyer desperately fought to get control of the weapon, but the Short Man was quick, and he slashed at Sawyer's chest and arms, the blade drawing blood in arcing slices. They broke apart and stood facing each other for several seconds, both of them winded and wounded. Sawyer knew that if he wanted any chance at confronting Rebekah, he needed to end this fight as soon as possible. He stepped back and braced himself.

The Short Man came at him again, but this time Sawyer did not try to dodge the strike. Instead, he met the knife at its lowest point, allowing the blade to sink deep into the muscle of his forearm. Sawyer roared in pain, but he kept his momentum moving forward, and he grabbed hold of the Short Man and dragged him to the ground. They struggled among the dead leaves and dirt for only a few seconds before the man realized that the boy would soon have him pinned, and he twisted like an animal and cried out in terror.

"Help me, Jeb! Help me, Rebekah!"

Sawyer did not give him another chance to call for help, and once in position he rose up and dropped a single devastating elbow across the bridge of the Short Man's nose, an explosion of blood splashing over his face as the skin split and bones broke. The man's arms fell to his side, but this time Sawyer could not stop himself, and he rained down blows until the Short Man was obviously dead, his head smashed like a pumpkin on the day after Halloween.

The man's knife was still lodged in the boy's forearm, and Sawyer pulled it free and shoved it into his belt, ignoring the pain. There was no time to do anything more than pack his wounds with dirt before he recovered the Mossberg and headed back in the direction he had come from, a patchy blanket of fog the Short Man's only burial shroud.

Sawyer returned to the roofless building and dragged the Tall Man's body around the corner, kicking a layer of dirt over the dark pool of blood near the doorway. He decided that his best chance to catch Rebekah was to wait for her to return, and with luck on his side, it was only minutes before he heard the faint sound of footsteps quickly approaching. Sawyer held his breath as a slight figure emerged from the darkness and stepped through the doorway. She quickly lit a candle, and she was about to walk back outside the building when Sawyer stepped out of the shadows and leveled the shotgun squarely at her astonished face. Rebekah went instantly white, and for the first time since the boy had known her, she fumbled with her words.

"Sawyer! My goodness! I can't—I mean, I don't—I mean, it's you. You're alive?"

Sawyer nodded and kept the shotgun trained on her face. Rebekah tried to compose herself before she spoke again.

"Where are the others? Is everyone safe?"

Sawyer said nothing, his finger poised just over the trigger, his eyes narrowed. Rebekah forced a smile.

"Please, Sawyer, for the love of God. It's me, Rebekah. Put the shotgun down. I know we haven't always seen eye to eye, but we need to talk and decide what to do. Please, let's work together. Now is the time for unity."

Sawyer had heard enough from her, and he shoved the shotgun into her chest, forcing Rebekah to step backward as he advanced.

"Shut up, Rebekah, and listen very closely. How many more men do you have with you? I want a number, and I want names. I need to know who is still out there."

Rebekah shook her head.

"Sawyer, I don't understand what you are asking me. What men? I heard the gunshots, and then I ran. That's all I know."

Sawyer growled.

"Sorry. Wrong answer, Rebekah."

Without warning, Sawyer whipped the end of the shotgun violently into her face, the heavy wooden stock splitting her lip as she crashed to the floor. He stepped over and grabbed her by the hair, dragging her out of the doorway. He let go and lifted her chin with the barrel of the Mossberg.

"Get up. We're going for a walk."

Rebekah staggered to her feet, and he shoved her forward down the trail, pushing her down to the ground once they were safely concealed within the tree line.

"Last chance, Rebekah. How many men are there with you?"

Rebekah held her hand to her mouth and looked down at her feet as she spoke, tears in her eyes, her voice shaky and weak.

"I don't know. It was Edward who made us do it. It was his idea from the start. He's gone mad. You can ask Benjamin when he comes. He'll tell you that it was all Edward's doing."

Sawyer let a dark smile flash across his face.

"Benjamin is dead, Rebekah. Jacob killed him. Blew most of his face clean off. I saw his body with my own eyes, or at least what was left of it."

Rebekah stopped crying and stared up at Sawyer.

"That is not true. I don't believe you."

"Believe whatever you want. But he's not the only one. Your other men—Jeb, Dawson, and the short one—they're all dead, too. Now, one last time: is there anyone else here with you?"

Rebekah let her head fall and whimpered.

"You have to ask Edward. He is the one you want, not me."

Again, the boy offered no warning, and he swung his boot directly into her face, splitting her cheek wide open just below her right eye. The woman was knocked backward by the kick, but even before she was able to sit back up, she raised one hand and pleaded.

"Please, for God's sake, no more. I'll tell you everything you want to know."

Sawyer pointed the shotgun at her face.

"Start talking."

"There were six of us, including Edward. Jeb, Dawson, Jesse,

Benjamin, and I. That's it, I swear to you. There is no one else."

"Where is Edward now? Is he coming to meet you here?"

Rebekah shook her head and wiped away the blood that was running down her cheek.

"I don't know where he is. I told you that it was his plan. I never wanted to be a part of it, but he forced me to. He said he would kill me if I were to try and warn anyone. Please, Sawyer. I beg of you. You must believe me!"

Sawyer was out of patience.

"This is the last time I ask you this question, Rebekah. Where is Edward?"

Rebekah reached out and pulled at the leg of Sawyer's pants.

"Please, Sawyer, I don't know! In the Lord's name, I don't know where he is!"

Sawyer stared at her for a long moment, and then he put the shotgun over his shoulder and took out the Short Man's knife. Rebekah's eyes grew big as she caught sight of the weapon.

"Please, no! I beg of you! It was Edward!"

"I don't really give a damn whose plan it was anymore. Edward is the last one of you left. If you can't tell me where he is right now, then you're worthless to me."

Rebekah shook her head.

"No, you're mistaken. I may not know where Edward is, but I am far from worthless to you. I can give you something worth much more than Edward."

"And what might that be, Rebekah?"

"I can take you to Edward's gold. It's no fairy tale like he told you it was. There's more than you can imagine, and it's not just the gold. Everything we need to start over is there. Food, water, fuel, generators—even weapons. It's all in an underground bunker on the base. It can all be ours."

Sawyer shook his head.

"I already told you that I couldn't care less about the gold or some fake story about a bunker. It's all crap."

There was an uneasy silence before Rebekah finally spoke, her eyes suddenly dry, the fear now gone from her voice.

"You simply do not understand, do you, Sawyer?"

Sawyer grabbed her by the back of the neck and pressed the blade of the knife against her windpipe.

"I understand everything perfectly well, Rebekah. I understand that you're an evil bitch who murdered Jacob and who deserves to burn in hell."

Despite the knife at her throat, Rebekah smirked.

"Jacob chose his own path, Sawyer. Those who offer a false witness to God cannot expect to escape his wrath, but that is beside the point."

"What is your point, Rebekah?"

She looked up into the boy's green eyes.

"Do you really think it will always be like this, Sawyer? Do you truly believe that the plants and animals will inherit the earth from man, and that you and Sara will go on living a fantasy as the last two lovers on the planet?"

Sawyer was not sure what she was getting at, and he let her go on talking.

"If you do believe that, then you are either exceptionally naïve or less intelligent than I have given you credit for. What you do not seem to understand is that humankind will rise again, Sawyer. There will be a time very soon when the righteous will re-populate this land, and God's chosen people will once again rule over all living things here on Earth. What you also do not seem to understand is that you and I are among those chosen few, Sawyer, and when God deems the time is right, there will be war between good and evil, and a glorious return to civilization will soon follow."

Sawyer still did not grasp what she was saying.

"What does that have to do with me?"

Rebekah's eyes grew brighter.

"Don't you see? It has everything to do with you. Wars require leadership, Sawyer, and in order to lead, one must first have power. And how does one come to have power? If history has taught us anything, it is that wealth brings power. And as it has been throughout history, gold will soon again become the common currency of man, and those who have gold will have power. Power that you and I can share. Do you understand what I am saying? We both know that you are a natural leader, and so am I. Working together, we can win the upcoming war against the Crows, and you and I can take our rightful place as architects of the new world. We can take our place as God's chosen leaders of the new era of humankind."

A smirk flashed across Sawyer's face.

"Together? As God's chosen leaders? You're even crazier than I thought. There is not going to be any war. There is no Cult of the Crow anymore. Besides, you've said yourself that only true believers will be among the chosen. If that's true, then why choose me?"

Rebekah looked up at the boy.

"I can see it in your eyes, Sawyer. Deep down, you do believe, and God always chooses his leaders wisely—even if they do keep the company of sinners, like your dearest, Sara."

Sawyer dug the tip of the knife into her throat, hard enough to draw blood.

"Don't you ever speak her name again, do you understand? Sara is ten times the person you will ever be. Never forget that fact. And as for your claim that God will choose who will be the next great leader—you might be too delusional to understand this, Rebekah, but the truth is that leaders are chosen by men, not by gods, and all the gold in the world couldn't get me to stand beside someone like you."

Rebekah hung her head, and as the tears began to flow from the corners of her eyes, she spoke quietly, her voice barely above a whisper.

"Everything I did, I did in the name of the Lord, and if you don't understand that, then there is nothing left to say. I am ready to enter God's Kingdom. Do what you must, Sawyer, but if even the smallest part of you believes in the one true Lord, please do it quickly. That is all I ask."

Rebekah closed her eyes, and Sawyer looked down at the woman. Her face was bruised and bloodied, her upper lip and cheek split and swollen. Snot was running from her nose. She looked utterly beaten-down and pathetic. Suddenly, he was reminded of the Bowman's daughter, and of all of the other lives that he had ended, and he knew right then that he could not kill the woman in cold blood. Instead, he pulled the knife from her throat and shook his head.

"I don't know what sick game you were trying to play here, Rebekah, but killing people in God's name doesn't make it right. And the truth is, who or what I believe is my business, not yours. But just so you know, I do believe in God, and you can thank him that I've had my fill of death for one day."

Sawyer tossed the knife into the darkness and stepped back. He bent down and growled through gritted teeth.

"Now get the hell out of here before I change my mind. If I even get the slightest feeling that you are anywhere near here ever again, I will hunt you down and feed you alive to the crows. Do you understand, Rebekah? Never come back to this Mission ever again. *Never* come back."

Rebekah wiped the blood from her quivering chin and stood up, her face a mask of disbelief.

"I understand. I won't come back, I promise. Thank you for your mercy, Sawyer. Whether you know it or not, God has chosen well."

Sawyer pulled the shotgun off his shoulder, and by the look

on his face Rebekah knew better than to risk saying another word. Instead, she gave Sawyer one last nod before she walked away, her dark form disappearing into the murky fog. As he watched her go, Sawyer could not help but think about his promise to Sara—to leave no one alive—but he understood now that it was a promise that he simply could not keep. He could not bring himself to take Rebekah's life like he had taken so many others, and he could only hope that the woman would keep her promise to never return.

Yet, even with Rebekah gone and her men dead, Sawyer was still concerned with both the whereabouts and the motives of Edward, and he knew that he had to get back to Sara as fast as he could. He had no idea where Edward was, or what the man was truly capable of, and all he could think about was that Sara might be in danger. He ran as fast he could, and he was only steps away from the main gate when he suddenly felt the presence of someone behind him. Sawyer slowly turned around, yet before he could make out who it was, a single gunshot rang out in the darkness.

The boy cried out as the shot tore straight through his side and exploded against the gate behind him, the white-hot sting of the bullet sending him to his knees. He tried to rise and swing the Mossberg into a firing position, but by the time he looked up, he knew it was too late. Standing over him was Rebekah, a small, smoking pistol in her hand. She whispered.

"You should have listened to me when you had the chance, Sawyer. What I told you about the bunker was true. Same with the Crows. Together, we could have done great things. Now, you are forsaken, and it is up to God to judge you for your sins."

The boy looked up at her and scowled.

"My father used to say that God doesn't judge the forsaken; he only pays for their ticket to meet the devil. So, go ahead and pull the trigger, Rebekah, just be sure to look me up when you get to Hell."

Rebekah shook her head one last time and hissed.

"I was wrong about you. You are nothing but a foolish boy. Goodbye, Sawyer, and may the Lord have no mercy on your soul."

Rebekah leveled the pistol at his head, and as the boy closed his eyes and pictured Sara one last time, a final shot pierced the night air, and everything went dead-still.

28

Sara had been anxiously waiting inside the dark confines of the shed when she heard the pop of the first gunshot, and a sickening feeling immediately washed over the girl. Despite the pain in her injured ankle, she used the 30.06 rifle like a crutch and climbed to her feet. She moved as fast as she could, but she was barely a quarter of the way across the courtyard when the second shot rang out, and, imagining the worst, Sara could not stop herself from screaming the boy's name at the top of her lungs.

"Sawyer!"

The girl's cry rose above the echo of the last gunshot, and as the sound of his name reverberated in the cool night air, the boy that Sara loved more than life itself suddenly opened his eyes.

For several moments, Sawyer did nothing but stare straight ahead. He did not move. He did not speak. He did not breathe. He could not believe what he was seeing. Lying on the ground only a few feet away from him was the body of Rebekah, her dead eyes wide open, the small pistol still gripped tightly in her hand. A single bullet hole was in the center of her forehead, and standing behind her, a smoking pistol in his hand, was none other than Edward. The man looked down at Sawyer and nodded one time.

"Hello, Sawyer. I can't tell you how good it is to see you."

The boy was almost too stunned to speak, but his instincts were still sharp, and he let his hand drift over to the shotgun resting beside him. He looked up at Edward and shook his head.

"I don't understand. You saved my life? You killed Rebekah? But why?"

Edward stood where he was, the gun still in hand, neither one of them venturing a movement or a word. For a moment, they sat like two ancient sculptures, Edward tall and menacing, a weapon of death in his hands, Sawyer the fallen hero, his existence hanging in the balance. Ultimately, it was Edward who broke the long silence.

"You want to really know why I killed Rebekah? Well, the straightforward answer is because she deserved it. She would have killed you had I not intervened, and I simply couldn't let that happen, not in good conscience. She gave me no other choice but to do what I did. So, I did it. Good riddance, if you ask me."

He spat on the ground beside her body and winked over at Sawyer.

"The only downside is that the devil gets another bride, but at least we know she's going to make his life a living hell."

If Sawyer wasn't in such pain he might have laughed at the man's unexpected jest, but instead he simply let Edward keep on talking.

"Look, son. There's something you need to understand. I've always been on your side, and I should have been honest with you since day one. Rebekah played us all. I always knew that she was hungry for power, but if I had even the slightest idea that it would come to this, to outright murder, I would have been the first to try and stop it. The fact is that she tried to kill us both tonight, and we're sure as hell lucky to be alive."

Sawyer hesitated another moment before finally speaking, not sure what to believe. His index finger had found the trigger on the Mossberg. The safety was already off.

"That's not what Rebekah told me. She said that it was you. She said that tonight was your idea all along."

Edward was unshaken.

"I had nothing to do with this, son. You know me, and you know her. Whatever she told you is just a plain lie. Not the first to come out of her mouth, that is for certain—but I think you know that already."

Sawyer took a deep breath. He calculated that it would only

take him a half-second to raise the shotgun and fire, but he was not quite ready yet.

"I know that Rebekah couldn't be trusted, but I guess that can be true of almost anyone, don't you think, Edward?"

Edward nodded. He looked down at the shotgun.

"I think that is true. But the real question here is whether you and I can trust each other. Am I right about that?"

Sawyer cocked his chin up and locked eyes with the man, answering the question with one of his own.

"You are right about that. So why don't you give me a reason to trust you? First off, where did you get the gun?"

Edward looked down at the pistol in his hand and slowly ejected the clip. He cleared the gun and tossed the magazine over to Sawyer. Both the pistol and the clip were obviously empty.

"I've kept this pistol with only a single shot in it hidden from Rebekah since the beginning. I wasn't sure who that one bullet was meant for, but now I'm starting to think that God had a plan all along."

Sawyer tossed the empty clip back to Edward. The man re-inserted the clip and threw the gun a few feet away. Sawyer nodded and leveled the shotgun at the man's chest.

"All right. I believe you, now why don't you also tell me everything you know about the gold? Tell me the truth about the bunker at Pendleton? And about the Crows."

The man allowed a small smile, the wrinkles in his face lining up one on top of another.

"So, it sounds like Rebekah's been busy spinning yarns once again. I'm not surprised. But the real question is, did you believe her?"

"I don't know. People say a lot of things when a knife is pressed against their throat. But then again, she was very specific. People also say the devil is in the details, and she gave me details."

Edward pushed out his bottom lip out and nodded.

"Fair enough, Sawyer. I do have a story to tell, but you're bleeding pretty badly from that gunshot wound, not to mention your arm. We should get you patched up, and then I will tell you everything that I know."

Sawyer shook his head.

"No. You'll tell me now. Besides, we're about as safe right here as we're going to get. Rebekah, and Benjamin, and all of her men are dead—all but maybe one of them. But that's what we're going to find out, aren't we, Edward?"

Edward raised his hands into the air just as Sara pushed through the gate. She took one look at the boy and let out a lengthy sigh, her bottom lip beginning to tremble.

"Sawyer! You're alive. I heard gunshots and I thought the worst. Are you OK?"

She hobbled over to Sawyer and helped him to stand up. Sawyer wanted nothing more than to grab the girl and kiss her a thousand times, but he kept the shotgun aimed at Edward.

"I'm all right, I think. At least for now."

Slowly, the girl looked down at the body of the dead woman

lying a few feet away. Her dark eyes went wide.

"Oh my god. Rebekah. She's dead. What happened?"

Sawyer glanced down at Rebekah's still open eyes and shuddered.

"She tried to kill me, but Edward stopped her before she could finish the job. I'll tell you everything else as soon as I can, but right now I need some information."

The boy took a step toward Edward.

"I want to know the truth about what went on at the base. I want to know everything about Rebekah, about the Cult, the bunker, and about your part in all of this. If I'm satisfied that you've been honest, then you have my word that I'll let you walk away from here. If not, and I think you're lying, you'll never take another step again. Do we have a deal, Edward?"

The man nodded.

"Yes, Sawyer. We have a deal."

"Good. I'm not going to lie, I've always liked you, Edward, but you better have a damn good story to tell."

Edward took a deep breath.

"I feel the same about you both, and I do have a story to tell. What Rebekah said to you on that first night was true. We did meet on the base, but it was no happy occasion. Up until about a few weeks before the blackout, I was working at Pendleton as a civilian consultant, but as soon as I was identified as immune to the virus, everything changed. Next thing I know, they are testing me like some damn lab rat, and they threw me in with Rebekah and her flock. You heard that it was called 'Paradise', but it was far from it. Not long after that, the grid went down, and by the time the brass declared the whole mission FUBAR and abandoned the base, Rebekah was already in full control."

Edward looked up at the sky and shook his head as if he were re-living every moment.

"You see, Rebekah had brainwashed her brother and the remaining survivors to believe that they were the chosen ones, and they controlled the food, the water, and the few guns that had been left behind. There were thirteen immune survivors at the beginning, but within a month, anyone who disagreed with Rebekah was either dead or disappeared somehow. The truth is, I was never one of her blind followers—she knew that—but unlike the others, I had something to bargain with. If not, Rebekah would have let her flock string me up long ago."

"Let me guess. You used the gold and everything else in that bunker to bargain for your life?"

Edward nodded.

"I did whatever I had to do, but yes. That bunker, and the rumor of gold inside it, was the best bargaining chip that I had. And that's what it was, a rumor—but it was one that people wanted to believe. Just after the base was abandoned, there was talk among the survivors that the military had secret bunkers stockpiled with greenbacks, weapons, fuel, food, vehicles, and even gold, all of it buried somewhere on Pendleton. Part of it was actually true, and I knew enough about it to make Rebekah believe I knew a hell of a lot more than I really did, and because of that, she kept me alive.

Alive, but on a very short leash."

Sawyer looked back at Edward, his eyebrows raised as he questioned the story for the first time.

"Rebekah kept you alive because of a rumor you told her? Those gold bars she gave all of us looked like the real thing to me. Where did those come from? And why didn't you just walk away if life on the base was so terrible."

"The gold bars she gave you were real, and there was always some truth to what I was telling her. The fact is, there is an underground bunker that was once filled with gold, and much more than just that, but it's empty now. The military made sure of that before they left. As for not walking away, well, some might say that I didn't have the courage to strike out on my own. Whether you believe it or not, Sawyer, not everyone can handle being alone."

The boy nodded, but he knew there was more to the story, and he waited. Edward looked down for a moment as if ashamed, but he continued speaking.

"In the confusion of the first round of evacuations at the base, I had the opportunity to access that bunker several times in the weeks before I was quarantined, and I took what I could. It wasn't right, and I'm not proud of it, but it in the long run it saved my life, and I was able to use the bars I took to convince Rebekah that there was more gold to be had—if only we could get inside the bunker, of course."

"And she believed you?"

"Well, let's just say that she definitely wanted to believe me.

Rebekah's entire world revolved around the idea of being chosen by God, and she saw herself as the only one who would rebuild his kingdom here on Earth. Not incorrectly, she recognized that gold would be the standard currency once society began to rebuild, and she was desperate to have that kind of power at her fingertips. Every day, I stayed alive by telling her that I was working to break the codes that we would need to access the lower levels of the bunker."

"And let me guess—you never did?"

"No. I don't know the first thing about code breaking, but neither did she, or anyone else, and as long as I scribbled numbers and algorithms in my notebook all day, she believed I was making progress. That worked for a time, but when our food and water started running dangerously thin, and things started getting desperate last summer, I knew that I was the next head on the chopping block."

"How did you know that?"

"She told me as much only days before we came here. She said that if I didn't get that bunker open by the end of the season, I was a dead man. But the next thing you know, we woke up to see a huge plume of smoke on the horizon, and just like that, she hatches a new plan. She never gave me any specifics, but I had no choice but to agree to come here with her. I'm a God-fearing man, Sawyer, but I'm no zealot, and Benjamin and the other men never trusted me. The fact of the matter is that it was only Rebekah, and her desire for the gold, that was keeping me alive in the first place, and I knew that if I stayed behind, one of those boys would kill me within the first hour that she was gone."

Sawyer took a deep breath. He still wanted more information from Edward.

"How much of her plan did she share with you? Did you know she planned on trying to murder us?"

"No, and I never expected her to take it this far. I knew that she would try and convert you all and assume whatever power she could, but I couldn't imagine that she would do something like this. I can only assume she must have sent her brother down to the base to collect those boys. Come to think of it, I hadn't seen Benjamin in a few days—just long enough to make it there and back again."

"OK. But that doesn't explain why you didn't warn us in the first place. Why didn't you tell us the truth about Pendleton?"

"Well, I guess I was being selfish. Once I was here, I wanted to stay at the Mission, regardless of what Rebekah and Benjamin were planning. Think about it, Sawyer. If I were to have told you the truth—that Rebekah and Benjamin believed a holy war was on the horizon, and that they were hell-bent on converting you at all costs—would you have let us stay? Not to mention the fact that there were also three more brain-washed whack-jobs back at the base, just waiting for Rebekah to summon them here. Would you really believe that I had nothing to do with it? You would have thrown us all out, if not worse."

Sawyer nodded, realizing that Edward was right as the man continued.

"I swear that I didn't know they had planned to do any of this. In fact, I was sound asleep in my bed when they came, but as soon as I heard that first gunshot and saw Dawson and Jeb standing outside my door, I was up and out the back window within seconds. It was Jeb that came after me, but I lost him in the dark and headed straight downtown. I knew all about their secret meeting place behind the old theater—and I guess you did, too. I waited for them there, but you showed up first."

Sawyer raised his eyebrows.

"You were there? But if you saw me, why didn't you say something?"

"I wanted to warn you right then and there, but I was tucked into the bushes, and before I could move, Jeb and Jesse showed up. Next thing I know, Jeb is dead, and then you disappeared after Jesse into the trees. By that time, I knew better than to follow you into the fog and get myself killed, too, so I stayed where I was, not altogether surprised when you came trudging back instead of Jesse. Even then, I figured that it was no time to come jumping out of the bushes, so I watched as you dumped Jeb and waited for Rebekah. To be honest, I thought you would kill her right then and there, and I was very surprised when you let her walk away. I will not ask, or pretend to know, why you let her live, but I do know exactly how that woman thinks, and as quick as you walked away, she doubled back and came creeping up on you, that tiny pistol in her hand. I tried to catch up to her before she caught up to you, but she was a step ahead. I'm just glad I got there in time to put that single bullet in her head before it was too late."

"So, you shot her only to save my life? Not because you wanted Rebekah dead yourself?"

Edward allowed another small smile to cross his lips.

"Well, I can't rightly argue that last point, but my guess is that, under the same circumstances, you would have done the same for me."

Sawyer thought for a moment before he answered.

"Under the same circumstances, yeah, I just might have. But let me get all of this straight. What you are saying is that the gold is gone, you had nothing to do with this attack, and that everything else that Rebekah told me is a lie?"

"Yes and no. I had nothing to do with this attack, that is fact, but the gold is something else altogether. Look, son, the story behind that gold has helped to keep me alive for all this time, but even Rebekah needed more than just a few bars to keep her satisfied. In the end, I turned over my entire stockpile to her: a leather satchel with fifty, one-thousand-gram bars in total. Rebekah did not trust anyone back at the base, and she had us cart it here with us when we came. I wish I could prove it to you, but to be honest, I don't even know what became of it. I think she buried it somewhere outside the Mission, but I don't have the slightest idea where."

Sawyer looked over at Sara. They were both surprised that Edward would mention the satchel so specifically, but the girl nodded as if satisfied. Sawyer looked back to Edward.

"But what about the Cult of the Crow? Was Rebekah telling the truth about them or not?"

Edward sighed.

"There is some truth in what Rebekah said, and the Crows do still exist in small numbers. I've seen them with my own eyes, and they're not to be underestimated. Rumor has it that some of them were not naturally immune like us, that the military was involved somehow, but as for any war between good and evil, that's something only the man upstairs can predict."

Sawyer kept his eyes locked on Edward.

"So, what now, Edward? I believe that you've told us the truth, and I do appreciate what you've done for me, but I'm not sure what else there is to say."

"Well, I did what I thought was right, but I should have never let Rebekah take it this far, and for that, I'm sorry. But before I go, there is one thing I might ask, Sawyer—something that you have every right to deny me, should you so decide."

"All right, Edward. What is it?"

"The past is behind us now, Sawyer. Rebekah is dead, and what I want is the chance to make it all up to you. Truth is, I've got nowhere else to go, no one else to call a friend, and I'd like a chance to be a part of something that is real and good."

"What does that mean, exactly? What are you trying to ask me, Edward?"

"I only want one thing, Sawyer. I want to remain here at the Mission. I want to stay here, until time, circumstances, or you say otherwise. I'm on your side, Sawyer. I always have been. I think you have something good going on here, and I would proud to be a part of it all. Please just consider it. I will respect your answer, even if it's not what I want to hear."

Sawyer stared deep into Edward's eyes, and he saw nothing to make him question the man's word. He looked over at Sara. She nodded at him one time, and he knew it was his decision to make. He looked back to Edward and lowered the shotgun.

"I appreciate that, Edward, and that respect is a major reason why I am considering taking a chance on you. But before I can do that, if you really do want to stay with us, there are two conditions, and they are both non-negotiable."

"Of course, Sawyer. What are they?"

"First, I need to tell you something that I am guessing you don't know. Jacob is dead. He didn't make it out of the house before it collapsed, and Mason has run away. For now, it's just Sara and I."

Edward looked stunned and saddened. He looked over at Sara and bowed his head.

"I'm sorry to hear that. My condolences for your loss, Sara."

Sara finally lowered her gun and nodded. Sawyer put his hand on her shoulder and looked back to Edward.

"This leads us to the first condition."

"Of course, Sawyer. What is it?"

"Sara and I are not looking for someone to take over for Jacob. She doesn't need a father figure, and I don't need someone telling me what is best for me or for the Mission. I know that I'm young, but I've been on my own for a long time, and this place is my home. With Jacob gone, it's my responsibility now. I need to know that you understand where I am coming from."

Edward looked Sawyer square in the eyes.

"I completely understand, Sawyer. I only hope that I can serve as a resource for you when you need it, but otherwise, I will be happy to follow your lead, no questions asked."

The boy took a deep breath and studied the man's face for a moment before he spoke again.

"Good. That's what I needed to hear."

"And the second condition?"

Sawyer shifted his gaze up and stared into Edward's eyes.

"Well, the second condition is simple, Edward. It doesn't have to be today, or tomorrow, but promise me that someday before too long, you will tell me the real story about the bunker, and the gold."

At that moment, Edward realized just how exceptional the boy truly was, and he could not help but crack a wry smile.

"Not much gets by you, does it, Sawyer?"

The boy shook his head.

"No, not much."

"Well, that sounds like more than a reasonable deal to me, and I promise to tell you everything you want to know—in due time, of course."

Edward stepped forward and extended his hand to Sawyer. Sawyer shook the man's hand.

"Thanks again, young man. I promise not to let you and Sara down."

The boy nodded and Sara looked up at Edward.

"And thank you, Edward. Thank you for saving Sawyer's life."

Edward winked at the girl and gave them both a look of genuine thanks.

"You are most welcome, Sara, and I can't tell you how much I appreciate you both taking a chance on me. I sure as hell don't claim to see the future, but with God as my witness, I see bright days ahead of us."

Edward smiled, but as Sawyer looked over at Sara's tear-streaked face, Rebekah's dead body, and the column of smoke still rising from Jacob's fiery tomb, the boy did not feel the same, and with the dappled light of the moon dancing in his emerald-green eyes, Sawyer looked up to the sky and sighed one final time.

"I pray to God that you're right, Edward, and that our future is bright. Because right now, with so much pain, death, and destruction all around us, all I can see is another dark tomorrow."

Acknowledgements

I would like to express my sincere gratitude to everyone who supported me in the development and writing of this novel; but above all I would like to thank my wife and best friend, Jodi, for always believing in me, and for giving me the opportunity to follow my dreams.

I would also like to thank all those who were with me from the beginning, the friends and family who were willing to read, edit, and offer their opinions when I needed it most. Specifically, I want to thank my mother, Janet, for her honest feedback, invaluable insight, and for instilling in me a life-long love of literature. I would like to thank my father, Jerry, and my brother, Gene, who took the time to read and offer their support during the long road to publication. I would like to thank my father in-law, Fred Flores, and friends Julie Hackney, and Kyle and Ericka O'Campo for their support as well. I must also thank my editors at Month9books, Shara Zaval and Michelle Millet, who provided astute commentary and top-notch editing of my book.

Finally, I would like to thank both my agent, Mark Gottlieb of Trident Media, and my publisher, Georgia McBride of Month9books, for believing in my work, and for taking a chance on me. This journey has not been easy, but it has been amazingly rewarding, and once again, thanks to everyone who helped make this book possible.

Jeremiah Franklin

Jeremiah Franklin is a former private investigator, arm-chair survivalist, and author of the *Dark Tomorrow* trilogy. When he is not creating thrilling post-apocalyptic worlds, or discussing himself in the third person, the author enjoys reading, staying active, and spending time outdoors with family and friends. He holds a Bachelor's Degree in Psychology, a Master's Degree in Education, and several other certifications that no one really cares about.

OTHER MONTH9BOOKS TITLES YOU MIGHT LIKE

YELLOW LOCUST
SUPERHEROES SUCK

Find more books like this at http://www.Month9Books.com

Connect with Month9Books online:
Facebook: www.Facebook.com/Month9Books
Twitter: https://twitter.com/Month9Books
YouTube: www.youtube.com/user/Month9Books
Tumblr: http://month9books.tumblr.com/
Instagram: https://instagram.com/month9books

Neither quick fists nor nimble feet can save Selena Flood, a fighter of preternatural talent, from the forces of New Canaan, the most ruthless and powerful of the despotic kingdoms around.

YELLOW LOCUST

JUSTIN JOSCHKO

WELCOME TO GEMINI CITY, WHERE SUPER BATTLES DISRUPT RUSH HOUR, CLAIM ADJUSTERS ARE LIKE ROCK STARS, AND VILLAINS STASH THE SOULS OF MURDERED SUPERHEROES INSIDE LITTLE CHILDREN

SUPERHEROES

SUCK

JAMIE ZAKIAN